OUR YOUNG MAN

Edmund White

ISBN HB   978-1-4088-5801-0
       TPB   978-1-4088-5804-1
       PB   978-1-4088-5800-7
       ePub 978-1-4088-5803-0

2 4 6 8 10 9 7 5 3 1

Typeset by Refinecatch Limited, Bungay, Suffolk
Printed in Great Britain by CPI Group (UK) Ltd, Croydon C

BLOOMSBURY

LONDON · OXFORD · NEW YORK · NEW DELHI · SYDNEY

Bloomsbury Publishing
An imprint of Bloomsbury Publishing Plc

50 Bedford Square   1385 Broadway
London   New York
WC1B 3DP   NY 10018
UK   USA

www.bloomsbury.com

First published in Great Britain 2016
This paperback edition first published in 2017

British Library Cataloguing-in-Publication Data
A catalogue record for this book is available from the British Library.

Printed and bo   R0 4YY

To find out   .com.
Here you will find extracts, author interviews, details of forthcoming events
and the option to sign up for our newsletters.

To Christopher Bollen

Then she remembered him, that he was there. All of him, with his hands, his eyes.

—LEO TOLSTOY, *ANNA KARENINA*, TRANSLATED BY RICHARD PEVEAR AND LARISSA VOLOKHONSKY

OUR YOUNG MAN

1.

ALTHOUGH GUY WAS thirty-five he was still working as
a model, and certain of his more ironic and cultured
friends called him, as the dying Proust had been called by
Colette, "our young man." For so many years he'd been actually
young; he'd arrived from Paris to New York in the late 1970s
when he was in his late twenties but passed as nineteen. He'd
been the darling of Fire Island Pines the summers of 1980 and
1981; everyone in the Octagon House was in love with him
and he was a good deal more egalitarian and participatory in
chores and expenses than he needed to be, splitting the grocery
and housecleaning bills down to the last penny, even when he
skipped meals or entire weekends.

Everyone adored him, so he could have skimped on his share.
He was making $175 an hour as a model for a whole host of beauty
products, which was a lot of money in those days; he made more
in two hours than his housemate, the young journalist Howard,
earned in a week, or Howard's lover the mustachioed Cuban
bartender Martin took in at Uncle Charlie's in tips on two or
three shifts. Even his heavy French accent made him all the more
desirable; one of their most besotted housemates, Tom, started
taking French lessons but could never master a whole sentence.

Nor was he stinting with his favors. He'd swallow an after-dinner concoction Ted would assemble of acid, tranquilizers, Quaaludes, and the odd yellow jacket. After a strenuous night of dancing at the Sandpiper he'd be found nude at dawn, splayed in the surf with three other amorous beauties or massaging a Croatian fellow model on the deck by the pool as they sipped big shaggy joints of Acapulco gold.

He liked the Pines, since the muscular men there were bankers or lawyers or surgeons and not just gigolos, as comparable studs would have been in Saint-Tropez, lounging around on the decks of moored yachts (or "laying out in the sun," as these American guys all said, though Guy knew from *lycée* English class back in France that it should be "lying"; the French, he thought primly, would never have made a similar mistake in their own language).

He was from Clermont-Ferrand, a big, dead, dreary industrial city in the heart of France, lava-black, cold in the winter and suffocatingly hot in the summer, and now he sent home a thousand dollars a month from New York to his pious mother, who arranged the flowers for the altar, and his Communist father, a Michelin factory hand who'd been laid off for twenty years, living on welfare and drinking too much red wine (his first *coup de rouge* he downed at eleven every morning, an old habit from his working days).

Guy had always known since his grandmother had told him that he was unusually handsome, with his jug ears, full inviting upper lip, and dark intense eyes the color of burnt honey; only the brightest sunlight discovered the amber spokes in them. He'd played soccer in the streets since he was a six-year-old and had the round ass to prove it, itself as firm and slightly giving as an inflated soccer ball. He was six-foot-three and towered over his friends but he was always disastrously skinny and his nickname had been "Sec" ("Dry") because that's what the French called those who hadn't an extra gram of fat on them. When he was seventeen he began to fill in, but just about then he turned moody (*boudeur*) and started smoking and skipped classes and resigned from being the crozier at church—in fact he slept in on Sundays and missed mass altogether; the omission made his mother cry and his father smile. His parents quarreled once a week and his father, drunk, broke furniture and his mother pronounced bitter reproaches in a soft speaking voice, precise, hateful condemnations which she'd devised to wound and which she muttered expressionlessly.

There were two younger children, a boy and a girl, the nearest, Robert, five years younger, and the girl, Tiphaine, a dozen—both of them presumably the result of Saturday night rapes visited on his outraged mother. The little kids were mousy and unattractive, although Tiphaine seemed to be gifted in math and Robert loved his father and was loved back; their companionship made Guy feel all the more isolated. In the autumn Guy's father and Robert always left on a weeklong hunting trip to the Sologne to which Guy was never invited.

Guy went with a girl, a friend from *lycée*, to a session with a professional photographer; she had her heart set on being a top model, though she was overweight and spotty. Everyone in France said "topmodel," as if it were a bound form. The bored photographer, to whom she was paying five hundred francs for her "portfolio," ended up taking as many pictures gratis of Guy as of Lazarette. He told Guy that he should pursue modeling. Guy stored that hint away; it might be his passport out of Clermont-Ferrand. Although he was a little rebellious, nevertheless he was a good boy and "projected" goodness—which later would be the downfall of many a person.

One weekend Guy went to Paris with some pilgrims from his church; although he claimed to be an atheist he wanted to see Paris and agreed to participate in the huge youth rally mass that was being held in the Parc des Princes. But on the day of the mass he snuck off and took the Métro to Saint-Germain-de-Prés, which he'd read in a magazine was the artistic center of the capital. He sipped a coffee and studied Le Soir at the highly recommended Café de Flore for two hours, and when he got up to leave a friendly-looking middle-aged man sitting by the window waved him over. "Hello, hello," he sang out in a loud voice in which Guy could detect just a hint of irony, or was he, Guy, being the provincial paranoid?

Guy had on his tightest black pants and most beautiful baby-blue sweater, though it was really too warm for a sweater. He'd spent an hour before the mirror at the hostel nursing his hair into little sheep curls and had twice gone through all three outfits he'd brought with him. Tiphaine always ribbed him for being more vain than a girl, but their grandmother, overhearing her, had said, "He's obsessed with his looks and clothes like any normal teenage boy." Although she'd retired to Clermont-Ferrand she'd been a cashier ("Madame Caisse") for forty years at a popular Parisian café. She kept her eyebrows plucked and lips painted magenta with a brush even now. From the waist up she was always impeccable, though her skirt was stained and twisted and her shoes worn down; on the job only her top half had been visible to customers and even now that was all she cared about. She chain-smoked Gauloises and drank a shot of cognac every night after dinner. She had a certain Parisian sauciness that the rest of the family lacked and a salty Titi Parisienne way of talking like the actress Arletty.

The man at the Café de Flore invited Guy to join him for a drink. He said, "It'll just take a second of your time and it could change your whole life." Guy's heart was racing but he thought no harm could come to him, could it, in such a public place. Surely he was safe here, wasn't he?

The man, who was bald but had very shaggy eyebrows to compensate and was wonderfully well dressed in a gray sports jacket the color of a cloud and a flamboyant red and gold silk pocket square, said his name was Pierre-Georges. As soon as Guy had ordered a Suze, which he thought was sufficiently elegant and its yellow color would work to enhance his brown eyes, Pierre-Georges said, "You're the best-looking man in Paris today. Surely you're aware of that." He handed Guy his card, which had the words SCOUTING AGENT printed in embossed letters below his name and above his details. "It's my business to know these things."

Guy was surprised, not because he doubted the man's verdict but because he hadn't picked up that anyone was studying him. His worldly-wise grandmother had told him only two months earlier that he had the sort of good looks that weren't dazzling but only slowly dawned on an observer.

"You could be a model!" the man said. "Are you already?" Maybe his grandmother was wrong and had just been quoting some striking Parisian observation she'd overheard.

"No," he said, deciding to set the bar very low and make himself sound naïve and folkloric. "I'm just a simple boy of the people from Clermont-Ferrand and this is the first time I've ever been in Paris."

Pierre-Georges pressed a smile away with his fingertips and asked, "Age?"

"Seventeen."

"*Lycée?*"

"*Terminale.*"

"So in a few weeks you'll be free to work?"

"Yes, sir."

"Do you have any objections"—again the fingertips pressing the smile from the lips—"to living in Paris and traveling to New York and Milan?"

He decided to play the ingénu (which in fact he was) and said, "Are you kidding? That would be a dream come true." He knew that a cool, blasé tone was beyond his means; he thought Pierre-Georges would prefer to discover an innocent (Guy was a born actor and could even consciously perform himself).

He took a bus up to Paris a week after the youth rally and Pierre-Georges arranged to have his hair cut and straightened and lightened. He was dressed by Pierre-Georges in loud plaids and a tight-fitting paisley shirt, with long collar points and darts in the back, tight puttees, and English winklepicker shoes, all the ghastly fashions of the early seventies. He learned right away to keep changing his pose. ("You're giving me repeats," the wiry little photographer had had to say menacingly only once.) Guy pivoted and smiled or frowned, touched his face or jumped in the air or stared shamelessly at a spot on the wall, all the poses he'd observed in *L'Uomo Vogue*. The photographer and Pierre-Georges discussed him as if he were more or less a desirable side of beef who could not hear them.

"Great bones," the photographer said.

"But his nose is a little shiny on the left side," Pierre-Georges pointed out. "And there's no notch between his nose and his forehead."

"But that's very ancient Greek," the photographer argued. "Very chic just now."

"He needs to work out," Pierre-Georges declared. "A little, not much, just some push-ups and curls and bench presses, high reps and low weights, just to fill out his chest and give his biceps some definition."

"Straight or gay?" the photographer asked.

"He reads straight," Pierre-Georges said. "That's all that counts. All the new male models are straight and married."

"Nice hands," the photographer added, "but he needs a manicure, no varnish."

"Guy, you should throw your shoulders back; the hollowed-out chest look is only for women. And stop smoking! Nothing ages your skin more. If you wanted to do some German catalogue work, swimsuits and underwear, bare-chested, I'd have to burn those two moles off your chest." Guy's hand instinctively rushed to his chest to protect it.

In Clermont-Ferrand no one seemed to be gay, or at least everyone he encountered was careful not to cruise. Everyone he knew except the priest was married. Like many teenagers, Guy was unfamiliar with himself. He didn't know what he wanted—except to see the world. He didn't know what effect he had on others, but everyone tried to please him, even strangers, and even middle-class men and women overcame their reserve to smile or speak to him. He never had to say much to make people open up to him. He liked to say he led a charmed life.

Guy could tell Pierre-Georges liked him but he didn't know in what way. He seemed to want to perfect Guy's look and sometimes Guy felt he was nothing more than a plastic doll that came with tiny outfits and a tiny clothes brush. But Pierre-Georges occasionally smiled at Guy in full complicity as if he knew what was going through the young man's head. Once, when the wiry little photographer was racing about taking shots of Guy jumping in the air as a fan blew his hair, Pierre-Georges winked at the boy. It was absurd! All three of them clustered together in the darkroom improvised in the bathroom: They watched Guy's features slowly emerge beneath the clear fluid under the red light. The little photographer whispered in awe, "*Magnifique!* A god." And Pierre-Georges even muttered his highest praise, "Not bad."

Guy's mother, wearing her black, most classic dress minus the lace fichu, which Guy had begged her to forego, accompanied him to Paris for his first runway show for Pierre Cardin. She was more nervous than Guy and must have told him ten times not to fall off the stage. He acquitted himself without embarrassment and each time stopped at the right spot for a second's pause, and the photographers loved him; at least more flashes went off when he took to the runway than for any of the other men. He wasn't prepared for the frantic changes of clothes backstage; the abrupt, hissed orders as the *maquilleuse*, smelling of cinnamon gum, kept dancing around him on one foot and dusting his face with her powder puff. Pierre-Georges told him he should look angry, even menacing, as if he wanted to punch someone: "That will give you the right look."

Inexperienced as Guy was, even he could see that Cardin's loud plaids and vests for men and polyester ties were in bad taste and that orange, the prevailing color, was offensive. The show was held in the immense new Espace Cardin next to the American Embassy. The great man himself was rushing about, muttering orders and folding back collars. Guy noticed that several of the male models had stopped shaving and showed black stubble. He'd never seen that before and thought it must hurt to be kissed by such a man. At the last minute, Cardin himself clapped horn-rimmed glasses on Guy's face. The lenses, fortunately, were just clear glass, and Guy could see perfectly normally through them. Guy felt a combination of fear and satisfaction on the runway in front of so many strangers. He felt the power of his looks, but it seemed a very limited power and he couldn't yet calculate its dimensions.

The next day Guy's face was splashed all over Paris and he was (sort of) a star (nameless). Pierre-Georges brought to his romantic Left Bank hotel with the view of Notre Dame a whole stack of newspapers. Guy wanted to seem casual and indifferent, but he couldn't help pawing through the papers, especially the regional ones he read regularly. He could see his cheekbones were so high they cast shadows on his thin face, but he thought he was too smiley and risked looking like a simpleton. Pierre-Georges told Guy and his mother that Cardin wanted to sign him up to an exclusive contract but Pierre-Georges thought they should say no. "I can get you a lot more money," he said, "by shopping you around."

Just as Guy was saying, "You're the expert," his mother was saying, "Is it wise to turn down a definite offer?" And they all three laughed at this spontaneous revelation of character.

Guy was excited about having his picture all over the papers and millions of readers looking at him. Would they speculate about who he was and what he wanted, or was the whole presentation so glossy it was impersonal? Would people long to know him? Had he already inspired a passion in some stranger's heart?

Pierre-Georges took Guy and three girls dancing at the Rock 'n' Roll Circus, a tuxedo disco. The tall skinny girls were decked out in horrible Cardin "space age" dresses of floating geometrical panels over body stockings. (Cardin, he learned, had lent the girls the new dresses from his latest ready-to-wear collection because he wanted his clothes to be seen in Paris hot spots.) Guy didn't feel confident about his dancing and he wondered if the black light was doing something facetious to his newly processed hair. But Pierre-Georges assured him he looked handsome in black-tie. From there they went on to the Élysée Matignon. When they all got hungry about midnight they went to the Club Sept, which was a table-hopping restaurant and bar upstairs and a small, mirror-lined gay disco in the basement. The music was a wonderful mix; the Cuban *disquaire*, whom Pierre-Georges called Guy Cuevas, was sitting in a Lucite box and kept playing Marvin Gaye and Dalida.

Guy was secretly thrilled by the blend of gay and straight, black and white, European and American, old and young at the Club Sept and the oddly shaped asymmetrical dishes, spotlit bouquets on each table and the towering wine glasses on green, twisted stems. It seemed very contemporary to him. All of his anguish about whether he liked boys or girls was suddenly resolved and pacified in the dizzying omnisexual pandemonium of the Sept.

He'd had a few sordid gay experiences. He'd wrestled with an obese neighbor boy in Clermont-Ferrand when he was fourteen and last year had been approached in the Clermont-Ferrand train station loo by an obscene old man who'd removed his dentures, wagged his tongue, and pointed to his open, pulsing mouth. *Dear God, please God, don't let me join that man's race of the damned.* But now here at the Sept he could see handsome men in coat and tie kissing at the bar, surrounded by their stylish, indifferent women friends.

Guy kept looking at his long, nervous, freshly manicured hand set off by the black sleeve above the heavy white linen cuff pierced by Pierre-Georges's borrowed silver cuff links. ("Silver in the summer, gold in the winter," Pierre-Georges had declared.) The girls, Guy noticed, ate large green salads of *mâche*, no bread, and only played with their *noisettes de veau* and drank just one glass of white wine each, though he couldn't resist taking a bite out of the delicious hard roll positioned directly on the napery, even when all three girls and Pierre-Georges raised an eyebrow at his lack of discipline. They excused themselves one after another and Guy wondered if they were vomiting their dinners. (He'd heard of such things.)

It was an exciting evening. Some young men at the bar stared over at their table and murmured remarks to one another with hard, mobile mouths. Had they recognized him? A bloated, loud American, stumbling drunkenly, shouting English, was swiftly escorted out to the street. For many long minutes he kept pounding on the street door in vain. "Jeem Morrison," Pierre-Georges whispered. "Sad. He's lost his looks—*bouffi*." Bloated.

A month later Morrison was dead and buried in Père Lachaise, the two moles had been burned painlessly off Guy's chest, and he was successfully weaned from cigarettes after fighting a real struggle (and gaining ten pounds). Pierre-Georges had helped him lose the weight by feeding him amphetamines and had finagled him some very lucrative contracts. Guy had learned that though Pierre-Georges liked to be seen in public with very young models and pretty ephebes, he preferred rough middle-aged brutes in bed whom he dragged home from a bar on the rue Keller. Pierre-Georges encouraged fashion insiders to think Guy was his lover, all the while protesting Guy was "hopelessly straight" and affianced to a silly girl back home in Clermont-Ferrand. Word got out that Guy was as heterosexual as the American guys Bruce Weber was flying over to the Hôtel Meurice and photographing horsing around in the Bois de Boulogne. Zizi Jeanmaire—her spiky hair dyed freshly black—stared at Guy meaningfully over dinner. "He's not straight," she said dismissively on her way out, as if no normal man could resist her.

A young American photographer, who lived at the end of a lane on the Left Bank, not far from the offices of *Le Monde*, invited him to pose for a catalogue of ski gear—he even had a simulated, snow-covered slope all set up. The photographer, Hal, was a *joli laid*, not really handsome, with kinky blond hair, big lugubrious eyes of faded blue, big dumpling ears, but he'd done everything to make his look streamlined, modern, effective; his hair was tamed with brilliantine, it seemed, and he lifted weights and was wearing a tight T-shirt to prove it. He had a collection of plates made from broken, colorful shards, which he called *pique assiette*, and the soaring walls of his studio were painted green in such a way as to look smudged and to leave traces of the brushwork.

They had to work quickly before the snow melted and there were lots of clothes to get through. There was no one doing hair and makeup, nor a dresser, but Guy was a good sport and half the time he was in his underwear as he changed.

Hal was unsmiling (did he think that made him more *soigné*, or was he really bored by life?) but he was friendly enough, though he stared too much and took too long to answer questions in his deep voice. It couldn't be a matter of his comprehension—he'd lived here five years, he said, and his French was good. He didn't even have much of an accent.

And then, as Guy was getting dressed to leave, Hal said, "I've got an idea. Let's do some nudes. You'll be happy someday to have a record of your beauty, your youth." When he saw a hesitant look on Guy's face, Hal said, "They'll be just for us. I'll give you the prints. And nothing pornographic."

A large brown envelope arrived in the mail saying NE PAS PLIER (Don't Bend) and reinforced with stiff cardboard. Inside, in glassine envelopes, were several full-color nudes of himself posed against the snowbank. He was naked except for a pair of skis he was holding straight up and a stocking cap. Guy looked at the pictures through a loupe. His uncircumcised penis was large enough. His chest was hairy and he had a clear treasure trail pointing down from his navel to his crotch. He liked the way he appeared, though he worried his forearms looked too small.

Three months later Pierre-Georges steamed into Guy's studio without knocking and slapped down on the kitchen table Guy's full-page nude in the American gay magazine *Blueboy*. "Slut, you've just sunk your career," he sputtered. "And it doesn't even look big." It took a long dinner and four glasses of Bordeaux for him to go from sputtering to simmering.

"You've spoiled all our good work," he said in a drained, tragic voice. "The whole game with models is never to let the public see everything. Make them dream, make them imagine! Let them see a haunch, not a strange little penis." He said the harsh slang word *bitte*.

Guy told him the whole story of Hal's treachery and Pierre-Georges hissed, "Idiot!" Then he relented and said, "Well, it's an American magazine. No one here will ever see it and he called you Ralph, of all things." He reflected. "But that is where we want to sell you, America. That's where the money is."

Guy had a new thought: "Anyone who buys this magazine shares our vice, and who would admit that?"

"I'm not talking about confession but about gossip."

Guy longed for a best friend, a confidant. He liked walking everywhere in Paris despite the sudden heat, but he wanted to discuss things with a friend, male or female, and his solitude made him melancholy. He looked at store windows on the Left Bank and across the river on the rue Saint-Honoré and tried to decide whether he liked best Hugo Boss or Kenzo or Lanvin. He coveted a pale gray silk bathrobe from Lanvin but he rebelled at the $1,000 price tag: He laughed when the disdainful clerk at Hermès told him the small pigskin valise with the brass fittings cost $6,000. He wasn't very sure about money. He didn't know how long people would want to hire him. He was a popular runway model but he'd have to wait until September for the spring collections to work again. The booking agent at *Vogue* liked him but editorial didn't pay much, and besides, they didn't want the same male faces to become too familiar to their readers. He had a big, well-paying yogurt account for print, and then he did a commercial for Brie where he had to dress as a starving young monk who fell on the cheese the second the older, chubbier monks left him alone. That spot ran ten times a day on TV for a month and the residuals kept rolling in.

He had grown up poor. They had a small, smelly trailer they drove around France for vacations; in the trailer park outside Montoire-sur-le-Loir they'd stayed for five nights. His father set up an awning and a grill and drank even more red wine than usual. That's where Guy had lost his virginity to a shy, lovely girl from Vichy named Violette. They were both fifteen. His family never ate in restaurants, not even cafés, when they were traveling. Guy had loved clothes but never had had money to buy them. Now, in Paris, he had money but was very practical about saving. Most of his clothes were given to him by designers at a severe discount.

For nearly a decade he was the darling of Paris. He bought an art nouveau apartment designed around 1910 by Guimard, the man who had done the Métro entrances. It was small, but Pierre-Georges declared it "distinguished" and approved that it was in the safe, serene, and nonhappening sixteenth arrondissement. Publicly Guy dated starlets and female models, who mostly were pleased he didn't expect them to put out. Privately he'd go off at the end of long, bibulous evenings with other good-looking young "straight" men he met at heterosexual pickup bars on the boulevard Montparnasse, guys who like him had been unlucky with lining up a girl for the evening before last call. But he never saw one of these men more than once and never gave out his real name.

Pierre-Georges said to him, "You're universally liked because you're such a black hole in space. You don't have any real traits. You're *sympa*, at least as much as a narcissist can be, but that means nothing. You're beautiful and everybody projects onto you what they're looking for, which is easy to do since you don't stand for anything definite. You're a black hole in space."

Then Pierre-Georges sent him to New York for a Pepsi commercial, where his Frenchness was of no relevance; in fact, he had to dress in jeans and a sports shirt and flip burgers among young Americans at a picnic shot on a rented estate in Far Hills, New Jersey. It was 1980 and suddenly male models, two years after women, were becoming "supermodels." Their names were known; the public gossiped about them. Their hourly rates went up. The public laughed at them for being overpaid, but Pierre-Georges pointed out that the career of a model was very short.

Guy worried about everything. The currency in America never made any sense to him since nickels were bigger than dimes, which were worth more. From all those Fred Astaire movies, he thought everyone in New York would be in evening clothes, but actually they were badly dressed and coiffed. Chicly dressed women wore sneakers (he was told they'd put on their heels at the office). Many men looked unwashed. He was shocked how obese some Negro women were and how unself-consciously, even sloppily, they rolled from side to side down the sidewalk. Portions in restaurants seemed comically large and he was puzzled that several places offered "all you can eat." The doggy bag was a new idea. New York struck him as dowdy and provincial but strangely electric. Everything was fast and careless, even the hurried way shopgirls wrapped packages. Oddly, waiters were extraordinarily friendly; at one place in the Village the waitress sat down with them and said, "I hope you folks don't have a complicated order. I'm completely stoned." Although Guy fancied he knew English well, he had to ask the photographer's assistant what "folks" and "stoned" meant. From then on Guy used "folks" as often as possible, as in, "They are very funny folks," thinking that meant they were amusing. Calling someone "amusing" just seemed to irritate New Yorkers.

Even so, he was a huge success in America. There didn't seem to be room, not even in New York, for several French models, but Guy quickly became the go-to French guy. He met all the top photographers, including Hiro, a very pure, quiet Japanese artist who would arrange a few objects and get ravishing forms and citrusy color combinations, and Richard Avedon, much smaller and younger than Guy had imagined, a very bossy, hardworking genius who told him, "These days I just shoot constantly and my work has all the excitement of confetti." Avedon was so slim and stylish even in his work clothes that he didn't seem American or even heterosexual, but he was famous for his celebrated women friends, including the legendary model Dovima, the one he'd photographed with an elephant.

Pierre-Georges told him that New York was very dangerous and when he took a taxi home he should have the driver wait until he was safely in the front door. He could be mugged crossing the five meters between the cab and his lobby. He lived in Greenwich Village (he had trouble pronouncing "Greenwich") in a floor-through of a brownstone on the corner, illogically, of West Fourth and West Eleventh. Pierre-Georges had found it and even furnished it for him, though Guy was allowed to place family pictures on tiny silver easels Pierre-Georges bought. Guy also draped an extravagant silk scarf across the plain beige couch, but Pierre-Georges teased him about it and he folded it and put it away the next day.

He joined a nearby gym upstairs at Sheridan Square. There was lots of loud joking among the folks working out; some of them were grotesquely muscular and one guy had to be helped up the stairs by his brother. Every day the guy ate an entire rotisserie chicken and drank a pint of bull's blood. Guy couldn't understand most of the gibes, but it seemed half the folks were gay and half normal and they were joking about which orientation was more amusing: "Just think of dick as pussy on a stick," one of the loudmouths guffawed. The population of the gym was at the tipping point between gay and normal.

In the cedar-lined sauna a polite flabby man with a bushy gray mustache and expensive sapphire eyes and the ruins of good looks struck up a conversation. His nipples were the size of erasers. In Paris Guy would have been curt, but here in America folks appeared to be vulgarly friendly. When the man, *un vieux beau*, heard Guy's accent he switched to a very good French. He said his name was Walt and he was from San Francisco, but he didn't really work because he had to be free to travel with his older friend, a Belgian baron and banker who was always in transit between Gstaad and Phuket and Venice and Mykonos, you really should meet him, and what do you do, oh, I suspected as much, I know you're not supposed to ask French people what kind of work they do, but hey, we're in New York, and Walt laughed at the funny coincidence of that.

By chance they got out of the sauna at the same time and headed down the hall to the showers. Walt cupped one of Guy's hot buttocks; Guy glared at him but Walt looked unfazed, as though he'd been innocently testing a melon for ripeness or as if someone else had done it. In the shower Walt continued smiling and chatting but he made a bit too much out of laundering his genitals. Although he was too fat, strangely enough Guy could imagine it would be fun to hold him. Walt had a body meant to be held.

When they were dressed and heading out, Walt wrote down Guy's phone number. Under his taut silk briefs Guy could still feel the shocking familiarity of Walt's hand, but it confused him. He'd never been attracted to anyone over thirty, at least not to his knowledge, but he was secretly thrilled by the infringement of that brazen touch. Maybe it was because such an obviously civilized man, who spoke French and skied at Gstaad, had done it—as if someone in evening clothes had knelt in the mud to suck his cock. After all, Walt vacationed in Thailand, he studded his conversation with references to yachts and international watering holes—and he'd also reached for Guy's ass.

Guy realized how lonely he was. How starved for affection. In Paris he'd met an older woman named Elaine in an English class they were both enrolled in. She was an anesthesiologist who lived and worked in Versailles and was sort of perky but fundamentally dull, though she was always free and treated Guy as a kid brother. They never got beyond the formality of calling each other *vous*. In New York he didn't even have an Elaine to share meals or movies with.

Because almost every man here in the Village stared at him, he'd learned to ignore them all. One had a nice torso but lady legs. Another had worked out his biceps but not his triceps. A third had a good body but ludicrous muttonchops. A fourth carried a man purse because his pale gabardine trousers had no pockets and looked sprayed on: In France only middle-aged bus drivers out on the town still carried them. Guy inventoried all these "faults" because he was just as critical of his own short-comings—or guarded vigilantly against having any. But he knew that if he could connect with even a very ordinary person he wouldn't look for that person's flaws.

If he walked though Washington Square past a lone guy sitting on a bench, eyeing him, Guy would find it harder and harder to breathe as he got nearer, almost as if he were passing through a dangerous force field. His first weekend on Fire Island with Pierre-Georges (who was unexpectedly hairy in a swimsuit), Guy slowly descended the wooden stairs from the dunes to the beach wearing nothing but a tight white swimsuit and sunglasses, and a dozen men looked up from their towels at him and he was afraid he might faint. He thought to himself, *I'll never be this perfect again*, an idea that made him sad. Something about being beautiful induced melancholy in Guy. He was aware of how brief his perfection would be—and then sneered at himself for being so narcissistic. Beauty was only a way of making money.

He thought he was like an expensive racehorse whom all the people around him kept inspecting and trotting not for his well-being but to protect their investment. Feel his withers . . . is he off his feed? . . . the grandstand seems to spook him, he needs blinders . . . his nose is warm. If he went out without sunglasses, Pierre-Georges came running after him to warn him against squint lines. If he gained an ounce, Pierre-Georges would pinch his waist and murmur, "Miss Piggy." If he wore tight jeans, Pierre-Georges would hiss, "You look like a whore," and make him change to something looser. Once, when he wore a filmy, sheer robe, Pierre-Georges whispered that most dismissive of French phrases, "Très original." If he concentrated while doing a crossword, Pierre-Georges warned him he was getting elevenses—those vertical worry lines above his nose.

He and Pierre-Georges took a public speedboat at midnight from the Grove to the Pines with a bunch of overexcited guys and they all rushed into the Sandpiper. Guy was stoned and taller than most of the other men, and as he stared out over them he experienced a distinctly Buddhist feeling of evanescence. He looked out over the shirtless, muscled, tanned men and realized that right here, on this disco floor, there was such a concentration of fashion, slimming, money, bleaching, plastic surgery, psychotherapy—and all for naught. In a few years they'd all be old walruses, and in a few more, dead.

Guy met some hunky guys who'd improvised an outdoor gym with weights on the sand in front of their house over on Tuna and they said he could work out with them. One day a small, slender, but perfectly formed blond drew him aside and said, "You should do gymnastics—you're a model, right? Do you want me to teach you?" The guy, wearing blue baggy shorts, jumped up onto parallel bars and walked down them with just his hands, then turned a somersault and extended his legs and pointed his feet. Guy exercised with him for an hour; apparently the man didn't expect anything in return—these Americans were amazing!

He'd read an article in a beauty magazine about facial isometrics and every morning in front of the mirror he hooked his fingers in his mouth and stretched out his lips toward his ears, trying to close his mouth at the same time. Or he tilted his head back like a goose and pointed his chin and pressed his tongue against the roof of his mouth to firm up his chin.

As he came out of the Sandpiper for a breather he ran into Walt, who was very solicitously shepherding about his baron. They were introduced and the baron, ugly as a commissar, held on to Guy's hand for an uncomfortably long interval. Of course they were speaking French, and rather loudly, and Guy worried the foreign language might irritate some folks, just as he became resentful when several boisterous Germans would speak their language loudly in a Paris café. Guy feared it might be a petit bourgeois trait on his part, but he didn't want to stand out as a foreigner, though most Americans said they loved his accent, it was so sexy.

The baron, whose name was Édouard, invited him to lunch the next day on his yacht—and he pointed to a massive boat moored and nearly extinct in the slip just beside them. Guy had noticed attractive men and women on the deck of the yacht just that afternoon. He asked, "What time?" Then he asked if he could bring a French-speaking friend.

The little gymnast sidled up to Guy and said, "I see you've met Spare Parts."

"Who, Baron Édouard?"

"We call him Spare Parts because he's had so much work done on him and still looks like a toad."

"Toad?" Finally Guy deduced he meant a *crapaud*: That was probably said out of envy and jealousy.

"Be careful of him," the gymnast added. "He likes violent sex; you don't want those pretty nipples stretched out. He's also into fisting. Actually, he's the slave, I think."

For once Pierre-Georges, whose instinct was to frown whenever Guy suggested an idea, smiled instead. "A baron? A yacht?" he asked, reassured they weren't that far from Saint-Tropez after all.

Guy had braced himself for a scary intimate lunch, but the yacht was flourishing with young hangers-on and the baron was only intermittently visible, fully dressed in captain's whites. Guy thought he must be a clever seducer and was determined to imitate him when he was old—to bait the hook with lots of shiny lures. Walt was very much in evidence, making sure the bong was circulating, that the icy daiquiris were replenished, and the hot blue cheese pastries were being passed around, as well as the crudités with the delicious crab claws.

Walt asked in a whisper, "Which of these boys do you fancy the most?"

Guy shrugged but Walt persevered. "Seriously," he said.

Guy had spent so much time rejecting even the most hand-some Americans that now it was difficult for him to pick someone. He was the one everyone else pursued; he was the commodity, not the consumer. But when Walt asked a third time, Guy murmured in a strangled voice, "That little blond in the neon-blue swimsuit."

"Jacky? He's the biggest slut on the island and a major masochist. He's always being chained to an abandoned refriger-ator in the Meat Rack and we have to send someone at dawn to free him. Not that he's ever anything but cheerful, whistling all the time. He's a wannabe deejay."

So, Guy thought, *the baron does like violent sex and surrounds himself with cheerful slaves*—and Guy looked to see if Jacky's nipples were deformed, and they did look sort of large and chewed-on, like cold gristle. *But hold on*, Guy said to himself. *If the baron is a masochist himself, then why would he entertain another masochist? I suppose he wants someone cute to attract other sadists.*

There were lots of women present—well, three. They were a bit coarse, but the men paid court to them, as if gay men had been cut off from women for so long they reverted right away to their high school sissy-boy gallantry.

After Guy's second daiquiri the baron emerged from the cabin. Guy had closed his eyes for the moment against the sun, and when he opened them there was Édouard in the captain's chair next to his deck chair. "You must be careful that perfect skin of yours doesn't burn," he said. "I could put some sunscreen on your back if you liked," and he held up a little tube from Kiehl's.

"That's extremely kind of you, but my friend Pierre-Georges has already coated me like a roast chicken in soft butter."

The baron didn't laugh, which made Guy feel uncomfort-able. He sipped his third drink, which he'd vowed not to touch.

Édouard seemed so somehow honored by Guy's friendship that he began to give all-male dinners for him—one in a three-story ferryboat that cruised up the Hudson at sunset with a hundred guests served by handsome waiters in short-shorts and orange work boots and black T-shirts silkscreened with the baron's coat of arms in silver. Édouard was careful to toast Guy, the guest of honor. Otherwise he didn't pester him. The ship didn't turn around and return to the Battery until midnight; by then many of the boys had paired off and mounted to the top, darkened deck. Guy stayed below chatting with two of his new friends. In America everyone called the merest acquaintance a "friend"—Guy had taken up the habit. It made him feel better about not having any real friends.

At another dinner, equally large and lavish, they were served again by the boys in micro-shorts and orange work boots, but this time their midriffs were exposed. Guy's mother was in town and she was the only woman present among a hundred A-list homosexuals, who were all courtly to her, though Guy got tired of translating their inanities: "Gee, oh, wow, it's really neat to meet Guy's mom," to which his mother said anxiously to her son, "What did he say? What did he say? Oh. Tell him it's a true honor to meet one of my son's colleagues."

"What did she say? Seriously, what did she say?"

At least the baron was unctuous with her and spoke to her his most ancien régime French; Guy's mother, in her neck-twisting, unsmiling way, was distinctly flirting with Édouard, though that was imperceptible to anyone not in her immediate family. She drank too many foamy grasshoppers and seemed not to register she was the only woman present; at least she didn't comment on it when Guy led her back to her midtown hotel, the Warwick, which they both pronounced in the American, not the English way.

Édouard told Pierre-Georges over the lunch he'd invited him to at the Côte Basque that he would give anything, pay anything, to sleep with Guy just one night. Of course, he realized Guy might be shocked by the baron's bodily disarray; Édouard was under no illusion about how unpresentable he'd become. Very few men of his generation could undrape becomingly, and he knew he wasn't one of them. Since Guy seemed to fancy Jacky, the boy could be introduced into the repast to make it more palatable.

The whole conversation, which excited Pierre-Georges as much as it made him uncomfortable, since he had no polite precedent for such an exchange, was duly reported to Guy. "I suggested you had your heart set on a sky-blue Mercedes convertible but that garage fees made contemplating the purchase of a car unimaginable, given that a parking space in Manhattan was as dear as an apartment in Paris."

"You just sold my immortal soul for a car and a parking lot without consulting me?" Guy wailed. Everything was rushing by. It seemed to him his life limped along and then went into unexpected spurts.

"I'm consulting you now. Did I do wrong? A Mercedes is fairly expensive."

Guy sipped his Diet Coke. At last he said sullenly, "No."

"What?"

"I said no, you did nothing wrong. What did he say?"

"Édouard just blinked and smiled. I suggested you had a saint's day coming up. Then we spoke of other things. Your career. He offered that Zoli is a personal friend and he could make an introduction."

"But you're my agent," Guy objected. He looked out the window at the gingko tree. It was July, but the summer evenings weren't as long as they were in Paris.

"He could be your agent and I could be your manager. Zoli's the top agent for men."

Guy worried that he'd have to give Zoli his statistics to be printed next to a new head shot—and would he give his real age: thirty? People said he looked twenty—maybe he'd say he was twenty-two, though Zoli was no fool and might call him on it. A little research would turn up all those French ads from ten years ago; of course, Guy could always say that had been a look-alike older brother, now selling sports equipment in a shop in Épinal.

Guy was groomed by Didier Malige, who Pierre-Georges said was the world's most exclusive hairdresser. New hair and a new facial regime by Mario Badeau and a new photo set by Bruce Weber—that might get him higher fees and stretch his image across the skies during what must surely be his sunset years.

As for the baron, he was kind and respectful and usually interesting and full of fun projects. For his parties he usually annexed Guy's guest list. He was always seated fully clothed and never exposed people to his terrible old body. He was always surrounded by the cutest young boys who would sit on the floor at his feet while he draped his puffy, jeweled hands over their shoulders—but innocently, innocently, as a grandfather might. The kids were like expensive borzoi snuggled against him. Walt was always around filling glasses, passing joints, putting on new party tapes. Walt always had the latest fashion icon in tow—he brought Christie Brinkley and Gia Carangi by and the makeup wizard Way Bandy. Gia complained there were no girls present—she was bi and preferred girls. But she also talked about her latest boyfriend: "He doesn't love me, not really. Would you believe he flew me to Milan business class?" Seeing the blank stares, she added, "And not first class." Walt made everything function smoothly. He hired the caterers, took everyone off to dance at Doubles in a stretch, remembered who was a vegetarian and who was a pescetarian. (Guy had the usual French impatience with picky eaters.)

Although they laughed freely and jostled each other playfully, most of the other male models had nothing in common and were easily bored. Most of them were living with a woman, usually another model. Several were athletes and tennis champs or went in for boxing or motorbiking or were ranked high by the International Ski Federation in the slalom and alpine categories. Several were swimming stars. Even if they were aristocrats who had gone to Le Rosey, the exclusive Swiss boarding school, they knew all the words to Donna Summer's hit "Once Upon a Time." Some of the guys were somebodies—Alain Delon's son (born and brought up in Beverly Hills) or Barry Goldwater's grandson—but some of them were uncultured thugs, raised in Brooklyn's "Ravioli Alley" and sporting a tattoo or two, bad teeth, and a thick Brooklyn accent. How much did that Brooklyn guy work? Guy wondered. He'd heard there was an agency called Funny Faces. Maybe they represented him. One guy was the national swimming champion of Spain and had an earring, a shaved chest, and fluffy armpits.

Most of them were interested in the Japanese chanting sort of Buddhism, maybe because it was hopeful and optimistic and was an exotic alternative to Christianity, which was contaminated with overfamiliarity and gloom. Buddhism sounded austere and nonproselytizing and kind of cerebral, but in fact this popular cult kind, Nam-myoho-renge-kyo, was one in which you chanted for a Cadillac or a go-see. You didn't have to meditate, just chant. It was very materialistic but the men who did it claimed it settled their minds, brought inner peace . . . lots of things. It was really cool how you could kneel in front of your own portable altar and say Nam-myoho-renge-kyo for hours every night instead of snorting coke or drunk-dialing. And it was fun to have a brass gong you struck every time you chanted Nam-myoho-renge-kyo three times, though the lotus position, granted, was hell on the knees.

Guy never opened up to the other models he worked with but he liked to joke with them. They had been discovered by Bruce Weber playing college football or mowing lawns. Guy only pretended to like girls, though he was very close to one girl, a makeup artist most recently from Ohio, or was it Iowa; she was the sweetest girl alive, an orphan who'd lived in one foster home after another. Her name was Lucie and she was close to forty but slender and she always wore black tights and her sort of kinky hair pulled back in a pigtail held in a pink rubber band and she looked really young but tired, as if she'd been awake for two nights. Actually the truth was the opposite: She slept too much and said she loved sleeping more than anything, curled up with her two stuffed lions. She usually wore a gray sweatshirt with the sleeves pushed up. Her hands were big and clean and mannish. She had very large, full breasts, which were only visible when she stripped down to a gray T-shirt. She wore no bra. She was very sexy in her full-figured way, though she didn't play the woman card. She wore no makeup except white lip gloss. She was all business and she always carried her fishing-tackle box loaded with eye shadow, eye crayons to cancel dark circles, pressed powders to contour and sculpt the face, a liquid foundation, lip gloss, highlighters, mascara, lipsticks, rouges, cold cream, and an astringent makeup remover to be followed by a soothing moisturizer.

Lucie had been born in Normandy. Her father was a black American soldier and her mother a Vietnamese refugee. Lucie didn't look Asian. The French orphanage had had an approved list of girls' names and they went through it systematically; Lucie had been her turn. Maybe the orphanage and foster homes were what had made her so independent, self-sustaining. Although she'd lived in America since she was eighteen (she had an American passport), she had the French way of only complaining about little things (the heat) and passing over the big things (beatings, hunger). She spoke French fluently but with a beguiling American accent (her *r* was atypical and her *u* more an *oo*). Pierre-Georges thought she was a bore, but he only approved of people who could help him.

Guy met Lucie on a set and she did his makeup in a minute, mainly powdering away that confoundedly shiny nose (only the left side).

She told him she liked his tiny jug ears, his intense eyes, his hollow cheeks and full upper lip, his hairy chest poking up above his T-shirt, and his ineradicable trace of a mustache, no matter how many times a day he shaved. His eyebrows were just two straight dashes and his hairline was low on his forehead. His nose was straight and seemed to be the prolongation of a frown, though he'd disciplined himself never to frown. Pierre-Georges told him not to stand around with his mouth open but his lips were so full they were hard to compress. Pierre-Georges said that full lips like Belmondo's were sensual when the person was young but grotesque when the person aged; he might consider having them surgically thinned. Lucie said that was crazy and she didn't know why, but Guy's strangely assorted features definitely "worked." (She used the English word.) Lucie seemed like a real friend—observant, loyal, tender.

There was something melancholy, veiled, wounded about Lucie. Guy just knew her childhood had been tragic but he didn't dare quiz her about it. He felt that once she started to unburden herself they'd never be able to push all her woes back in again. She liked to eat unbuttered popcorn with Guy and watch television in her bare feet; she stayed over twice and hugged him in bed but seemed to expect nothing more. Guy would go to Studio with Lucie. Or he'd take a model he'd just met on a shoot. It was fun to sweep in past that line of clamoring New Jersey kids with their horrible haircuts and tacky *Saturday Night Fever* clothes. ("I know Steve.") It was fun to dance under the giant spoon lifting cocaine to a silver nostril. He was now surer of his dancing. The waiters were striking—and often were hired by Zoli or Click as tomorrow's models. The biggest thrill was when Steve invited one upstairs to the VIP lounge. It was exhilarating to be among the in-crowd along with Lisa, Halston, and Andy. Guy didn't really like to get high, no more than Andy did; he noticed Andy was always taping people or taking Polaroids of them as a way of avoiding talk or even contact. Maybe it was Guy's altar-boy childhood or his petit bourgeois fear of ending up broke, but he liked being in control and he feared jeopardizing his looks. Dancing was good exercise but the drugs that fueled it surely took their toll, though people said coke was harmless and not at all addictive.

It wasn't that he exactly lied about his age, and with real friends like Lucie he'd freely admit how old he was, but in the business he was coy or actively dishonest. No one wanted a middle-aged French fag kissing the girl in a Kellogg's commercial.

One September day, Guy's saint's day, the baron gave him an intimate dinner party in his East Sixtieth Street apartment—and a small beribboned white box containing the keys to a Mercedes 450SEL. Guy gave him a peck on the cheek, which was the most demonstrative he'd ever permitted himself to be with the baron. He wondered when Édouard would try to collect his pound of flesh. He noticed that Jacky was present and was wearing a white shirt nearly opened to the navel with puffy pirate sleeves. Walt was always hovering in the background, organizing the waitstaff.

Saint Guy of Anderlecht was the tenth-century Belgian saint of animals, stables, workhorses, and bachelors, and Édouard had as the centerpiece of his immaculate table a white *faience crèche* in Saint Guy's honor, the exquisite figurines placed on a mirror as if they were drowning in a placid pool. Everyone was a model or might as well have been, so there were several salads, three vegetables, a sliver of fish on every plate, and unsweetened raspberries, no bread, though as a Frenchman Guy found it hard to eat without a baguette slice as a scooper. Vintage champagne was served throughout. The models kept leaning over the centerpiece so they could check themselves out in the mirror, Guy noticed. Édouard made several jokes about Saint Guy being the bachelor's saint. Walt passed a joint.

Guy was ordinarily paranoid in company; was it because he didn't feel at ease in English and was afraid he'd missed an allusion to *Charlie's Angels* or *The Brady Bunch*? These Americans thought their TV series and their pop singers were universal and eternal. When they talked about them they got big moist eyes like Bambi. Of course they'd never heard of Dalida or Véronique Sanson. Tonight he thought he should get high, just in case they all ended up in bed. The more he smoked, the more his fantasies were unleashed, as if he were rubbing the magic lantern with every toke. He looked at Jacky with an almost uncontrollable desire. (He was afraid that he, Guy, might at any moment fall to his knees and crawl across the room and bury his head in Jacky's lap.) Jacky looked so desirable, with his full purple lips and ash-blond crew cut which begged to be brushed with an affectionate hand and turned to wheat or silver. The muscles in his neck stood out. Although there were dark circles under his eyes, he looked unbearably young—how did he do that? Wasn't Jacky what Americans called the "bottom," indicated by the keys he wore clipped to the right side of his white painter's pants? Maybe Jacky was like Pierre-Georges, who wanted his bed partners to be grizzly brutes, not the pretty boys he liked only as arm candy. There was Pierre-Georges, over there on the love seat, speaking French to Lucie and looking bored. She'd put on a pretty party dress for the occasion, cut so low he could see she was, unusually, wearing a bustier laced with pink ribbon; she had on silver-threaded blue *bas résille* stockings. Now she got up to leave.

"I have a six A.M. call tomorrow," she said. "Top of the newly finished Citicorp Building for Italian *Bazaar*. I'm working for Von Wangenheim."

He stood and kissed her on both cheeks. He knew she was really leaving out of discretion; she was the only woman still present. "Thanks for the gift," he said. She'd brought him a used hardcover of *Zen and the Art of Motorcycle Maintenance*, which he'd always meant to read. She'd told him that she chanted and it had brought her the job for *Vogue Patterns*, which had the world's most daring editorial pages. Lucie had painted a Japanese model's face pale green and dressed her in a skin-colored, sleazy vintage ball gown she and Guy had found in a secondhand store on Greenwich Avenue. It had started a revolution, the sick look.

With Lucie's departure, Walt turned down the lights. Pierre-Georges took his leave and winked complicitously at Guy. Guy was dying to run down to the garage and drive his new car around; the parking space the baron had rented was in his, the baron's, building, which wasn't convenient to Guy's place in the Village, but the baron no doubt hoped to lure Guy even more often up to the East Side. Guy wondered if the title of the car was also in the baron's name.

Now that there were only four handsome guys left, all gay, he noticed, the music was no longer disco ("Higher and Higher") but Peggy Lee ("Is That All There Is?"), Édouard's idea of mood music. Two joints were making the rounds and the champagne was replaced by sweet, deadly stingers. The Ravioli Alley guy, who looked like the young Elvis, was rubbing his crotch through his trousers. He would, Guy thought. It looked half hard and very big. Then Walt, who was sitting next to Elvis, put his hand on his knee and Elvis moved it closer to his dick. Jacky stood and made a show of refilling his drink, but a second later he was sitting on the other side of Elvis and was kissing him passionately. The baron had left the room. Guy was so stoned that he was magnetized to Jacky's side. As soon as an idea popped into his head he was doing it. There seemed to be a skip between every series of actions as if it had been edited out. Guy looked at Walt; they smiled hopelessly and each said, at the same moment, "Gosh, I'm stoned." Walt added, "I think that shit was sprayed with PCP." And Guy nodded meekly, though he had no idea what that meant. Guy's own erection was so hard it ached, as if it were an angry dog begging to be let out and pawing at the door. He felt a little silly, possibly intrusive, sitting next to Jacky as Jacky kissed Elvis, a bit like an importunate extra man who wants to cut in on a woman perfectly happy with her dancing partner. But then Walt had extricated the thug's big, uncircumcised, ropy cock from his trousers and Elvis was sprawling back on the couch to get sucked. He pulled away from Jacky, who turned without missing a beat to kiss Guy. Jacky's mouth tasted metallic, which Guy imagined was from the thug's saliva. Jacky's eyes were closed. Did he know whom he was kissing? Jacky's hand unzipped Guy's fly and pulled out his rigid, leaking penis. As though drawn to it like a sunflower to sun, his mouth descended and engulfed it. Guy trembled from the warm, liquid enclosure, all alive and squirming, the tongue. *Oh, God, don't let me shoot right away!* Now Jacky was grappling with Guy's belt and unbuttoning him—Guy lifted his hips slightly and Jacky tugged his trousers down. With a flicker of anxiety Guy hoped his crotch didn't smell, hoped his wallet didn't fall out. But Jacky liked it; Guy thought of the French word *pervers* and then the English word "manhood." Jacky had unfolded his manhood and had it on display and isolated as if prepped for surgery. He had pulled back his foreskin and was licking Guy's balls and now the stretch of skin beside them. His tongue was as rough as a cat's.

Guy looked over at Walt's gray mustache beavering away on the thug's big penis, which was so adolescent it was pressing up against his soft stomach, fish-belly white, and Walt had to pull it down fastidiously between thumb and forefinger in order to suck it.

Where was Édouard? The wall beside them was covered with gilt bosses and Louis Seize knots in plaster and Guy thought he could see an eye—liquid, shifting, sensitive as a quivering sea urchin—blinking at the center of one of the ornaments. Was Édouard just a voyeur? Was he back there jacking off? Poor Édouard, deaf even with two hearing aids and his bald head painfully seeded with implants. Could he even get an erection?

Knowing that they were being watched excited Guy, who moved his arm out of the way as men do in porn to make the focus of excitement more visible to the viewer. Was a glimpse of his cock worth a Mercedes?

After it was all over, Édouard rejoined them and chuckled. "I am like the Cardinal de Bernis, who spied on Casanova and a nun." Guy knew who Casanova was but not the other guy. He was happy to see that Édouard was highly satisfied with his dinner party and orgy. Ever prudent, Guy decided he was too drunk to drive. He and Édouard took the elevator down to the garage to look at the Mercedes. Guy stood with his arm resting on Édouard's shoulder, then kissed his forehead and took a cab home.

"Gay men," Pierre-Georges said over the phone, "pay more for boys who don't put out. Straight men pay for women who do fuck them. I don't know why that should be so."

"Maybe boys are too plentiful and available, whereas pussy is scarce." He said the French word, *con*, and Pierre-Georges laughed even to hear this mild profanity in Guy's mouth.

"Scarce? Hardly. Not now. Just troll any of those Second Avenue singles bars in the Fifties. If you're not too picky, young fat girls are very available."

"So do you think I should play hard-to-get for Édouard?"

"It's worked so far."

A year went by and Guy submitted every month to Jacky's attentions while Édouard watched through the mosharabia.

Once, after a very stoned Christmas dinner, Jacky was kissing Guy deeply and Guy felt a new mouth on his dick. It was Édouard's, no doubt; he'd removed his dentures and Guy remembered that old guy at the Clermont-Ferrand train station. How old had he been then? Seventeen? Now it was sixteen years later. Guy pulled down Jacky's trousers, releasing his stubby erection. The baron took turns sucking them off. Guy noticed that Jacky had shaved all his pubic hair—was that some master's whim or was it aesthetic? Guy had observed the same practice once when he'd made love to an Arab.

He heard distant rumors of the new backroom bars where some French tourist friends had been turned away by the doorman for wearing cologne, cashmere sweaters draped over their shoulders, and Gucci loafers, no socks. Apparently they wanted only "real men." America had no images for masculinity that weren't working-class.

At one bar, the Mine Shaft, there were two floors of horrors, naked men sitting in bathtubs being peed on, a whole wall of glory holes where guys were serviced anonymously, a sling where "bottoms" could get fisted. There was no way Guy could visit that place or the leather bars in the West Twenties. What if someone took his picture? He'd even heard of society people going to the baths on the Upper West Side to hear singers while men in towels stood around. A Polish princess had taken off her rings to fist a go-go boy down on Fourteenth Street.

Édouard had a glory hole installed in the doorway to his bedroom. It was just a piece of plywood, easily removed, with a large, optimistically large hole cut through at waist-height. They had a light dinner à deux; a butler served them and called Guy monsieur and Édouard Monsieur le Baron. After dinner, which was slightly tedious with its six changes of plates and tableware and its three wines, ending with a delicious Chateau d'Yquem, Édouard sat back in his chair and lit a joint. He talked about the gloomy castle in which he'd grown up where it was always raining. "Then in Brussels we lived above the bank, just a block from the royal palace. My father died when I was nine—gossips said he shot himself because he was gay. My mother was a delicious woman who surrounded herself with artists. There's a portrait of her." He pointed to a life-sized painting of a blond woman in a ball gown. The painter had shown more interest in the candy-striped silk dress with its frothy lace bodice than in the subject's face, which looked fairly generic. "She was a saint—but a powerhouse, too. I've tried to follow her example by surrounding myself with beauty and sensitivity." He winked. His newly installed hair was dyed a *Death-in-Venice* black. Suddenly he grew silent and left the table. Guy knew what was expected of him and after a few minutes he headed for the glory hole. He "betrayed" Édouard by imagining the toothless mouth on the other side of the door was Jacky's.

Édouard relaxed around Guy. They always spoke French; an old man appreciates slipping back into his native tongue. Guy was becoming more and more famous. He was in a widely seen music video lip-synching a song about a sharp-dressed man. He was photographed in black-tie getting out of a limousine with a dowager in a tiara; the photograph was an allusion to Weegee's photos of New York society people in the forties. It was for a men's cologne in *GQ* as a full page during the three months leading up to Christmas. American scents smelled like bubble gum and were all vile, Guy thought, except for Perry Ellis's. A "nose" in Paris had once told him that the best perfume was Ivoire by Balmain but it was priced too low. Guy used it as a room spray.

Guy was in commercials for A/X, Banana Republic, Barbados rum, and he did runway shows in Paris, Milan, and New York for Sonia Rykiel, Valentino, and YSL. He didn't have a perfect six-pack or the chest for a Tarzan poster or hooded eyes or pillowed lips—nothing distinctive, no trademark trait except his little jug ears—but he was a perfect size and his very anonymity meant that he could be used in runway shows one after another without drawing attention to his redundant appearances. Even though he didn't have rugged good looks or a hooked nose or a high-profile girlfriend like Elle Macpherson or Andie MacDowell, he did have his jug ears, small dark eyes, and a hairy chest, and everyone in the business thought he was surprisingly friendly and (America's highest and weirdest compliment) "down-to-earth," and *Forbes* listed him as the world's fourteenth most successful male model.

Édouard liked Guy's combination of celebrity and anonymity and gave him a large emerald ring for Christmas. Guy could look at it for hours, especially in the twilight, when it glowed darkly. He could imagine a wizard fondling it and gazing into its mysterious depths. People always remarked on it, which he liked. It was a lightning rod for their attention; better it than him. Not that he wasn't insecure if people ignored him, but that seldom happened. A drunk girl at a party told him he was of a different species, that surely someone as beautiful as he had lived an enchanted existence. Wasn't it correct in America to call a man "handsome" rather than "beautiful"?

A new illness called "gay cancer" or "gay-related immune deficiency (GRID)" broke out and wiped out a whole house of five on Fire Island. Guy decided not to renew his share for the following summer. He loved the rapturous, lyrical nights there, no care greater than the exact moment to leave the Botel and to migrate over to the Sandpiper or what to prepare for his housemates for dinner, something that they could all afford and that wouldn't run afoul of all their strange allergies and food dislikes. He never saw those guys off-island but he liked the way they all adored him—and he was amused by their "ass stories" (*histoires de cul*) told over morning coffee at noon about their exploits the night before, and he liked that Édouard stayed on his yacht and never visited the Octagon House where Guy lived.

But with this new disease it was safer to go to the Hamptons this summer (safer but more expensive and less fun). On Fire Island everyone was in a Speedo pulling a wagon of groceries across the bumpy boardwalk; you couldn't tell the houseboys from the bankers. But in South Hampton servants were in pickup trucks and their bosses in Jaguars and there was no place they mixed except sometimes on the beach. (But the help often weren't permitted to swim, or they preferred to get together in a coffeehouse on their day off.) Only very evolved employers had their chefs tooling around in shorts and answering to first names. ("What's for dinner, Jeff?" "Well, Dick, I found the most incredible spare ribs.")

One day Pierre-Georges came for a coffee at Guy's apartment in the Village after he'd had lunch at the Côte Basque with the baron.

"He wants you to participate in his S&M activities. As a sadist. I said that was completely against your gentle nature, though you did have a violent streak that I'd witnessed twice and that could be cultivated. But only if you felt completely secure as a man . . ."

"What on earth! You talk as if I were a child. I'm a grown man of thirty-two."

"Professionally you're twenty-three. But I like your outrage—we can build on that."

"Build?"

"Wait, wait," Pierre-Georges said, making a calming motion with both hands and looking perfectly calm himself, even smiling. "I told him that your building was up for sale and if you owned it and had two income properties . . ."

"What?"

"If you owned the whole building, you could rent out—"

"And what did he say?"

"He asked me to test the waters."

"He'd buy me the building and I'd switch his butt?"

"More than that and more than once."

"*Berk!*" (The sound for revulsion in French comic strips.)

Pierre-Georges let a long silence accumulate. He who was always voluble didn't mind showing his tacit impatience or disapproval.

At last Guy took a new tack: "You're adept at all things hard"—he used the English word "hard," the *h* suppressed, newly imported into French for sadomasochism—"but I know nothing of . . . all that. Would you tell me how it's organized?" They both liked the cool, cerebral tone of "organized." Normally Guy never asked questions. He didn't like to admit he didn't already know something. Like all French people he didn't say, "*Je ne sais pas*," but "*Je ne sais plus*" ("I no longer know").

The only thing that slightly irritated Pierre-Georges was the dismissive "all that" (*tout ça*). He said, "It's partly my fault you've reached your great age and are so naïve. I haven't wanted you to come across as a slut"—*une salope*—"especially now that

there's this new *saloperie* going around"—he meant gay cancer—
"but sadism"—and he laughed, surprised at his own thought—
"is bizarrely safe. You don't even have to touch the slave! And if
the slave is a very distinguished old man . . . who's very particular . . . and who's slowed down forcibly with age . . ."

Everything Pierre-Georges was saying set off a small deton-
ation in Guy's mind. Did disease specially spare distinguished
old men? Did it affect only riffraff who had problems of . . .
hygiene? Did a single exposure to it suffice (that would be too
unfair!), or was it cumulative, was it like Russian roulette, in
which only one chamber out of six was loaded but the odds of
being eliminated increased with each turn of the barrel?

"No touching?" Guy said. "But don't you have to penetrate
the victim?"

"Rarely. It's all mostly verbal menace and gestures of domina-
tion. It's verbal and mental, in fact."

"Convenient if true."

"Of course, you wouldn't be alone. The baron likes scenes,
orgies with a narrative. There'd be other young men there,
attractive ones, experienced."

Guy's thoughts, usually imperturbable, ricocheted now like
a panicked bird inside a closed room. "So," he said. "What's the
difference between me and a whore?" He swallowed. "Am I a
whore?"

"No more then every married woman. Or heir. They all
benefit from wealth they haven't earned. But whore, if you like.
The trick is to be a clever whore"—*le truc est d'etre une putain
rusée*. Pierre-Georges laughed his barking, unfunny laugh. "It
would be agreeable to own a house in Greenwich Village,
n'est-ce pas, and to be a rentier, especially in a profession like
yours with such a short shelf life, no?"

Guy reasoned with himself that night as he tossed and turned in bed, surely there was something pure about him; he'd never slept with someone as a brutal transaction. Then he turned the emerald ring around in the dark. He laughed at himself. It was true he hadn't directly negotiated for the jewel, but after he'd received the *petit cadeau* ("little gift," to use a whore's euphemism), he'd thrust himself through the glory hole for the first time. Why did he dream of more and more wealth? He had plenty, didn't he, which Pierre-Georges had invested for him? Maybe because he'd grown up poor, just spaghetti sometimes three nights in a row, never a franc to buy candy, always hand-me-down clothes, never enough to buy schoolbooks—that had seemed like reality to him. And now that someone wanted to take care of him, he was . . . grateful? Was that the word?

He switched on the light and picked up a copy of a novel by Alphonse Daudet that Pierre-Georges had given him, a book he couldn't get into, for some reason. It was old, he thought accusingly. From some other century. He didn't like old things. He closed the book.

All right, so he'd already acquiesced to the baron for one big gift—why not a bigger one?

He phoned Pierre-Georges and said, "I can't sleep. Would he buy me the building outright?" He looked at himself in the large wall mirror over the bed, one he'd positioned there to reflect his "pigginesses" (*cochonneries*). Of course, his hair was a mess, but he thought he looked pretty good, though his neck, still firm, was threatening to give way, like a dam after ten days of rain. Nothing visible yet, but he could just tell that that would be the first area of devastation. And his elbows were getting leathery.

He turned his head from left to right. Would he give that guy in the mirror a building?

He wasn't his own type.

"Yes," Pierre-Georges said, "I'm certain he'd let you sign the deed. It would all be done through lawyers so you wouldn't have any embarrassment."

"What would I wear?" Guy blurted.

"At the lawyers'? Your dark blue suit, the Armani."

"No, I mean, at the orgy."

"We could go to a shop on Christopher Street, where they'd fit you for black leather shorts—"

"*Berk!*"

"And a harness."

"I'm not a horse. And I thought I would be the master."

"That's what the master wears."

"Why?"

"That's like asking why English words are spelled the way they are. Because. Just because."

The line was silent with just Guy's audible breathing. "I hope I didn't wake you."

"No," Pierre-Georges said. "I was watching an old movie on television."

"Oh? Which one?" Guy and Pierre-Georges often watched movies at the same time, each one at home before his own television. Sometimes thirty minutes would go by without either of them saying anything beyond, "Isn't that weird? Is that a shovel he has in his hand? What is she doing? Is that a pancake?" Guy's English was better and he often filled Pierre-Georges in on the plot.

"Well," Guy said, "I've been thinking about my future. I'm thirty-two. Time I had some steady income."

"You have your Paris apartment rented out."

"For a pittance. No, tell the baron it's a yes."

"He wouldn't want it to sound like a transaction. He helps his protégé out, and then one night, spontaneously, the protégé explores his dark side in Édouard's dungeon, just because he wants to."

"Dungeon?"

"He has a dungeon on West Twenty-sixth Street, two rooms, quite spacious, really, with a Saint Edward's cross and everything."

"You've been there?"

"Yes. You'll see—it's all exciting and effortless."

"What if I can't get it up?" Guy wailed.

"That's of no importance if you're on the right end of a whip."

The building was transferred to Guy. He dressed up in his Armani suit and drove in the Mercedes down to the Woolworth Building near Wall Street and visited the very high-end lawyer. There were so many documents to sign, but at the end of it all he was given a copy of the deed. Guy's own lawyer, a balding bewildered man from the Zoli agency, looked it over and nodded. A nod for which Guy was paying a hundred dollars. But no matter. Pierre-Georges met them there for the signing. He, too, looked very elegant in his boxy Kenzo suit; the lapels were wide and his tie a silk the color of an old bruise. He invited Guy to a Christopher Street restaurant that was calm and empty, next to the Theater de Lys—and, on the other side, to the leather store.

Guy found it very exciting to have Pierre-Georges, the tailor, and a middle-aged clerk watching him as he stripped down in the back of the shop behind a blackout curtain. Guy got an erection from the bright spotlights, the man measuring him, the smell of the leather, the focus and intensity of their stares. He decided not to be embarrassed. The tailor pushed it gently, respectfully, to one side as if it were a familiar though awesome problem. Guy started to say to himself, "Cow-cow, chicken-chicken," his usual command for going soft, but he stayed hard. Outside on the street, Pierre-Georges, in an unusual gesture of warmth, put an arm around him and said, "You'll be just fine."

It wasn't more than five days later when Édouard phoned him in the afternoon and gave him the address on West Twenty-sixth. He said it wasn't the main entrance to the building, which was protected by a doorman, but a completely anonymous side door to the right with a buzzer and an intercom. "A woman will answer and you'll say you're there for Ed. That's what they call me: Ed. Tonight at eleven o'clock. I think you'll find it amusing."

A fat young woman with a synthetic shiny red nylon-looking pageboy, dressed in black stockings with red garters, a leather miniskirt, a tightly laced bodice from which spilled her large globular breasts, let him in. He did not find her very appetizing. Guy asked if there was a changing room. He had his new leathers in a gym bag. The louvered door in the hallway led to a changing room. "Don't leave your clothes in there." Then she said, "Ed's party is in there," and pointed to a heavy metal door, the sort Guy imagined was made to contain a fire.

Guy changed rapidly and looked in the mirror to check his hair and outfit. His legs looked skinny and white below the shorts, he feared. But overall he looked frightening—you wouldn't want to encounter *that* in a dark alley. He was a long way from Clermont-Ferrand.

He decided not to knock on the metal door and say, "Pardon," the way he'd been taught but to barge in like Genghis Khan, some big terrifying conqueror. Unfortunately he had his street clothes in the gym bag, which mitigated his sadistic allure.

He walked in and saw four tall men in chaps, asses exposed, standing together with their backs to him, almost as if they were at a *urinoir*. He put the bag down and drew closer and they were pissing on the baron, who was crouched on his knees, glorying in the rancid urine. He was wearing a strange leather full-length coat, open to expose his chest, belly, and pitiful little erection. The coat was very Wehrmacht. Guy hoped the liquid wouldn't cause a short in his hearing aids.

Guy knew not to say hello or greet his host. He pulled up beside the man farthest to the left. They seemed to have an inexhaustible supply of urine and they were painting Édouard's face and chest and belly with the liquid, which wasn't so yellow. Guy could see a dozen beer cans lined up on the ledge and he imagined that that was what was being recirculated so abundantly.

He was sure he'd be piss-shy, but he tugged his leather shorts down, and out flopped his tumescent dick. Édouard (he tried to think of him as "it," the piece-of-shit slave, as Pierre-Georges had taught him) crawled over to Guy; he was dripping and barking like a seal. Guy resorted to the usual French banalizing thought: *But it's completely normal*, he said to himself, though there was nothing normal about it. Guy was a good enough actor that he felt challenged by this new role. The other folks were muttering the same stupid words, "Yeah, now you're getting there, yeah, pig, now you're sucking that big uncut cock, go for it, piggy, yeah, you want that hot young piss, you know you want it . . ." Guy didn't dare say anything, with his accent and his ignorance of the right words; he'd be bound to say something like, "Yes, pig, that's truly excellent," and they would all laugh, evaporate, like vampires at dawn. He might say something funny. Pierre-Georges had told him humor was the great enemy of sadism. At the sound of the first laugh the whole dungeon would collapse in a puff and vanish.

The baron reached behind him and turned on a faucet that poured water directly onto the raw concrete floor. It flowed into a drain, an industrial-looking drain. No doubt the baron hoped the sound of water would sympathetically induce Guy to pee, but no such luck. He should have gulped three Diet Cokes before coming.

Guy wondered what the scenario was for tonight. Hadn't Pierre-Georges said the baron liked his orgies to have narratives? It seemed tonight the baron was a bad dog, who kept racing forward to bite his masters on the leg until they whipped him and drove him back into a kennel. The baron actually was uttering, "Gr-r-r," in an amateurish way that Guy found *attachant*; at least, mercifully, he was no longer begging for Guy's piss.

The other men were all of a type—tall, balding, skinny, pale, tattooed, almost as if they were vagrants who slept rough, smelling of old cigarettes and beer, their asses wrinkled and flat like deflated balloons but their dicks big and bridled with shiny cock rings. They all had nascent beards and one man, who looked as if he were in his forties, had a broken tooth. He was the only one wearing a motorcycle jacket and no shirt. His ribs were countable, his stomach flat as a drumhead, his chest stringy with sparse, long hairs.

The bad dog made a rush for Guy's calf and bit into it. It was painful and released enough adrenaline to power an angry outburst from Guy, who lashed the cur back into its kennel; a second later Guy wondered if he'd actually hurt Édouard and broken the skin, but there was no way to ask.

The dog bite hurt; he could see he was bleeding and he tried to remember if he had any runway dates this week where he had to wear shorts. (He didn't think so.)

Now that the dog had been sufficiently subdued, all the masters drew a tighter and tighter circle around it and forced it to suck them one after another as dogs will. Then the man with the broken tooth made the dog lie paws-out, faceup on the cement floor. He squatted over it and strained and shit in its mouth. Its mouth was a black hole and it was weeping and chewing. Guy knelt down to Édouard and Guy whispered with concern, "*Ça va, Monsieur le Baron?*"

2

"'*MONSIEUR LE BARON*'?" Pierre-Georges said angrily. "How did you know I said that last night?"

"Édouard phoned me. He was very irritated and disabused."

"I felt sorry for him. I was worried about him."

"So he said," Pierre-Georges said acidly. "The scales fell from his eyes and he no longer thinks you're a real man but some sort of mama's boy."

"I knew it was a blunder but I felt genuine compassion for my friend—"

"A blunder? I'll say. That's what he wanted; he'd paid two hundred dollars to each of those types. Since his childhood, he told me he's dreamed of being disciplined as a bad dog and then forced to eat a turd—*un étron*."

"No one has that fantasy. Little boys want to be cowboys or fireman—no one wants to be a bad dog forced to eat shit. Not even a Belgian baron."

"*Chacun à son goût*," Pierre-Georges said philosophically.

"What should I do when I see him the next time?" Guy asked. "How should I act?"

"It's finished. He won't bother you again. No more intimate or name-day parties. No more amazing gifts. You might be invited as an extra on a crowded stage if you're lucky."

"But we're friends!" Guy objected.

"Oh, sure. Do you think he invites you because he likes your scintillating conversation about the ups and downs of the rag trade? Do you think he has a burning interest in the rag trade?"

"We have other subjects, serious subjects."

"I forgot: Your sad childhood. Your Buddhist chants. No, it's finished."

Guy thought for a while. "He talked about his sad childhood, too."

Pierre-Georges snapped, "The only thing sad about his childhood was that he couldn't convince any of the footmen to shit in his mouth." Pierre-Georges was warming up to his role as the disabuser. He'd come over to Guy's for the emergency. He smiled for the first time today. He opened a white paper bag and pulled out a croissant, found a plate in the cupboard, and ate it. As Guy's manager he of course didn't offer him anything to eat; Guy's breakfast was always a cup of black coffee, which he was sipping now while looking sheepish.

After a solitary lunch (a third of a chicken salad at the Front Porch, a neighborhood restaurant where he liked the campy waiter), Guy felt absolved and talked himself into a storm of irritation. He was tired of feeling foolish for a simple act of human kindness. He'd been brought up by a sainted mother. Was it his fault that he couldn't despise a kind old man, even someone as deeply perverted and depraved as Édouard? Guy imagined most aristocrats were decadent. He was proud of his humble origins. His instincts were still unimpaired. A decade in fashion hadn't spoiled him. He was still a good person, a simple boy of the people from Clermont-Ferrand and, thank god, not a shit-eating Belgian. He tried to feel sorry for Édouard, for making a mess out of his life.

He decided he'd invite Édouard to dinner. He knew how to cook eel in green sauce, which Édouard loved. And Guy would wear his leather harness and shorts and have *menottes*, cuff links—no, handcuffs!—dangling on his left side. After a bottle of Gewürztraminer, the baron would end up on his knees begging for it. He'd always been fond of Édouard, who'd been so kind to him, who'd bought him this house, who'd celebrated his name day. He was strange, but then they'd had some good conversations.

But when he phoned Édouard the butler told him once, then twice, that *"Monsieur le Baron est sorti"*—not at home. He decided to phone at eight A.M. before the butler, who'd never liked him, would have arrived and he'd get the cook, who adored him. But Marguerite for some reason was very cold, too, and told him *"Monsieur le Baron est sorti."*

"Ça va, Marguerite?" he asked cheerfully.

"Ça va, Monsieur Guy. Et vous-même?" She'd said *tu* to him for ages, and Guy felt rebuffed. He said, "I'll call back," and she said nothing. He hung up.

A week went by. At last Guy received a creamy envelope embossed with the baron's coat of arms (two books surrounding a lion and the words MON PLAISIR), inviting him to a large reception honoring the Belgian king's birthday with the note, "Business attire." Oh, it would be a straight evening, a champagne reception for dozens of business associates and their wives. No opportunity to flaunt his leathers there!

He made sure he'd look better than everyone else and took a long time with his toilette. His Armani suit, his lace-up Churches, his classic white shirt, and the solid maroon silk tie—and, of course, the emerald. He felt sure the baron would melt when he saw the emerald. It would bring back so many memories.

But the party was a rout, all Belgians (mostly speaking Flemish), toasting the king with American champagne, none of the usual crowd of hot guys, nothing to eat except pretzels (which for some reason the baron thought elegant), several awkward conversations with slow-talking businessmen who wanted to find out how Guy knew the baron and did he work for one of his suppliers, then a sudden general departure at eight engineered by the hateful, tight-lipped butler (the invitation had specified six to eight), and Guy had only caught a glimpse of Édouard, and when he tried to talk to him, the baron had brought forward a fat man in a sports jacket and said, "Oh, good, you two can speak English. Fred, Guy," and the baron rushed off to kiss an old woman's hand as she entered the room. Guy waved at Walt, who pretended he didn't see him.

It turned out this Fred was a very nice man, not a Belgian, not even linked to the baron's brewery, like all the others, but a film producer from Hollywood who invited Guy out to dinner. They went to Casey's, a place in the Village, all candles and mirrors, which Guy had walked past a million times but never entered, though it was only four blocks away from where he lived. After the cold douche of the baron's reception (he hadn't even said goodbye as Guy was being ushered out in the general stampede), this Fred's kindness and obvious interest and openness was a balm. Guy felt he'd been slapped in the face and looked at the mirror almost expecting a red hand mark on his cheek, but no, his skin was perfect. Never had Guy been insulted like that, but was the baron, he wondered, freezing him out for his thoughtless kindness? Would he give Guy a second chance? Maybe he was just provoking Guy, hoping to be punished later. (Guy had heard masochists were good at needling their tops.)

At first Guy didn't say much, nor did he have to. Fred wasn't exactly a braggart, but he was quick to fill Guy in on his life and work.

"Where are you from?" He'd learned that was the standard question in America, not an impertinence, as it would be in France.

"Oregon."

"What kind of films do you make?"

"Blaxploitation."

"Pardon?"

"Movies for black audiences."

"Oh," Guy said, losing interest.

"It's mostly for export. Not something we'd go see, but they love it in Accra."

"What are they about?"

"Get whitey."

"Who's Weddy?"

"Where are you from?"

"Paris."

"What brings you to these shores?"

"Work. I'm a model."

"Hands? You have beautiful hands." Fred smiled.

Guy looked at his hands as if he'd forgotten them. "Oh, really? Do you like my hands?" Did he say hands because he couldn't think of anything else nice to say? Then he was afraid of thinking like an airhead model and asked, "How do you know Édouard?"

"We have the same taste in boys," Fred said, lifting his eyebrows significantly.

"You met in some dungeon?"

"Oh, no, I'm a romantic. I like to kiss. I'm looking for a partner."

"A business partner? For a new African film?" Guy wasn't paying attention—there were too many mirrors.

"No, a partner in love. A life partner. Someone to share my life with. You see, I just came out."

"Really? What did you do . . . before?" The unfamiliarity of the topic made him focus for a minute and to raise his hand to his forehead to block out his own multiplied reflections. He couldn't concentrate in front of so many mirrors.

"I was married. Three kids. You won't believe this, but two grandchildren," and he pulled out his wallet to show their pictures.

Guy didn't like children but he smiled, not with tenderness at the pictures but out of politeness. "Was it a hard transition?" Guy asked sympathetically. His main course, which Americans for some reason called an entrée, arrived; it was beef Wellington, rare and in a crust that for once wasn't soggy. He vowed to eat only half of it.

"Coming out?" Fred was tucking into his dish, which was flounder stuffed with crabmeat and shrimp—Guy should have taken that, it would have been lighter. Oh, well, nothing but yogurt for lunch tomorrow. Damn, there was his reflection again. He looked very young in candlelight, he thought, though he usually blew candles out, they hurt his eyes. Like all Frenchmen he preferred a well-lit restaurant and no background music.

"Yes, it was agonizing, but it had to be done." Fred made it sound like pulling an infected tooth.

Guy realized with a start it was his turn to say something. "Was your wife very hurt?"

"Ceil?" Wasn't a seal an animal, a *phoque*? But then Guy realized it must be short for Celia. "Angry? Livid. Ceil had thought for years she must not be desirable, that was why I was shunning her, but when she realized I was gay from the get-go, boy, was she pissed, I'd condemned her to a loveless marriage, ruining the best years of her life."

"But you gave her children—and grandchildren," Guy reminded him, "and probably a nice house."

"A showplace. But she has that famished look of a woman that hasn't been touched in years—you know the look."

Guy wasn't sure he did know the look.

Fred said, "And to come out at sixty-three—okay, sixty-six—is no joke. If you're a romantic and looking for love." Fred expected Guy to say something—but what?

Guy pointed out, "There are plenty of other available gay men in their sixties."

"Nah," Fred said, and actually shuddered as if he'd seen a ghost. "Older guys have too much emotional baggage. They've already lived their lives. I'm only just starting out on mine. I want another youngster, if that makes sense."

"Perfectly," Guy said, though he didn't quite understand.

"A young, handsome guy—a masculine, muscular one. *Masc-musc*, as we say in L.A."

Guy wondered if he qualified, though he wasn't at all attracted to Fred. *The minute someone announces a casting call*, Guy thought ruefully, *I always wonder if I'll get the part.*

Fred was on his third martini. "All my life I've been staring at those guys, wanting them, never daring to talk to them, volunteering to coach Little League—"

Little League. *Oh, dear*, Guy thought, *isn't that children?*

"Going down to the beach and staring at the surfers. Say, we've got to get you out to L.A. for some screen tests."

"Aren't I the wrong color for your films?"

Fred laughed. "Put a little slap on you. Seriously, I'm co-producing a wonderful art-house movie about a schizophrenic who falls for an anorexic."

"Schizophrenic? So you thought of me?"

"I can't stop thinking of you," Fred said in a lower, sexy voice. "No, the schizophrenic's confidant, a pastry chef."

"And this pastry chef is French?"

"Why not? We need some textures."

"Do you have a director?"

Fred sat up in his chair. "We haven't signed anyone yet, but this is such a high-end property we're talking to some of the European and experimental guys in the business."

"I'm not sure I'm much of an actor." Guy flashed on his recent debacle in the dungeon.

After dinner Fred invited Guy up to his place in a new building overlooking Washington Square.

"I thought you lived in Los Angeles."

"I'm bicoastal," Fred said suggestively. "Nah, I was born in Brooklyn. I need New York the way a fish needs air."

Guy tried to work that one out.

The apartment, which was a dusty neglected penthouse with dead plants and a view of the graffiti-covered Washington Square arch and the seething, dangerous park beyond it, was glitzy-Oriental, with three gilt life-sized statues of the meditating Buddha at the entrance, low black-lacquered tables with pagoda trim, blood-red silk couches with heavy tassel pulls, a spotlit abstraction that some decorator had obviously chosen for the color, a terrazzo floor with glitter buried into it delineating—oh, a dragon lounging on the Great Wall of China. "I'm a sort of Buddhist myself," Guy said, to be agreeable in case the décor was an expression of Fred's beliefs rather then his tastes.

"This is something Ceil concocted with that pansy decorator of hers—I'm going to clear it all out and put in something simple and modern and classic, maybe with a Pompeian motif or a Moorish."

"Don't be too hasty," Guy advised.

"Maybe I'll go all antique. Édouard has that handsome young antique dealer he's so crazy about. What a body that kid has! Gr-r-r . . ." and he made the sound of an angry dog, which reminded Guy uncomfortably of Édouard's excesses.

"I haven't met him," Guy said coolly.

"Really? Édouard's besotted with him. He's clearing out all that boring-ass white furniture of his and going all Chippendale or something, but I'll bet you it's just so he can be with young Will, who's going to supply him with lots of priceless lumber with a fifty percent markup, you can bet."

That was quick, Guy thought, panicking to think he'd been replaced.

Fred turned a dial and lowered the lights. "It's nice to see the city from here, if you can glimpse it between all those goddamn Buddhas. Sorry," he said.

"I'm just the chanting kind of Buddhist," Guy hastened to say, "not the begging-bowl kind." Fred had refreshed their drinks and now was sitting next to Guy. He said, "Isn't that the kind where you chant all day for things you want? I had a friend who chanted who was bi and kept by rich men and women one at a time. He chanted for a Rolls and got it. He said the only disadvantage of being a live-in gigolo is that you have to be willing to play canasta at three A.M. with some ancient insomniac lady."

"I wouldn't know," Guy was quick to say.

"But what are you chanting for?"

"A beach house in Fire Island Pines."

Fred, who'd been leaning forward, now sat back. "Whoa! I'm not that rich. I'm a millionaire, but a very minor millionaire," and he held his finger and thumb apart to indicate two inches.

Guy laughed. "But I wasn't asking you for anything. That's what I chant for. I pray to Amida, not to you." But after Guy went to the toilet he said he was tired, he had an early call, and he thanked Fred, who looked devastated.

"You can't just walk out of my life like that."

They exchanged phone numbers, but when Fred tried to line him up for lunch or dinner or a movie, Guy said, "I don't have my schedule yet for this week. It would be unfair to you to make a date and then have to break it."

"Don't French people kiss each other goodbye on two cheeks?"

"Fathers and sons. When you get the Légion d'honneur. Silly Parisian queens and society people."

While Fred was pondering this, Guy shook hands, thanked him, and left.

Guy needed some time alone to absorb how the baron had turned on him. All that talk about how they were soul mates, about how Guy had a rare gift for transcending nationality, class, age. Had he said class? Did that mean he thought Guy was beneath him, low-class? Pierre-Georges had insinuated he, Guy, was a bore, with just his looks to offer. Was he a bore?

On his way home he cruised a hot kid who turned out to be a nineteen-year-old dancer named Vladimir. Guy took him home, gave him a drink, and fucked him. *Enough old men!* Guy told himself. But after the adoring, rapturous Vladimir had left ("Sorry, I can't sleep with another person in bed," Guy had said drily), he still felt bruised and insulted.

He wondered the next morning if Édouard would phone him, but Vlad and Fred did. He agreed to have a quick lunch with Fred, who was in some sort of golfing clothes minus the cleats.

"I couldn't sleep all night," Fred said. "I worried that I'd said something wrong, that I'd turned you off somehow."

"Not at all," Guy said, turning on a thousand-watt smile. He smiled like that when he wanted to appear inaccessible. "I had a delightful evening."

"Really? You're not bullshitting me? Because, honestly, I'm completely dazzled by you." He sighed heavily and ran a hand across his baldpate. "Coming out in your sixties is no joke. I mean, you're so vulnerable. It's like being a pimply fifteen-year-old all over again. I'm a whizz at picking up birds." (*Oh, he means women.*) "Birds are easy, at least in L.A., if you have a nice car and you say you're a producer. They're all like Lana Turner waiting to be discovered at that drugstore." (Guy didn't get the reference, but he thought he'd heard of that old actress).

"I guess you must be quite the stud," Guy said, and wondered if Fred would detect the irony. From his decade in Paris, Guy had learned how to insult people sweetly.

But Fred didn't pick up on the irony. "I'm not saying that. It's just that wealth and influence count more with women than they do with men. You see, men want to be the top dog, not attract him."

Dogs again, Guy thought. "It must have been a relief to come out finally."

"Yes and no. I was in terrible shape. I had to go on a diet and lose fifty pounds. Now I go to the gym three hours every day and my personal trainer is a real demon. Then"—here he dropped his voice—"I'm only telling you this 'cause I trust you—I had a face-lift." He showed him the scars behind his ears. There were whiskers growing there—some of the beard skin had been tucked back there. "That's why I look so young."

"Oh, that's why," Guy said.

"And I had liposuction—they boiled down ten pounds of gut fat. I had to wear a corset for a month. I'm having hair implants, but boy, are those painful. I had my eyebrows and my ears lasered clean of hair. I had the age spots burned off my hands with an acetylene torch. When the scabs fall off, your hands are white."

"In French," Guy said, "we call those spots cemetery flowers."

"Gross. I had my elbows sanded. My teeth are all new." He smiled to show his new teeth.

"Is it worth it?" Guy asked.

"I want to be an A-list gay. I want people to say, 'Who's that young stud?'"

Guy didn't know what to say, so he just smiled. The campy waiter stopped by to chat for a few minutes; they were the last lunch customers. Talking as two masculine men with one who was so flamboyant formed a kind of bond, and after the waiter tripped off, Fred said, "I feel really good with you. You know how to make a guy feel good. I don't know why I trust you."

Guy looked at his own beautiful Beaume & Mercier watch, which he'd bought at duty-free at Charles de Gaulle, and exclaimed, "I've got to be running." He was trying to head Fred off from making an embarrassing avowal.

"Run, run," Fred said in a friendly way, though the color drained from his face and his eyes went extinct.

When Guy called Pierre-Georges to relate all his recent

news, Pierre-Georges said to him, "You see, Americans aren't realistic like us, even the old: They want to be loved for themselves. They want to be young. They don't recognize they have to have something to offer—money or power or a title."

"Would you check this guy out—Fred Hampton—and see if he's legitimate?"

The next night Fred invited Guy out to a musical (Guy despised musicals, but didn't say anything) and to dinner in a Russian restaurant complete with blinis and caviar, lamb shashlik on skewers, and a caterwauling baritone who accompanied himself approximately on the piano. ("Memories light the corners of my mind . . .") Fred drank quite a bit of one of the twenty-three kinds of vodkas on offer. (He chose bison grass, whatever that was.) "So tell me—gosh, you're handsome! What's the secret of being a successful male model, other than being fabulously good-looking?"

Guy decided to ignore the compliment and to answer the question seriously. "It's like acting—knowing how you look to other people." He'd thought about this and talked about it with Lucie. "Most people can't see themselves from the camera's—or the audience's—point of view. They just do what feels natural. They don't know how they look, how they're coming across."

"For example?" *Anglo-Saxons*, Guy thought, *always want examples. So lowering. They're incapable of thinking abstractly.*

"Bad actors, if they want to look anxious, wave their arms a lot, which feels right but looks absurd."

"And models?"

"You might hold up your hand to suggest protest or resistance, but an open hand thrust forward is the size of a head—it feels right but it looks wrong. A hand should never be seen except in profile."

"How interesting," Fred said, looking uninterested. *He wants to talk only about his love for me.* "Go on."

"A model selling a new typewriter might look directly at the camera, especially if he's been told he has beautiful eyes."

"You have beautiful eyes," Fred said sadly, possibly anticipating Guy's indifference.

"But a model, if he's selling a product, should look at *it*, never the camera." Suddenly Guy felt shocked by the childish insistence in his voice and disheartened by how trivial the knowledge of his "craft" sounded. For different reasons both men were sad, and they lapsed into silence.

Suddenly Fred brightened and said, "You know, that house on Fire Island you keep mentioning?"

"That I'm chanting for," Guy corrected, smiling.

"I think we should go out there this Sunday now that it's getting warmer. I've lined up a real estate agent who could show us some houses." Fred smiled. "I wouldn't want you to chant in vain. We can stay over Sunday night."

When Guy told Pierre-Georges that night his news over the phone, Pierre-Georges exclaimed, "You see! I've always claimed you get more if you're a man by not putting out. Women succeed by sleeping with men, but men do better by not sleeping with them."

"Have you always said that?" Guy said, teasing him. "I've never done anything through calculation. I just chant."

"She just chants—Little Miss Innocent."

"It would be nice to have a house right on the beach. Wake up at noon, pull back the blackout curtains, open the glass doors, cross the dunes . . . just wear a smile and a Jantzen."

"That dates you!"

"You're right. I wish we could just wash our brains clean of everything from the past. What are you eating?"

"White beans and sardines and chervil."

"I love that! But it's better with red peppercorns."

Lucie came by to show off her new burnt-orange sweater, which stretched attractively across her tits and looked like a radiant mango against her light brown skin. She twirled around to show it off but she was so little an exhibitionist that she ran out of steam after a half turn and deflated self-consciously onto the couch.

"Look, I've only got ten minutes," Guy said, "before I go off for a Banana Republic go-see way uptown, but I want to talk about something with you. Then I have a Bacardi rum shoot midtown."

"Fine," she said. "Tell me." He was never this serious and she felt flattered and hoped to be worthy of his confidence.

"This chanting thing is sort of creepy."

"How so?" She chanted, too, and always defended Buddhism.

"Just for fun, I was chanting for a beach house in the Pines, and now this old guy seems to want to offer me one."

"Bravo!"

"Do you think I'm just a big whore?"

"None of us is getting any younger." She reoriented herself and said, "Americans are always so cheap. They always want to split the bill. Of course, the younger girl models never pay for anything, but they have to go out with horrible Russian gangsters. You're the only one who gets an apartment"—she looked around—"or a house out of the deal. How do you do it?"

"Chanting."

"I've been chanting for a Cadillac convertible and I'm still taking the IRT."

They laughed. Guy took her hand between both of his. She was surprised by the gesture. "Do you think I've become a gold digger? I've already got plenty of money saved up. But I can't stop myself."

"Look, it's nothing you're doing. You're gorgeous—that's your only fault."

Guy decided to believe her. It was simpler.

But what was he going to do Sunday night when Fred would want to share his bed? He could always say he had a big job Monday early, that he was doing a whole shoot for Perry Ellis.

It was a cool March day in the Pines as they crossed the bay in a powerboat Fred had hired in advance. (The ferry wasn't running yet.) Big gray clouds chased one another like fat, playful puppies in a pet store window, except the enclosure was immense, all of outdoors. It was fairly cool and there was a stinging hint of rain in the air, what the French call "spit" (*crachin*). Fred squinted at the wind and rain reproachfully, as if it were conspiring to ruin their day, but Guy said, "I love it. It reminds me of Brittany."

They were shown a gray-shingled house from the 1950s a block from the beach with a rotting wood staircase. Inside, the house smelled of kerosene and septic tank. "Did some old couple just live here and die?" Guy asked.

"How much does this cost?" Fred asked, raising and lowering his jacket zipper nervously.

The agent—a prematurely tanned middle-aged man—smiled and held out his hands jokily, miming as if he were trying to juggle several balls or answer both questions at once. "Yes! An old couple lived here. They haven't died but they need the cash. Their winter house is in Sayville. This is a fixer-upper; that's why it's only a million and a half."

"Only!" Fred shouted. "It's run-down, it's off the beach; even fixed up, the rooms are too small. And you can't get flood or hurricane insurance out here, you told me that yourself." The agent shrugged and Fred zipped his blue windbreaker shut so it held his stomach as in a sling. He walked out on the stairs and flicked open his chrome lighter, cupped the flame, and lit a Camel, squinting into the blowback. His jaw muscles were working; maybe he hadn't expected such high prices.

Next they saw an architect's house right on the dunes with glass doors and turrets and a great room two stories high, but a screen door was banging in the wind, the rubber insulation around the kitchen windows was rotting, and the parquet floor was buckling. "How much is this one?" Fred asked.

"Just three million. You'd pay that much for an empty lot in this location."

"We'll take it," Guy called out, then looked at Fred and said, "Right, Daddy?" Then he bent over laughing at his little joke.

Fred smiled a sour little smile.

As they walked along Atlantic, they battled a cold wind, which raised goose bumps on their legs. They were both in shorts. "I know some of these kids get into calling their older boyfriends 'Daddy,' but I think that's sick." Fred was holding on to Guy as if to keep him warm and grounded in the wind. He had a strong arm across Guy's back and was whispering into his ear, "I don't want to be anyone's daddy. I already have three kids and two grandchildren—you'd never guess it, would you?"

"No, you don't seem the type." But then Guy realized Fred was referring to his youthfulness, not his paternal image. "You look too young."

Fred brightened. "I do? Honest?"

"Honest," Guy echoed, feeling depressed.

Because he'd inadvertently cooperated with Fred's sense that he was an A-list gay, Guy went to bed with him that night in the suite he'd rented in some Potemkin-village "palace" an old queen had pieced together according to her fantasies of luxury and history. It was all falling apart, but at first glance it did seem baronial-Liberace, especially compared to the humble dwellings that surrounded it, with names like "Lickety Split" and "Atta Gurl." It was all gray and white like some comic-book version of a stately home, except inside it smelled of Kools and roach spray and the potted ferns were turning brown. The "velvet" bedspread was some flimsy synthetic that clung to their bodies and didn't breathe.

They sat down to a big porterhouse steak, creamed spinach, and a quart of sour red wine, all topped off with a brandy alexander pie in a graham cracker crust. Their "romantic table" was positioned under a dusty chandelier missing lusters. The whole place felt dirty, greasy. Guy had swilled three Rusty Nails over shaved ice and then willingly, drunkenly presented Fred with his asshole, with a full-sized replica of the David in the corner, apparently carved out of soap, its penis no more erect than Fred's. But what Fred lacked in turgidity he made up for in passionate utterance. "I'm the luckiest man in the world," he mumbled into Guy's crotch.

It was all over in five minutes and Guy was drunk enough to sleep through Fred's scary-sounding roller-coaster snores—his chain-saw breathing, then his disturbingly long silences and his sudden, panicked gasps.

They woke up early and Guy hurried to take his shower and dress before Fred began with another blowjob, this one with halitosis. In fact, Guy hurried off to the breakfast nook with its goblin-and-leprechaun motif for a first cup of coffee and a squishy croissant. Fred looked reproachful and slightly uncertain.

They saw three more houses before heading back to New York; Fred decided to rent a new house right on the beach—a cool $60,000 for the four-month season. Guy said, "I'm sure you could buy a house somewhere for that sum."

"But it wouldn't be the Pines," Fred pointed out, "and no one would visit. Not even you."

Guy was impressed by his take-charge attitude; he hadn't seen that side before.

3

F RED BOUGHT THE house after they'd road-tested it for the summer. Guy, following Pierre-Georges's advice, hadn't put out to Fred once after that one drunken night, and Guy's indifference or coldness, though he was always scrupulously polite, had brought Fred to his knees. Maybe Fred was so much in love because he was used to women caving before his assaults, in particular starlets and cute unpaid interns, but Guy was a man, French, well paid, not striving to get into the movies. Guy was an A-list gay, young, buffed, a head-turner, everything Fred wanted to be. Although Guy didn't do drugs very often, most of the youngsters hanging around their pool did, and when stoned they weren't exactly interesting but strangely tender and considerate. It was as if these beautiful, fit boys, usually so wary and disdainful, suddenly shed a constricting shell when they were stoned and became both vulnerable and expansive, capable of looking with humanity and genuine curiosity at a much older man, normally a pariah. A couple of times some A-listers, who were high, had even started making out with Fred, but he didn't dare go all the way with them in case that would suggest to Guy that he, Fred, wasn't single-minded in his devotion.

Pierre-Georges had researched Fred and called up with a full report: "First of all, Hampton isn't his real last name. It's Gershowitz. Before he became a movie producer he owned a chain of shoe stores in malls up and down the East Coast. His wife is the daughter of the smoked salmon king of the Bronx. He's made forty-seven movies. He's declared bankruptcy twice. That's all I could find."

In the morning Fred would get up early, shave, and shower, and slip into bed beside Guy; the young man would permit that much. Fred would then force himself to go on long walks to Water Island with his red setter, Sandy. Anything rather than to lie with a hard-on wide awake beside Guy. A gay friend of Fred's from college days, someone he'd never known well but now confided in when they re-met on Fire Island, asked him after he recounted the whole saga with Guy, "But what do you love about him? What's so great about him except he's handsome, and French, and sought after?"

They walked in silence for a minute along the beach, both of them sort of boxy and chunky in their loose trunks, but handsome, with worn, seasoned faces. "You know what I think?" the guy, who was named Vito, said. "I think you're having problems coming out. I've seen that before."

"No, I'm not. I've left Ceil, the kids are furious with me—"

"Yeah, but a lot of guys, when they're coming out, keep clinging to the first man in their lives, the more unavailable the better. That way they can say to themselves two things—'It's not that I'm gay, it's just that I love Guy,' and the other thing, 'Oh, if only Guy loved me I'd be gay, but he doesn't.'"

"That's a low blow," Fred said, scuffing his feet in the sand, hoping the abrasion might wear away the calluses on his heels. He wasn't really paying attention, but he didn't like the sound of Guy not being in love with him. Guy was so "binding," to use a word his shrink had introduced only last week, precisely because he was so mysterious. Maybe that was just the famous French discretion, the don't-ask-don't-tell of those fellows. (Guy had mentioned that.)

Fred looked over at Vito. He didn't like to be seen with an old guy—okay, someone his own age, but Fred had just lost twenty years with all his surgery, yet if he hung out with Vito people might start noticing his leathery elbows and his too-perfect replacement teeth. No one was up yet, however, at this hour. They had the beach to themselves and Fred felt safe.

"But what's so great about Guy?" Vito persisted.

"He's fresh, young, unspoiled. He makes me feel young."

"You look older with that face-lift and tummy tuck and those skinny legs and those hair plugs and that harsh black dye."

"Do you think you look so great, with that bald head and big belly? It's hard to believe you're the same age as I am. Guy couldn't believe it when I told him. You've really let yourself go."

"Personally, I like a face that's not so lifted it can't still smile. A natural man's face. Guy's just humoring you—he's a gold digger."

Fred thought about what he loved in Guy. Guy was beautiful. Guy was classy. Guy was sophisticated. Guy was kind.

Was he bright, inquisitive? Guy could speak two languages and he'd lived here—what did he say?—only two years, and for someone in his early twenties he'd really boned up on old pop songs and old movies, though, like most foreigners, Fred guessed, Guy didn't know anything about old TV shows except *Colombo*, which they saw in France, for some reason.

Was he really a gold digger? He made a fortune out of modeling. He didn't need anyone else's money.

When it came down to it, Fred had to admit he liked being seen with Guy, and Guy always leaned on his shoulder in public and whispered in his ear—well, it was nice to have some arm candy like Guy around. It was good for his image. Whereas a companion like Vito was bad for business—it was like an old whore walking an old dog, it led to invidious comparisons.

Fred suddenly announced he was going to jog and he took off running with his dog down the beach. What if some early riser in one of these houses had been watching them through binoculars?

Guy liked Fred around because his presence meant he wasn't tempted to sleep with any of these hot boys hanging around the pool. This new gay cancer was dangerous—four more of Guy's friends were dying. Guy didn't want to sleep with Fred, though he didn't mind if Fred slipped in beside him in bed for an hour at dawn. One time he'd awakened at midnight to see Fred with a flashlight looking at Guy's cock. Guy was sleeping on his stomach as he usually did. Fred was pushing the mattress down at Guy's crotch level and kneeling and studying his penis in the soft light. Guy shouted and sat upright and ordered Fred out. They never discussed it and it never happened again, but Fred was sheepish and silent for a day and he bought four bottles of Cristal for the boys around the pool.

When he told Pierre-Georges about it that afternoon during their daily phone call, Pierre-Georges said he found that "disgusting."

After Labor Day, Guy was due to go to Paris and Milan for work. Fred was sad, especially since he'd not been able to secure a trip with him or plans of any sort to be together. Guy was also beginning to see a young man, Andrés, who was a Ph.D. student of thirty at Rutgers, a Colombian he'd met on the beach. Andrés was hanging around the pool for hours and often stayed for lunch or dinner. Fred had hired a full-time Sri Lankan cook named Nili, who lived in the maid's room with his wife and four small children. The family stayed out of the way, though they probably had the run of the house when no one was around. They were all a bit too servile for Fire Island, but at least they no longer bowed or performed that namaste thing.

Guy and Andrés spent hours by the pool or on the couch looking through expensive art books Guy had bought for Andrés. He was getting a doctorate in art history, something to do with that fraud Dalí. Andrés had a soft breathy way of talking. They seemed smitten with each other, and more than once Fred had seen a big erection in Andrés's green Speedo as he stared at Guy. Fred had never suggested Guy take a vow of chastity or fidelity; he didn't need to. He knew Guy was scared shitless of this gay cancer thing as long as it lasted, maybe another year. Fred knew that if Guy hadn't been so bored by the Hamptons he would have never dared to come back to Fire Island.

What could Fred do to secure his future with Guy? If he bought the house, they would at least have that in common, and Guy wouldn't be able to exclude him, Fred, from a place he'd paid for. But he couldn't really afford it, not if he was going to produce that new hip-hop film in the coming year. And then Ceil was taking him to the cleaners. He didn't want to be forced to declare bankruptcy again. Fred could sell the New York apartment and rent a studio, but that didn't make sense. Guy might despise him if he saw how abject or poor he'd become. Why buy a showplace on the beach for a kid you've only fucked once?

He watched Guy and Andrés flirting with each other from deck chairs around the pool, Andrés's green Speedo always filled with an erection no matter how lofty the talk about surrealism might get to be. They were both dark and hairy, though Guy had those small intense eyes like bullet holes drilled through a sheet and Andrés had large green eyes and a smile that was beguiling but slightly tarnished and a dime-sized bald spot. Andrés, though Colombian, could speak some French (his parents were both profs in Medillín and his mother taught French and Italian), and when they were murmuring together they leaned in to each other until their bodies almost touched.

The Elvis Presley look-alike thug stopped by for a free drink. His body was white and hairless and out of shape, but he had an unusual degree of confidence and he zeroed right in on Fred. His name was Gerritt, for some unlikely reason, and he sat next to Fred on the deck and began to feel himself up in his canary-yellow bikini. Fred's eyes kept darting back and forth from Guy and Andrés on the other side of the pool, laughing together with obscene complacency, and the rapidly growing anaconda in Gerritt's bikini. Gerritt said, "Neat tattoo," but then he realized he was staring at burst blue veins on Fred's arm and looked away. Gerritt sipped a doobie that some hanger-on had assembled and leaned in and whispered with his gin-soaked breath, "I'd fuck you for two hundred bucks." Fred didn't say anything, but he just wipered his hand in a signal suggesting erasure or "not for me." He was offended that Gerritt assumed he had to pay for it. Gerritt got up out of the deck chair with some difficulty and stumbled off drunkenly with not so much as a "so long," headed for the Meat Rack, no doubt, and an afternoon freebie with a young size queen. (What was the saying, there were two kinds of gays—size queens and liars?) Fred couldn't help reflecting that he could get laid cheap with any of these fellows around the pool—cheap or gratis, since several of them wanted to be in the movies.

That night Fred got sloppy drunk on vodka and tonic and headed for the Meat Rack. He loved (as one loves slow, sad music) the sound of the surf pounding on the sand, the feel of the salty wind blowing through his clothes, and the look of men darting through the low bushes and pausing to glance back. Fred guessed he must look good in his tight jeans and plain white T-shirt, which turned his new pectorals into bluish, glowing dry-ice mounds. He was in such despair as he mentally pictured Guy and Andrés nodding and laughing together, Andrés shamelessly displaying the bend sinister of his hard-on. And then that Gerritt insinuating that Fred was so obviously a john!

Fred was drunk and stumbling through the sand down unmarked little paths. Next thing he knew, he was in the big warm embrace of a giant in a scratchy wool shirt who put a yard of tongue down Fred's throat, and then they were groping each other. Fred needed his hands and kisses but worried they might belong to a B-list man past his prime, but then the man turned him around and inserted a wet finger followed by a slick prick into his ass. A few thrusts later and the man had squirted, heaved a sigh, pulled out, and disappeared into the brush.

Fred sobered and had the panicky thought: *I've just signed up for a death sentence in exchange for five dirty minutes in the dark with a stranger who wasn't even hung.*

The next day Fred felt lonely, humiliated, and deeply repentant. Although Guy didn't know anything about his visit to the

Meat Rack, Fred was as guilt-ridden as if his foolish submission had been thoroughly documented on film. Without thinking it out, he made an appointment with the real estate agent. As he walked to his office at the harbor on a late August day that was sultry and windless, past houses that for the moment were for the most part deserted (it was Wednesday and the garbage was smelling foul in the heat—it wouldn't be collected till Friday), he wondered if this was a terrible idea. He couldn't really afford it and his flushed face burned with shame and anxiety.

It was all over in five minutes. He bought the house and wrote out a check for a down payment of $250,000.

Just as Guy was about to leave the Pines (Andrés had decided to go along for the ride to JFK) and was handing Fred the key to the rented house, Fred squeezed his hand shut around the key and said, "Now it's yours."

"What is?" Guy asked with a sweet, dazed smile; he was mildly confused, but his smile anticipated an as-yet-unspecified happy surprise.

"The house is yours for next summer. I bought it."

"You did? You're not joking?" The uniformed chauffeur had come for Guy's bags. They'd walk to the harbor, take a waiting boat to the waiting limousine.

"I've never been more serious," Fred said. "I hope we'll have many a happy summer here together," he added. "I bought it yesterday."

Guy grabbed him by the neck and gazed into his eyes for a second.

Fred said in a low voice, "I hope you'll invite me out once in a while."

Guy said, "Silly." He never knew if that word was a good translation for *stupide*, just as he never knew if naughty meant *mauvais*. He'd once made Americans laugh when he had said, "Hitler was naughty." Andrés was standing off to one side, his head lowered deferentially, as if Guy were receiving a benediction from Signor Fred, their venerable host.

Guy held Fred's head between his hands and kissed him on the lips, no tongue: The $2.2 million kiss, Fred thought bitterly. A second later, Andrés, slender and elegant and very tanned in a crisp white shirt, open at the neck and the sleeves rolled back, hurried off down the boardwalk behind the uniformed chauffeur and beside Guy, who looked back and blew a kiss.

The next few days Fred was in a state of anguish over Guy. Had Andrés flown off with him to Paris? These grad students seemed so idle, and Andrés was always resting. Once Fred had tried to fill in his résumé in his mind and noticed a blank of a whole year. "What did you do in 1982?" he asked. Andrés replied innocently, "I rested."

And then Fred obsessed over the risky sex he'd had in the bushes. He kept feeling the glands in his neck and under his arms and looking for telltale brown patches on his legs. There was no test for gay cancer and no treatment. Oh, what a fool he'd been! No wonder Guy was so puritanical; you couldn't trust anyone, least of all a sleazeball in the bushes.

He couldn't think of anyone he could discuss his twin obsessions with, Guy and GRID, other than the baron. They had dinner in the baron's library, where his new lover the antique dealer had installed a tapestry of a bewigged king on horseback pointing gleefully to a distant city on the banks of a river—"in honor of a peace treaty," Édouard explained vaguely. The room, which Fred remembered as white and sterile but spacious, now seemed crowded with heavy window treatments, potted palms, lots of bric-a-brac, spotlit oil paintings of smiling despots, and even a fire, though it was only late September and still warm out.

"Guess your new lover is responsible for all this?" Fred asked, making a sweeping gesture with his hand. "Classy."

"Yes, Will has worked miracles," Édouard said with a timid smile.

"Guess you have all the luck with the young boys—first Guy and now Will."

"Boys!" Édouard said, guffawing into his sole amandine. (Even the plates looked old and crazed and stained, Louis somebody.) "Guy's no boy! Walt snooped around and found some pictures of Guy in French *Vogue* going back to the early seventies. We figured out he must be nearly forty if he's a day."

"But he looks so young."

"He must have a terrible painting in the attic."

But Fred was too appalled to laugh. He felt someone had socked him in the stomach. He began to sweat and breathe faster, as if he might panic any moment. He'd been fooled, made to look a fool. Panic or maybe vomit. No one pulled the wool over his eyes. He was the cynic, the skeptic, he was fraud-proof. And yet, and yet, he'd been completely hoodwinked. And all that money! He'd spent so much money on Guy, the house—and all for a forty-year-old man who must clip the hair in his nose or yank it out and set off a fit of sneezing. *A middle-aged man who's probably down to jerking off every other day. A weary man of forty who's already seen everything come around twice, who let me fuck him that once in a hole where whole armies of men have doubtless passed. What a pretentious queen, pretending to be fresh and naïve, whereas he's long past his sell-by date. I could have been investing all this time and energy and money in a real kid who might have fallen for me, who wouldn't have known how to work me so expertly. Kids are*

emotional and reckless, whereas a man of forty is cold and calculating.
I've been duped.

"Guy has really upset me," Fred said, choking up. "I'm afraid
I had unsafe sex. Not with Guy—but with a stranger."

"They say you should know your partner's name. Do you
know the man's name, the man who you were . . . indiscreet
with?"

"No, it was in the bushes, in the Meat Rack."

"Oh, dear." The baron patted his hand. "I'm no one to talk.
I specialize in anonymous sex. Though Will is making me
mend my ways."

"Do you think we're all doomed?"

"Surely not. We eat well, we exercise, we never have a
venereal disease for long. We have regular checkups—don't
you?"

"Yes, but I don't trust my gay doctor. He's a feel-good
doctor and a major masochist."

"Really?" the baron asked, rustling his neck like a mating
partridge. "What kind of masochist is he?"

"He had his testicles removed by a surgeon as his master
looked on."

The baron's eyes glittered. "That's irreversible," he said with
satisfaction. He blinked and said, "In any event, I believe this
gay cancer only hits men who've had repeated venereal diseases.
Their immune systems are compromised, overloaded. We're in
no danger, especially a straight guy like you, I mean ex-
straight."

"There we were, Guy and me, surrounded by some of the
great beauties of the day, and both of us as wise as virgins. We
were both afraid of GRID."

"What?"

"Gay-related immune deficiency."

Édouard nodded vigorously.

They went quiet after Will came in wearing beige calfskin suede trousers molded to his muscular thighs and butt, the fruits of thousands of squats. He seemed a bit drunk and more expansive than he'd been the only other time Fred had met him. He leaned down and pecked Édouard on the forehead and reached deliberately to pinch Édouard's tit through the soft blue Egyptian cotton of his monogrammed shirt. The baron winced for a second and then smiled timidly up at his young-master-antique-dealer. "It's nice to know a cutie like you is my property," Will said. The baron darted a nervous glance at his guest—and then smiled at his owner. "Yes," he said awkwardly, "very nice indeed." He was such a social creature, produced by centuries of breeding, but nothing in his rich experience had prepared him for this moment. (He'd never mixed his evenings on the rack with entertaining his friends.)

Back home, surrounded by staring, life-sized Buddhas, Fred made himself a scotch on the rocks and nervously rubbed his fingers together. Ceil had always hated that tic, the constant whispering sound of his fingers, and had put her hand over his at the movies when he started "pilling."

4.

I N P A R I S , G U Y felt relieved. He could speak the language
with all its nuances and not endlessly play the part of the
interesting foreigner. At the same time his accent didn't prompt
a discussion. He was just another Frenchman. He had lost his
primary accomplishment—the ability to speak English (which
he spoke better than he understood)—and the oddity of his
identity, of being French in America.

He was just one more handsome man in a whole city of handsome men—handsome if you liked skinny guys with big noses.
The Parisians looked at each other constantly but were more
curious about each other's shoes than their sexual availability. It
was raining a cold rain but never for long, and you could duck
from one awning to the next or from an expensive café to an
even more expensive shop. It was hard to believe that just two
weeks before, he'd been lying in the warm September sun in a
deck chair. Now he'd been repatriated to Paris's eternal mists.

Andrés had come with him and was staying with him at the
Crillon in a room that looked out on the place de la Concorde,
a "square" only in the abstract sense that it was a huge space
excavated out of the city around it but was curiously open on
three sides.

Andrés liked to have sex four or five times a day. Maybe because Guy had resisted him all summer long and had just stared at that big erection in the green Speedo, now that it was released it was relentless. They kissed so much that Guy's lips were red and swollen and he had to shy away—he had to be camera-ready in the morning.

But it was pure pleasure to lie in bed with this lithe young man who was so in love. He had a patch of long black hair like an emblem on his lean, defined chest. Guy could circle his waist with two hands. He was as elongated as a Christ carved out of wax but as flexible as a whip. He had a vaguely acrid odor, as if his deodorant weren't strong enough or as if the hot, empty oven were burning spilled food from the day before.

Guy liked to sit opposite him in an outdoor café, where they were kept warm under giant overhead heaters. Andrés was shy, that must be it, though Guy preferred the French word *sauvage*, which sounded more fierce than timid. Andrés had a hard time looking at him and would train his eyes on some distant spot in the sky. He would lean his face on his big open hand as if he were absorbed in new music, though every once in a while he'd shake himself out of his reverie and steal a glance at his companion. Was he tired, jet-lagged, was that why his head seemed too heavy for his neck? When he was looking at that mesmerizing point in the sky his whole face would be drained of color and expression, but when he'd dart a glance at Guy he'd smile a warm, timid smile and his upper lip, bruised from kisses, would pull back to show his wet, tarnished teeth. Andrés avoided sitting in a corner where there was a mirror behind him because he hoped Guy wouldn't notice his bald spot or at least not dwell upon it. Guy understood the strategy.

They walked across the river and up the boulevard Saint-Germain, stopping to look in all the store windows. Guy took Andrés's arm, which made the Colombian self-conscious. He kept interrogating the eyes of every passerby, though no one seemed startled, except, perhaps, by Guy's orange Doc Martens. Andrés was self-conscious but also proud, and he wondered if in people's eyes he measured up to Guy's beauty, or at least didn't look like a member of a different species. They murmured to each other in French, with Andrés inserting an occasional word in English. One word he said in Spanish was *siempre*, though it was *toujours* in French and, of course, "always" in English, but Guy didn't correct him because he liked his accent.

Guy's whole body was humming. Normally he thought only of his head—his eyes, his smile—and was aware of his body as merely the principle of forward propulsion trundling him along. But now he was all these bright pools of sensuality—his nipples, his half-hard cock, his tingling anus, even his feet. (Andrés had fellated each toe.) He was glowing all over and he felt the animal in him was longing to shed its clothes.

Back in the hotel they did shed them and he lay with his head on Andrés's belly watching TV, which bored the Colombian because he had trouble following the rapid-fire dialogue; it was a show where they were all discussing the merits and drawbacks of something—could it be incest?—and the young male presenter with his big boyish head, almost purple lips, and huge eyes (was he wearing mascara?) was just on the border between gay and straight, with his small bony hands in the air and a smile or even a smirk on his dark lips and his voice pitched as high as a twelve-year-old's and his constant quips capping everything the other guests said, the old actress or the fat, unshaved buffoon or the blond boy—and provoking the studio audience into rapid bursts of laughter, a quick chorus of barking, followed each time by a single tinkling laugh of one person slow on the uptake.

And then here was Andrés with a new erection that had to be appeased. The *place* beyond was suddenly immersed in night streaked with the headlights of circulating cars and the brilliant articulated facade of the National Assembly. They kept flipping back and forth, but it wasn't clear which was the more exquisitely pleasurable pain, to penetrate or to be penetrated. At the end Andrés's mouth, forbidden to kiss Guy's swollen lips, was just an open vowel of ecstasy as they both spilled on his muscly stomach in the dim, shifting colored light of the television and its maddening banter.

Guy had been in America so long that the French struck him as either coiled up and suspicious or absurdly sweet, with an eye out for profit—either paranoid or sycophantic.

He knew what they were up to, he'd been that way, too, with strangers, but in the intervening years he'd become as naïve, as kind, as childish (*bon enfant*) as Americans, which he definitely preferred now. Why waste all that energy being suspicious or syrupy? In America photographers and their assistants and the hair and makeup people thought of him as a good guy, but here, he noticed, friendliness was considered troubling. He enjoyed talking to his old French friends on the phone and with them he could joke and tell stories with no point, but if he tried to make conversation during a fashion shoot the strangers on the set went about their jobs briskly and greeted his American-style garrulousness with a sharp, derisive look, an intake of breath, and an "*Et alors?*"

Making love to Andrés was a full-time job. Whenever they went for a walk or a meal he could feel the impatient desire building up in the boy; at a table he'd rest his heavy head again on his huge cupped hand and look out the window, his mouth open. From time to time he'd surface from his thoughts and the racing images, no doubt, of remembered or projected couplings. Then he'd smile and say something amusing, but it almost felt as if a grieving man were trying to make small talk during a wake; he was definitely downshifting into a different speed. Only when they returned to their hotel room did his thoughts and actions seem to converge. He became more and more passionate and Guy thought of the Greek word *agon*, wasn't it at once an athletic contest and a style of suffering, an agony? Wasn't it the name of that Balanchine ballet he liked so much?

When he called his mother she sobbed into the phone and said, "Thank God you're back in France. Your father is going quickly. Come home right away. Tonight."

Guy said yes, of course, but after hanging up he sank into the bleakest resentment. He felt as if the last twenty years had just been a rosy chimera. He felt as if his parents were dragging him away from his glamorous, cosseted life in which so many men loved him. He knew his father had been fighting emphysema for years, though he wouldn't give up his pack of Gauloises a day and would even turn off the oxygen in his tent so that he could smoke another *clope*. He was now so bad he couldn't talk on the phone without gasping, and his mother said he couldn't walk fifty meters without sitting down to catch his breath.

"What's wrong?" Andrés asked, a crease across his lovely smooth forehead.

"I've got to take the train down to Clermont-Ferrand. My father's very sick. I think he's dying."

"*Oh, mon petit,*" Andrés said folding him into his arms. "Tonight?"

"Yes, I guess."

"I'll come with you."

"No, that wouldn't work. They don't want a guest at this time. And there are no hotels nearby. You can't believe how . . . poor it is! How poor they are. And how would I explain you to them?"

Andrés was Latin enough to understand the sacred rights of the family and the inconvenience of a same-sex lover. He looked pained, as if someone had turned off his oxygen, too; Guy remembered that in a crisis Latins don't know how to be stoic. They wear their emotions on their sleeve, and their lips, far from being stiff, are quavering with self-pity.

They had only two more hours before the train but Andrés managed to squeeze in another orgasm. Guy couldn't concentrate on sex. The concierge was arranging his train ticket, but he had to cancel tomorrow's shoot and tell his mother when he was arriving and he had to pack a few things. And call Pierre-Georges. Then, on top of everything else, he had Fred's daily phone call to deal with. He always called at four Paris time and ten P.M. New York time. Fred was always mournful because Guy had admitted that Andrés had flown over with him to Paris, but this evening, even while Andrés's sperm was still drying on his stomach, Guy was able to jolt Fred by announcing he was going to his father's deathbed.

"Oh, baby, what terrible news! Well, we saw it coming. He just wouldn't stop smoking—" And then Fred cut himself off, knowing that it was not in the best of taste to blame the dying. "I wish I could be there with you. I always assumed your father must be in his fifties, since I thought you were in your twenties. But now I know your true age, I guess your dad must be—"

"He's seventy-three," Guy said coldly, then he let a long silence install itself over the crackling wire. Guy had learned how eloquently uncomfortable a silence could be.

"Well, that's young," Fred babbled, completely disconcerted and aware that Andrés could probably divine Fred's faux pas from Guy's end of the conversation. Or if not, Guy would repeat it all to him soon enough. Best to change the subject. "So, how's the work?" Fred asked brightly.

"I've called it all off."

"Oh, no."

"Would you have me prancing on a runway while my father was dying?"

They hung up a moment later and Guy, who could see another of Andrés's erections developing, raced about packing a few things, checking the train schedule with the concierge, and then phoning his mother to confirm when he'd arrive. At least the seriousness and urgency of the moment made Andrés go soft, though he prolonged their "final" embrace and became erect again. Guy was just a bit disgusted and he did a quick inventory of what he'd packed while feigning rapture in Andrés's arms.

His first-class seat on the train was comfortable and Guy liked the smell of the carpet, which must have been steam-cleaned recently. He had remembered to stamp his ticket in the machine before he boarded and now the conductor was nowhere in sight. There was only one other man at the far end of the car, reading under a spotlight.

Guy was full of resentment against his parents for some reason, as if they were interrupting his new life (not so new now)—his New York pampered life of wealth and no responsibilities and lots of sex and eternal youth. They were dragging him back to the dirty lace curtains masking the windows giving directly onto the bleak, usually empty street, the view of the dirty white and gray uninterrupted facades of the houses across the way almost never lit from within, ghost houses in a ghost town. They were pulling him back to the space heater glowing red and then dimming, the freezing bedroom with the torn *toile de jouy* wallpaper and the matching slipcover on the one armchair, the dingy bathroom with the leprous mirror above the old-fashioned sink, and the mildewed shower curtain shrouding a shower no bigger than a sentry box. He couldn't bear the ugliness and the poverty, the mouse-shit-in-the-corner horror of it all, the reminder that ordinary people get old and die, that they get thicker and stiffer with age, that they gasp for air.

He went into the large bathroom on the train and locked the door and masturbated. Logically more sex was the last thing he should want, but he felt compelled to spurt, *gicler*, as perhaps a way of reclaiming himself from his importunate lover and from the cold neutering embrace of his parents. His mind raced between remembered images and those he made up as he sought to keep the divining rod bobbing and dipping above the buried stream of hot liquid. When it finally surfaced he was only half hard; jerking off had been more therapeutic than erotic.

His mother was wearing a cheap scarf and her old tan rain-coat and snow-stained flats as she stood out of the rain outside at the train station beneath the metal awning. Everything in France was so organized. He'd told her which train car he'd be on, and here she was in the exact place and at the exact time. She looked pale and as untweezered as a nun. She ignored his flowing, fashionable coat and his dark silk suit from Browns in

London and his new Vuitton luggage; she clung to him fiercely in one quick embrace and he felt a reproach in it, as if he'd handed a copy of *Vogue* to Medea.

His mother drove them swiftly and surely to the house as if she daren't spend an extra minute away from her dying husband. "I'm so glad you made it in time."

Guy said, "Is he that bad?"

His mother glanced away from the wet road unspooling before their headlights, illuminating corners of familiar old barns and houses as they swerved around corners. "Yes," she said with simple finality.

"Is Robert here? Tiphaine?"

"Yes, Robert drove up from Vienne, where he's working in a garage, and Tiphaine took the train down from Lyon, where she's a court stenographer."

Guy thought of things to ask about his siblings but he didn't feel that sort of chitchat would be appropriate; he also didn't want to draw attention to how out of touch he'd become with the basic facts about his family. So he just looked out the window at the rain, the passing lava-black buildings, and the glassy eyes of an attentive dog standing in the drizzle. There was the Dumoulins' dingy house and their old trailer parked on the front lawn. "Do you have a full-time nurse?" Guy asked, thinking that was the kind of no-nonsense question a real person might ask—his brother, for instance.

His father was so pale he looked as if he'd been copied in limestone. He was inside his oxygen tent dozing and his face was blurred behind the clear plastic. Guy didn't know if it was better to let him sleep or to tell him he'd come home to see him. His mother solved the problem by saying, "*Chéri, notre Guy est là,*" which caused his father's eyes to flutter open and his lips to produce a sketch of a smile. He'd gotten so much thinner and his features were stronger, more marked, so that he appeared younger in spite of his pallor. Guy could see that he'd once been handsome, the way he looked in that old picture from the fifties.

Guy realized he'd always been afraid of his father and now he tensed up, which was absurd faced with this pallid, skinny copy of his heavy-drinking parent, this shrunken facsimile smiling his sketchy little smile. "*Bonjour, Papa*," Guy said in a low voice the way he imagined Robert must sound. (His voice had always been much lower than Guy's; when they were teenagers Guy could hear him in the next room talking to himself, forcing his voice down a few notes.) His father reached with his nearly transparent hand for Guy's—something he'd never done before.

He realized that he always thought of Robert when he thought of his father. He'd always been jealous of the way they sat out Sunday morning mass while he attended with his mother and Tiphaine—the men and the women. His father had never been proud of his good grades and usually hadn't even glanced at his report card, though he'd been there at every soccer game Robert played, even some of the practice sessions, despite the fact that Robert had been a very mediocre player. If Robert took a girl out to the movies, his father, even if he always claimed to be broke (*fauché*), could usually find a blue folded note of fifty francs in his pocket. When his father was so drunk he couldn't get up the stairs to bed, it was Robert who took off his shoes and propped him up, dragging him along and whispering sweet nothings in his father's ear, while Guy and his mother, pretending to read, sat rigid and unsmiling under the bright floor lamp, almost embarrassed to be witnessing out of the corner of an eye such a tender, intimate, shameful moment.

But now his dying father had opened his eyes wide and was trying to say something. Guy bent down so that his ear was next to his father's lips, which were whispering, "Water." Guy held up his father's head with the matted white hair and looked at his long white nose hairs and tilted a glass to his papery lips. Guy was embarrassed by his expensive Creed eau de cologne, but he was sure his father couldn't identify it. Tiphaine, who'd been napping in her room, came down the stairs, plumper than before, her hair crushed on one side, her cheap dress ill-fitting. She whispered, "Guy," and kissed him on both cheeks, but for some reason she was smiling at this little drama of filial piety, as if she knew how insincere and out-of-character it was. Guy resented her smile but overcame his surge of hostility toward her.

Guy's mother heated up a daube and spooned it out for her children. It wasn't half bad, Guy said to himself, and then hated himself for even noticing. This was hardly a moment to be handing out stars for cuisine. Robert came home after they'd been served and spent fifteen minutes washing grease from his hands and arms and lingered five minutes looking at his sleeping father. He said he had a kayak and spent a lot of time boating and paddling. He checked out Guy's wasp waist and muttered his teenage nickname, Sec ("Dry"). Robert's neck, however, was cross-hatched with tiny squares—the sun, no doubt. Real men don't moisturize.

While their mother was in the kitchen fetching the dessert, Robert said, "You seem to be prospering."

"Can't complain."

"You know, at the garage I have a chance to get a good price on an '82 Opel. Mom needs a new car."

Guy said, "Sure." He felt guilty because he hadn't thought

about her car; New Yorkers weren't part of car culture, though he had his Mercedes. "How much is it?"

"I think I can get it for thirty-two hundred francs."

"Thank you for arranging it."

"What do you drive?"

"Mercedes SEL."

Robert winced, the way he always had. "I'm sorry I haven't been contributing my part to help Mom. But at the garage . . . and with three kids . . ." (*gosses*, he said, a word Guy had almost forgotten). "And I make all the repairs around here. You're never here."

Oh, dear, Guy thought. "That's our deal," he said smoothly. "You look in on Mother"—he glanced at Tiphaine—"and you do, too. Money is the easy part. I'm so grateful to both of you." He didn't want to sound hypocritical; they had never been this polite, this deferential around each other before. He smiled forbearingly at his siblings with a look that pleaded, he hoped, for sympathy and, if he'd somehow offended them, for forgiveness.

"What's this, what's this?" their mother sang out in a forced, cheerful voice as she brought in the chocolate mousse. It was his favorite, at least according to family legend, though he hadn't eaten a dessert in twenty years. But he'd heard her whipping the cream in the kitchen and he knew he couldn't refuse it.

"We're going to give you a new-old car, an Opel," Guy said. "Robert's arranging it."

"But that's too extravagant," their mother cried. "The old one—"

"Robert's getting it at a good price. And he'll make sure it runs well."

Guy worried that Robert would resent this last assertion, that Guy was being a busybody, but Robert was smiling and saying Guy would pay for it out of his New World riches. "And I'll wash it and vacuum it once a month," Tiphaine threw in light-heartedly.

Their mother seemed overwhelmed. She had tears in her eyes and looked at Guy. "You already do so much for me. How did I deserve such a loving son? If I'd economized better—"

Guy held a finger to his lips and shushed her. "No one else could make so little money go so far. I'm the one at fault, I've been thoughtless. I haven't taken into account that the dollar's been getting weaker. I will double your allowance *and* buy the car if Robert will be so kind as to handle the transaction and do the maintenance—that's the hard part."

As was her nature, their mother cleared the dishes before everyone was done. When she came back in she said, "How is that nice . . . Baron Édouard?" she asked, uncomfortable with his title but fearing, no doubt, that a simple "monsieur" would be rude or sound presumptuous. Tiphaine and Robert exchanged glances and a smirk, as if they were privy to a private joke.

"Oh, Édouard?" Guy said lazily. "He's always the same, never changes. I guess rich people don't change as much as the rest of us; we have to hustle. Except now he's crazy about antiques and is pawing through everyone's attic or barn, looking for a treasure. He asks after you . . . often." Seeing that his brother and sister were still smirking, he hoped to defuse their satire by asking, "Do you think he's a real baron? Or a Jew ennobled by the prince of Lichtenstein for making a big loan? Or do businessmen just use titles for prestige? I read that one quarter of all titles in Europe are fake."

"Fake? Fake?" their mother shrieked, horrified as if he'd questioned the authenticity of the Shroud of Turin. "He seemed to me authentic and a charming, generous man."

Guy wondered if she'd think him so charming if she could see him naked and barking.

Robert at least had stopped sneering. "I guess you must meet a lot of phonies in the fashion industry?"

Guy wondered how he could respond calmly to this remark. "I suppose all worlds have their fakes. Even garage mechanics. But strictly speaking Édouard isn't in fashion. He's a brewer."

Robert nodded solemnly. Their mother muttered, "In any event a very charming man, truly elegant."

At that moment they heard their father—whose bed had been moved downstairs into the salon—groan, and their mother rushed to his side and the three children followed her slowly, timidly. "We're here, my darling," their mother cooed. "We're right here, *chéri*, your whole family, your three children and me, you're not alone," but Guy thought that was a lie, you're never so alone as at the moment of your death.

Their father was gasping and their mother turned up the flow of oxygen and was patting down the sides of his square, transparent tent as if sealing a leak. Now he was sitting up and coughing and his face looked as red a baby's when it starts to cry.

I wonder who will be with me at the hour of my death, Guy wondered, then he mentally slapped himself for being morbid and self-pitying. With a trusted servant, he hoped, chuckling at his own frivolity. A servant who would know just how to arrange the pillows, tilt the lampshade, administer the opiate. A servant who would mourn, but only ceremonially, while speculating how generous her legacy would be. Guy knew how to deal with calculated kindness.

The next morning Tiphaine drove him to the train station after Guy had written down Robert's bank details for a transfer of funds for the Opel. He kissed his father goodbye, who was sleeping now and blue, not red. His mother was crying silently, seated beside his father; she herself was so frail she scarcely indented the mattress.

He and Tiphaine stopped by to see their grandmother, the one who'd worked as a cashier in a Paris café. She'd become almost feral and slept with three big dogs, more for the warmth than out of love for the animals. She who had always been so chic in her way now wore a dirty old bathrobe covered with dog hairs and slippers too big for her feet. She didn't have her teeth in and her eyebrows had grown in, big heavy caterpillars. Guy had always felt closest to her; after all, she was the Parisian, and she was the one who'd first told him he was handsome. But now she was a grinning savage, and her eyes didn't reveal if she recognized her grandchildren.

A day after Guy returned to Paris, his father went into the hospital with pneumonia. Guy volunteered to return home, but his mother said that the doctor had told them that this could go on for months, and besides, his father was seldom conscious now. They'd turned up the morphine and turned down the antibiotics and were hoping he'd just slip away.

Two days later, the phone rang at two A.M. and his mother was saying tonelessly it was all over. Guy wanted to ask her if she was relieved but he didn't know if that was what human beings asked. So he asked instead what he thought Robert would say: When was the funeral mass going to be held, and did she need any money?

He was glad, a moment later, that he hadn't asked her if she was relieved, because he realized she was already rescripting the past. "We had our differences sometimes," she said, "but he was a good man who was kind to me and very proud of you kids." Guy couldn't believe his ears—their father was a bitter drunk when he wasn't violent, and the only people he was pleasant with were his bar buddies, the other unemployed drunks of Clermont-Ferrand. Guy remembered distinctly that his mother had said to him maybe ten years ago (he was already in New York) that her husband drove her wild and that she'd kill herself if it wasn't against her faith. Divorce was even more unthinkable. Guy was cursed with a nearly geological memory in which each time stratum was clearly demarcated from every other and in which memories never blended, and they could always be located with precision. The levels of the past did not bleed into each other in Guy's mind, nor was the past "color-corrected" to match the present hue. Everything retained its original shade and he could never revise the cruel, barren past to substantiate some sentimental new evaluation. He'd hated and feared his father then and hated him now. His father had seldom talked at home except to mutter something sour and brief, but Guy had heard him at the bar expatiate on his political theories and racist prejudices and anti-German jingoism when he'd gone to collect him late at night at the bar. His father was also obsessed by Arabs. No one was paying much attention to him, but there he was haranguing the void, denouncing the *beurs* (Arabs born in France) and the *Bosches* (Huns). (Had he inherited his Germanophobia from his father, who'd fought them in the Great War and had had his eyelids burned off, or did he resent them because their industry was still thriving—or was it just a conventional prejudice, an indication that he was a thinking

man and had opinions?) Guy was tall but frail and as he sup-
ported his thick, smelly father through the dark, empty streets
he longed to slip out from under him so that the hateful man
would fall and crack his angry, mumbling skull and die. If they
encountered anyone in the streets, especially a brown skinned,
big-nosed Arab or a stranger who could be mistaken for an
Arab, Guy dreaded the filth that might pour forth from his
father's mouth. When they got home his mother would cluck
angrily, "*Oh là là*, what's this?" and hold her needles and half-
finished knitting and say, "If you think I'm going to share a bed
with—that—heave him onto the couch." But by then his father
was already snoring and Robert was coaxing his slumped body
up the stairs to the bed in the spare room.

Now, on the phone as their mother said sad affectionate
things, Guy assumed an impenetrable silence. *How could people
lie to themselves like that?* he wondered.

And then he thought, *What should she do? Admit that that man
ruined her life?* Was that what Guy expected or wanted: that his
mother should admit that she'd lived a ruined life?

And what was so great about his own life? He had to remember the names of three hundred people in the business whom he'd
greet with a smile, he could never go outside with baggy jeans
and a dirty T-shirt, he had to listen to hours and hours—
centuries!—of talk about clothes and photographers. "Yes, he
sleeps in the same bed with her every night, but why?" someone
might say of a photograph. "Does he ever touch her, or is it just a
New York marriage?" He had to listen to everyone's gossip and
schedule, where they'd been and where they were going, how
their astrologers warned against this or counseled that. And then
the daily facials (hoping the creams and astringents wouldn't
produce pimples), and the absolute trauma of changing a hairstyle.

(Was it ahead of the curve or behind it?) He wondered what his real hair color was. And then the hours and hours of chanting— should he have been chanting for his father's recovery? he wondered guiltily. What should he buy as a gift for Lucie? He'd seen an expensive blue lizard-skin wallet at Céline's—you wouldn't find that in New York, would you?

And what did his life add up to? A portfolio of pictures that was almost instantly démodé, a "beautiful" face with a "masculine" expression and stubble. He was living his life between quotation marks, every inverted comma a proof of inauthenticity—linking his looks to the fleeting moment. When people by accident looked back at his portfolio in fifty years would they say he looked "so eighties," just as he respond- ed to pictures of Valentino by saying he looked so "twenties," with his blackened eyebrows, his nostrils black as raisins, his hair shellacked, and his mouth unsmiling. People paid Guy a lot, advertising men projected onto him their own fantasies of "youth," "innocence," "sophistication," or "depth," but at the end of the day he'd have just a sheaf of glossies and a bitter lined face like a half lemon that had sat in the fridge too many weeks.

It was nice not to have to talk to Fred every day, who assumed he was with his parents. It was nice to lie in Andrés's arms; the poor boy had been trained to just brush Guy's lips with his lips, never to gnaw them. Now Guy had to teach him to wash his hands and not to sniff them at dinner or at a movie, fingers that had been knuckle-deep inside Guy, though it was a sweet failing. Guy felt that if he didn't watch out, Andrés would devour him. Andrés resented the waiter who delivered their breakfast. He would sigh, even moan, if the man took too long. Guy had to purchase Andrés new underthings and shirts and a hooded green rain slicker, *un ciré*, because the boy had bought his first-class plane ticket at the last minute. Did he have any money? Was his family rich?

Andrés never answered Guy's questions about money but just looked away and smiled mysteriously.

Guy had never felt so loved. Perhaps because Andrés was so handsome, perhaps because men and women stared at him as often as they stared at Guy, Guy felt Andrés was valuable, enviable, rich with options. Poor Édouard and Fred, they were desperate because time was running out on them. In the apartment of the Buddhas, Guy had seen a photo from the 1950s of Fred in which he was presentable, but he'd never been a beauty, though absurdly he aspired to be one now.

Andrés was intelligent, too, and could talk about Dalí for hours and hours and the surrealists in general. Apparently Dalí was on his last legs now, with a nose tube feeding him oxygen, all mixed up with his trademark wax mustaches. Dalí was Catalan. (They spoke a kind of Catalan as far south as Valencia, Andrés explained, and as far north as Perpignan.)

"I guess it's like Gaelic in Ireland," Guy said, just to be pleasant. He liked seeing Andrés getting worked up, his skin flushing red. Usually he was like the dead Christ in his loin-cloth being lowered from the cross into his mother's arms, and Guy enjoyed draping a sheet over his loins to underline the resemblance. He could imagine blood-black nail holes in his body.

Andrés would lie on his stomach practicing Dalí's signature for hours. His buttocks would always tense when he felt Guy was looking at him.

"Why Dalí?" Pierre-Georges asked over the phone. "He was a complete fraud and would even sign blank sheets of paper for sixty dollars a pop. His greedy wife Gala would put them in front of him; he was completely gaga and she thought she at least would live forever."

"How do you know all this?" Guy asked.

"There was an article in *Marie Claire*. But he's a complete fraud. When he was shown some lithographs of *Don Quixote* he declared them fakes. 'How can you tell?' someone asked. 'They're fakes because Dalí hasn't been paid for them.' Most of his so-called lithographs are just posters of photographic copies, he doesn't even know how to make lithographs."

"Andrés is doing his Ph.D. on Dalí."

One day Andrés went out by himself (which was unprecedented). He said something about meeting a friend for lunch, though there had been no exchange of calls. When he came back late in the afternoon he had a bundle of yellowing blank paper under his arm.

"What's that for?" Guy asked.

"It's paper from the 1950s. I found it at a *bouquiniste*," Andrés said. But when Guy pursued the matter Andrés just shrugged. Later he said, "Modern paper contains chemical brighteners that glow under infrared."

And then they were back in New York. Guy caught himself speaking to waiters in French; for him French had become the language of servants (though he'd learned Americans with their fussy egalitarianism preferred the word "help").

Andrés moved in with him and, when Fred or Pierre-Georges or Lucie came by, sat right next to Guy with his hand on his knee. They must have looked like a queer version of that painting *American Gothic*. Guy had to admit to himself that it made him uncomfortable to have someone so visibly stake a claim on him, and yet he found the idea reassuring, too. At least he knew that the usual tension in his neck and shoulders was melting away. Belonging to someone felt like being held in someone's arms, like being shielded from death. His father's death had caused him to feel more vulnerable, a flimsy transparency held up in the wind, a twist of paper dancing in an air shaft, but Andrés's embrace stopped him from twisting. Andrés was warm flesh, though he was painfully thin; he was flesh and stubble and his slightly sour odor. He was a thick, veiny penis, uncircumcised like Guy's, and a loose sack of balls. He was a bald spot and bad teeth. He was so physical despite his slightness pumping Guy full of hot spurts of vitality.

Guy's mother hadn't expected him to come back for the funeral. Pierre-Georges had arranged for a florist to deliver a big, standing wreath of red and white carnations and a blue silk ribbon stretched across its empty thorax reading, "Didier remembered always in the loving hearts of his family." Guy was shocked that Pierre-Georges had filed away his father's first name, Didier. Pierre-Georges was impeccable!

Guy spoke to his mother every day. She sounded subdued and a bit worried. She'd never written a check in her life. Tiphaine was teaching her how to keep a checkbook and work out a budget. Guy resented this intimate brush with poverty and mortality. He knew that someday soon he'd be old and infirm— but he repeated the words "old and infirm" precisely because they were a formula and held the reality at bay. They were prophylactic words, a sting of the same venom, an antidote like homeopathic medicine. His kind of Buddhism instructed you to live in the moment, he vaguely remembered, and that suited him fine. If you chanted twice a day and made love three times and always wore beautiful clothes and stayed away from dreary people, you could just hover in the present, couldn't you? Or had he gotten that completely wrong?

5.

FRED ANNOUNCED THAT he had Kaposi's sarcoma, but it wasn't always linked to AIDS, it was something older Jews and Italians got just naturally, older Mediterranean men, but it used to be very rare and it had been seen just in Jersey nursing homes or in Florida retirement villages. "We're going to beat this thing," he said, his voice breaking. "I've got the best goddamn team of doctors on the globe, the real McCoy." Then he thought about it for a day and he phoned: "But what if I infected you that one time I fucked you?"

"Don't worry about that," Guy said. "I haven't had any other STDs, so my immune system hasn't been compromised. And besides, you came on my stomach, not in my ass. I don't think it's in precum. Anyway, we only did it once—and you need multiple exposures, don't you?"

"Hey, maybe you gave it to me," Fred said. "That's a possibility, isn't it? Should I sue you? Can the top get it?"

"Not usually," Guy said. "Anyway, don't worry. You'll be fine. You're as strong as an ox."

"Do you know if you're clean?"

"Clean?"

"I guess I'm not clean now."

"Don't worry. Do you have any other symptoms?"

"A tubercular cough. Night sweats. Swollen lymph glands. Weight loss. I'm a goner, right?"

"I didn't realize it was that bad."

"C'mon!" Fred shouted into the receiver. "You're supposed to reassure me," he said, disgusted.

"What do the doctors say, the real McCoys?"

"They don't know shit. They don't even know for sure what causes it, do they? Poppers? Mustaches? Pork?"

"How about sex?"

"Isn't it ironic that I came out now? It's like moving to London during the Great Plague."

Guy wondered, could he have given GRID to Fred? Could Fred have given it to him?

Guy promised to shop for and microwave him dinner that very evening, something nourishing, chicken Parmigianino and broccoli, say.

Fred said, "The house is a mess. There is an inch of dust on the fuckin' Buddhas."

"That doesn't matter."

"It'll be great to see you. Don't be offended if I don't eat much. And if I look like hell. Is Andrew coming?" That was what he called Andrés.

"No, no, I'll come alone. You probably just have a bad case of flu. It's the season."

But Fred really did look frail and diminished when he opened the door, a little defeated old man. He was in a ratty old bathrobe over baggy boxer shorts and a torn T-shirt marked "Colorado State," where he'd studied and wrestled a century ago. "Don't touch me!" Fred warned. "Don't kiss me. I may be contagious. Disinfect your hands when you leave here. You really should be wearing a mask."

"I'll do no such thing, let me hug you."

"Guy, I'm not fooling around, stay away."

But Guy did hug him and felt how skinny he was under the robe, his ribs as articulated as a washboard or a xylophone. He smelled bad, like dirt and old sweat.

Guy worked hard at being cheerful; it was December, and Fred was trembling slightly like an expensive dog, though the apartment was toasty and smelled like sandalwood for some reason, maybe joss sticks burned before the idol.

Once the food was twirled and warmed in the microwave, Guy watched Fred eat, or rather dabble his fork in the sticky contents of his plate.

"Don't use so much salt," Guy said.

"Fuck it! I'll be dead long before a salt buildup in my arteries. Nothing has any taste."

Guy was staring at the quarter-sized brown spot on Fred's thigh where his robe had fallen open. Fred intercepted his glance and said, "Pretty bad, huh?"

Guy knew from his mother that you couldn't discuss mortality simply, nobly, honestly with the dying or the mourners, that the visitor was obliged to be cheerful. He also knew that Fred worshipped him so much he'd believe anything Guy would say. "You'll outlive us all," Guy promised. "You're an ox."

"I feel more like a calf being led to slaughter."

Guy could see the doomed look on Fred's face, like the pallid, resigned look of a drowning friend only a few meters out to sea but caught in an inescapable undertow. Fred had already given up. "What are my kids going to say? 'Daddy, we told you so.' What did I have the face-lift and the tummy tuck for? The mortician?"

"Stop, Fred, you'll feel fine in a week."

"Really?"

"Really. Trust me. A week."

"Carbolic acid," Fred said. "Wash all the exposed surfaces of your skin with carbolic acid."

"Shut up," Guy said playfully, and then he courageously embraced the sick man again. "I'll be back again tomorrow."

"You will? When?"

"We'll see." Then he added spitefully, "You have a heavy schedule tomorrow?"

"I've got nothing planned but worry. I don't even feel up to putting together this new movie deal." He thought about it and said, "I should do the first AIDS movie—something very romantic, with two hot young macho studs dying."

"How hot would they be," Guy asked, "if they both had AIDS?"

"The lead would have to lose thirty pounds for the last three minutes. We'd cast a famous straight father of nine. Makeup would cover him with black spots—an Oscar, he'd get an Oscar for kissing a man. Boffo box office!"

Fred seemed cheered up by his new product. It was a way of mastering the disease. It was a way of turning tragedy to farce for profit.

It was a depressing winter and spring. Fred kept succumbing to one disease or another. One day he couldn't write and he sat bemused in front of a few doodles. That turned out to be a parasite in the brain, toxoplasmosis, but they'd just discovered a way of routing it. Then he succumbed to PCP, the gay pneumonia, and he was put on a ventilator and an antibiotic drip.

He lost sensation in his feet except for occasional stabbing pains: neuropathy. Guy was learning a new vocabulary. Fred would get better and would go on long walks with Guy, though he was a skeleton in baggy clothes. Everything his eyes landed on he wanted to buy. Soon the spare bedroom was full of ostrich eggs nesting on branching coral supports, storage otto-mans, a signed first edition of *Huckleberry Finn*, a huge poster for the Italian version of *Gone with the Wind*, lots of bad paint-ings in gold frames. Everything went on his American Express card and Guy got a call from a hysterical Ceil; the kids had told her after a visit with Fred that Daddy was laying up treasures like a pharaoh furnishing his tomb. Guy, who wondered how she'd found his number, mumbled that he couldn't intervene. He didn't even know Fred that well. She started sobbing; "I don't care if he's gay. Gay, schmay. It's the children's inheritance I'm worried about."

"Aren't they already grown up and married, with children of their own?"

"You bastard, trying to rob my children, you filthy French harlot and . . . husband-stealer."

Guy just hung up and shrugged. He didn't pick up the ringing phone. It was sure to be the seal, the *phoque*. Two days later he received a letter in the mail poorly spelled and hastily written, calling him a Jezebel switching his little homo butt before the dazed eyes of a pathetic, dying old man. She knew all about the house on Fire Island and their drug-fueled orgies where gullible Fred had been deliberately infected with a fatal disease. She knew all about vicious fag home-breakers and gold diggers.

Guy just slapped the letter in front of Fred, who read it silently, intently, then looked up at Guy with a saturnine scowl. "The bitch will stop at nothing. We've got to transfer the ownership of the Pines house to you. I've heard stories of the family seconds after a death clearing out an apartment and changing the locks. The vultures! You can bet your bottom dollar Ceil will contest the will. We've got to put it in your name now and make it foolproof. I've heard of wills where if someone who's getting a bequest contests the will, he gets nothing. That's what I want."

"In France you can't disinherit your own children. Napoleonic law."

"Well, lah-di-fuckin'-dah, it's my money and I'll leave it like I want to, to the great love of my life."

As Guy walked home through the snow he felt bad he'd only put out that one time for Fred. If he'd only known Fred was going to *die* so soon, he'd have been less tight-assed about it. Coached by Pierre-Georges, Guy had been playing a deep game for long-term stakes, but there was going to be only the short term, as it turned out. Oh, well, he thought, maybe the great loves are always unreciprocated; did Beatrice put out for Dante, Eloisa for Abelard? Didn't Abelard castrate himself or something extreme? If love worked out, it was just dull and normal—Guy had done Fred a favor by rejecting him, and Guy had avoided the disease.

Andrés was commuting out to Rutgers on a bus three days a week; he was in the last year of coursework for his Ph.D. The bus was cheaper than the train. He'd rented a studio nearby on Weehawken Street where he spent two or three days a week, just a room next door to a taxidermist storeroom: Everything smelled of naphthalene. He was away from home almost too much, though at first Guy had welcomed the time alone. What was he doing in his studio? Taking tricks there? Why did he need a studio?

And then Guy paid a surprise visit to him one day on the pretense that he was in the neighborhood and wanted to take him to lunch at a new restaurant on Greenwich Street. The room was very bleak, just a chair and a desk and a floor lamp. And everywhere prints by Dalí, or at least very faithful copies— horrible robot women and crucified Christs seen from a strange axonometric perspective, and vaporous, mounted Don Quixotes, melting watches and forks. All with pretentious, far-fetched surrealist names and big Dalí signatures.

"These must be worth a fortune," Guy said. "Are they real?"

"They're part of my research for my Ph.D.," Andrés said, not looking Guy in the eye.

"Not every art history student can afford originals by his topic," Guy said.

Andrés looked uncomfortable. "Let's get out of here. These fumes are disgusting."

"They smell like mothballs."

"That's what they are. Let's go to that restaurant of yours— my treat. I've got an appointment at two-thirty."

"Who with?"

"Uh, my professor."

"I thought you said he was on leave in France."

"Well, a dealer, if you must know. My treat today."

Although Andrés had been poor or stingy when they first met, now he'd become a big spender—he covered Guy with expensive presents (seashells dipped in silver, a gold seal ring with an absurd coat of arms he'd invented, three parakeets on an apple, a white fox fur throw for the bed, first-class plane tickets for a weekend in San Juan, where he'd lodged them in El Convento, built around a courtyard, noisy all night with riotous birthday parties or business conventions). And he

bought himself designer clothes which looked silly on him—
skinny light blue Dolce & Gabbana trousers and an Hermès
jacket of a beige canvas with big red darts, dozens of monogrammed shirts, old-fashioned lace-up shoes from Brooks and
fur-lined black suede space boots, three good suits, and a Kenzo
gray overcoat. Where was all the money coming from? His
father had been laid off from his air-conditioning repair job,
Andrés told him when Guy read an article about unemployment in Colombia. All this senseless spending made Guy
uneasy, and whenever Andrés was about to purchase some new
silly extravagance, Guy would say, "Do you really need it? Will
you ever wear it? Why not save up and buy one really perfect
blazer?" It was as if Andrés were buying as compulsively as
Fred, as if he were embarrassed by all the cash stuffing his
wallet. Mysterious people (a lady, a man) called and asked for
Andrés; Guy overheard Andrés's end of the conversation, which
was all about delivery dates. "I can't do it that fast," Andrés said
curtly. His hands were often stained with coffee; there'd been
two hair dryers on his workshop desk—two? What for? Andrés
never blow-dried his hair. Then he saw a scrap of paper on
which Andrés had written the address of an art gallery in
St. Louis—Drew Fine Arts. What was going on?

He knew what was going on but chose to ignore it. Andrés
offered to pay Guy's rent.

"Are you mad?" Guy said. "Maybe when I owe some real
estate tax in March we can split it. It's only a few hundred
dollars. But you're my husband." And the word "husband,"
which Guy pronounced with an ambiguous smile, so thrilled
Andrés that he had to unbend his sudden erection that was
folded uncomfortably in his pale-blue shorts under his jeans.
He bullied Guy into the bedroom and then gently smoothed

him out on the bed like a paper dolly. He tugged their trousers off without unbuttoning them—they were both that skinny. In his haste he spilled some of Guy's pocket change on the floor. He didn't even bother to unbutton their shirts, and reached up to pinch his nipple. Nothing excited Guy more—he joked that his tits were his primary sexual organ—but he'd forbidden Andrés to inflict that sweet torture on him for fear his nipples would become grotesquely enlarged and he'd no longer be fit for bathing suit modeling. No tit-pinching, no long, bruising kisses—the merchandise had to be respected.

Never had Andrés been more ardent. Something about the word "husband" had roused him to new heights of ecstasy. Guy felt for the first time that he was understanding the meaning of each kiss, each hug, each thrust; it was as if in a dream he'd suddenly mastered sign language and could read it effortlessly, fluently. After they both climaxed, first Guy, then Andrés, they lay side by side, panting. Andrés got up and staggered a second and went into the bathroom. His ass looked boyish and white and unimportant under his dark shirt. He wiped them down with a wet washcloth. He almost swooned beside Guy. They turned on their sides facing each other. Guy just hoped Andrés wouldn't be caught by the police—it was a serious offense, wasn't it. Jail time?

"I like it that we both look alike, thin and hairy and tall, except you have these cute little ears"—he touched them— "and that perfect skin."

Guy laughed. "And I'm ten years older."

Startled, Andrés propped himself up on an elbow and said, "You're kidding."

"I'm thirty-eight. Look. I'll show you my passport."

"I always assumed you were six years *younger* than me."

"As Pierre-Georges would say, professionally I'm twenty-three. But chronologically I'm thirty-eight."

"I've always seen you as a little brother, someone I had to protect."

"Let's go on pretending. I like that role."

"It's crazy, how do you do it?"

"Genes, I guess. My brother Robert is another Dorian Gray, though my mother looks her age. Maybe I'll be struck by a *coup de vieux*." He sang the Beatles' line, "'Will you still need me, will you still feed me, when I'm sixty-four?' and when I look it?"

"I'll always love you," Andrés blurted out. And Guy looked at him with a sad smile, as if doubting and believing at the same time this eternal pledge.

"Anyway, it's all an illusion," Guy said. "Here you can see crow's feet." He pointed to his eyes. "And here my chin line is giving way no matter how many isometrics I do or how many sticks of gum I chew in private. And my nose is getting bigger every year, though luckily I was born with little jug ears. But the secret of looking young is always darting about, never staring at a fixed point, being the first to leap up and fetch the milk." He was very proud of the word "fetch," which had no equivalent in French. Lately they'd begun to speak mostly English to each other. Guy had no Spanish and Andrés's French was rusty. Besides, Americans resented foreign languages being spoken around them. Americans thought foreigners were like impertinent kids speaking pig latin to mock their elders.

"No," Andrés said, "it's your face! Nothing to do with being constantly in motion, though you do that, too, my little hummingbird. Your face is just so perfect and unlined and beautiful."

"*Autant que ça dure.* As long as it lasts."

"You're just gloomy because your father died."

"When a father dies, the son sees himself approaching the edge of the cliff: Next!"

"You always make everything into a general principle," Andrés said, teasing him, looking at how the black hairs on Guy's legs grew darker and denser as they approached his crotch and started to swirl as if being drawn into a vortex. They were such strong legs, strong like a bow strung with powerful muscles. Andrés could feel himself growing hard again and was afraid of annoying Guy with the persistence of desire—maybe Guy was too old to go at it multiple times! Andrés lay on his stomach to hide his erection but propped himself on his elbows so his bald spot wouldn't be right under Guy's nose.

"We Frenchies are just like that," Guy said, smiling. Guy buried his face in his hands, then lowered them slowly, as if peeking at Andrés: "Are you shocked that I'm so old?"

Andrés just rolled over on his side, revealing his erection.

"Very eloquent," Guy said. They made love again. The phone rang and rang. "Why doesn't the service pick up?" They took turns fucking each other. To Guy they enjoyed an almost oneiric freedom with each other, something he'd never known, which had nothing to do with role-playing and everything to do with abandon.

When Guy phoned his service the operator said a Mr. Fred had called and was back in St. Vincent's. Guy showered and dressed rapidly and walked over to the hospital. Guy faintly resented these constant emergencies, as if Fred had designed them to trap Guy into seeing him more frequently. He stopped by the front desk to ask which was Fred's room and zigzagged down the polished marble corridors to the elevator in the far southeast corner. His irritation melted away and he realized that all along it had been anxiety about what he'd find in Fred's room.

St. Vincent's had more cases of AIDS than any hospital in America, Guy had heard. Now he was walking past so many rooms housing cadaverous men on drips, it was as if Auschwitz victims were being resuscitated. Some seemed unsalvageable. They were like those concentration camp prisoners whom other inmates called "Muselmanns" because they just rocked back and forth, their eyes vacant, waiting for the end.

Fred wasn't one of those. He must have been given some sort of upper because he chattered incessantly and licked his dry lips. He winced under Guy's light touch when Guy bent down toward the bed. He was squinting—could he see Guy? Surely he must recognize his distinctive cologne. There were two other visitors when Guy arrived, cronies, childhood friends from Brooklyn, two old, portly men with liver spots on their hands and wattles under their chins. Fred would probably look like them if he hadn't had the spots blowtorched off his hands and a surgical lift of his chin. But how much more natural and comfortable these men seemed, with their hands folded over their bellies and their lived-in faces. Jews, Guy thought, and wondered why he'd never met any of Fred's childhood friends before, out on Fire Island. He'd heard that Jews were good family men who didn't drink or gamble or play with boys. Was Fred a tragic exception?

Fred made the introductions and the visitors gave him a limp handshake and tilted their faces in attitudes of suspicious inspection, as if Guy with his youth and startling good looks were the very embodiment of the Christian Gay Plague.

Guy said, "What's wrong with you now? You don't look sick."

"I'm blind. CMV in the eyes."

"How horrible. Are they curing it?"

"That's why I have the drip," Fred said wearily. "They're going to implant a pellet directly into my eyes with Something-Acyclovir in it. But it's irreversible." He looked tired. Guy wondered how long his friends had been here.

"Is it permanent?"

"Yes, I'm blind," Fred said bitterly. "Great for a film producer."

One of the guests had brought Fred a murder mystery, not even a new copy, which he suggested might be a good property for Fred to develop. "You could get your friend to read it to you."

"Just because you finally got around to reading a book, Marty, is no reason to turn it into a fuckin' movie."

"It's a sort of a Cagney film," Marty said defensively.

"Great. How long has he been dead? Nah, I probably won't be making any more films. I certainly won't spend my last days listening to Mickey Spillane. Keats, maybe, or Tolstoy. Or James Michener. Something classy."

Guy was reeling from news of the diagnosis. "You're really blind? You can't see me?"

"I'm blind!" Fred shouted, then he paused and smiled. "But I can remember every detail of your face. Sit here," he said, patting the bed, "so I can read your face like Braille."

Guy was embarrassed in front of the other men; he was a *fegala*, wasn't that what they were thinking, a gentile *and* a faggot and the angel of death. But he couldn't deny poor Fred anything, so he perched on the edge of the bed and lifted Fred's hands to his face, and Fred's hands roamed ravenously over his perfect features and even thundered over his ears. It was too much of a display of affection for the visitors; they stood and bade farewell. "Thank God these nudniks are gone, real schnorrers, always wanting something. That Marty always was a putz."

"Speak English," Guy said, laughing.

Fred's fingers, tasting of rubbing alcohol, traced his teeth and his lips, even caged his fluttering eyelids for a second. Guy thought of fireflies.

"My darling boy," Fred said. "My beauty."

"Since you've gotten sick," Guy said to be nice, "you look thinner and twenty years younger."

"I do?" Fred asked eagerly.

"Yes," Guy said, wondering how far he could go, "you look like that A-list gay you've always wanted to be." Tears sprang to Guy's eyes; luckily Fred couldn't see them.

"Perfect, and I can't even look in the mirror." He paused. "I don't want you to think you gave it to me. I went out to the Meat Rack last summer and got fucked."

"Without a rubber?"

"Yes, goddamn it, without a rubber."

"Just one time?"

"You're meshuga," Fred said, "with your multiple exposures, just one time you can get infected. I'm the living proof; that's the only time I ever bottomed."

Guy suddenly wondered if Andrés was clean. Was he faithful? That's why Guy thought he must always be available sexually for him—and passionate—or else he'd look elsewhere for that necessary fifth orgasm a day. Was he using his studio to trick?

Fred, as if reading Guy's mind, asked, "How's Andrew?"

Guy said, "He's fine. Do you want to sleep? Should I leave,

or should I sit over here and read a book while you nap? Tell me. I'll do whatever you say."

"Stay. Stay. Do you have a book?"

"I'll step out and buy the paper and get a coffee and come back in half an hour. Do you want something from the outside world?"

"Nothing, some wintergreen gum. Promise you'll come back?"

"I promise."

"That Marty! You could read the fuckin' Mickey Spillane."

Guy felt exhausted when he left Fred and walked past all those somber, silent men in their identical rooms—young, he supposed, but looking ancient, with their gaunt faces and their open mouths. He wanted to flee—he wished he could shoot a commercial in Tahiti, someplace sunny and distant from all this.

The rooms were identical but filled with grief and disease, flowers and stuffed animals and ranks of get-well cards.

People kept saying, "AIDS is not a death sentence," and they spoke of fighting it, but that was all nonsense; American puritans acted as if everything were just a matter of willpower. It did kill its victims, one after another, relentlessly. If Fred's indiscretion was in the Meat Rack, then that must mean he was infected *after* he fucked Guy last spring; that was a relief—although all this effort to pin down the exact occasion was futile and silly. No one knew precisely how it was transmitted and it seemed everyone, men and women, straight and gay, was vulnerable.

Guy got a phone call from Andrés one morning in February at nine A.M. His studio had been raided by the cops and the FBI and he was being retained at a federal prison, and they'd confiscated all his forgeries and were holding them as evidence. Two of his dealers in New York had also been rounded up in the same sweep. Guy wondered if he himself was a person of interest. He called Pierre-Georges.

"I wonder why Andrés was taking such risks?" Guy asked.

"He thought he needed more money to keep up with you. He told me so. What a careless guy, getting caught like that. And he's a risk queen—he used to have a motorcycle. These young men always get killed. The best source for organ transplants. Don't they call them 'donor cycles'?"

"Why didn't you tell me he was worried about money?" Guy asked, annoyed with the callous chatter.

"As your manager I didn't want to see you lavishing a fortune on that Andrés. I know you don't care about money, but someday—someday soon—you'll be grateful to me. And by the way, make sure your friend Fred transfers to you the title of 'Petticoat Junction.'" (That was Pierre-Georges's nickname for their Fire Island house.)

"Please don't bring that up. I've got to help Andrés. That's the thing."

"He was caught red-handed," Pierre-Georges said, interrupting. "He'll be in prison and released in six or seven years and deported for good. In prison he'll be raped, a pretty boy like him, and he'll catch AIDS. And die. Be a realist."

Guy said, "You're insufferable," and hung up on Pierre-Georges, who immediately called back and said, "I'll find you the best lawyer."

At last Guy muttered, "Thank you."

True to his word, Pierre-Georges found a lawyer later in the day whom Guy rushed to Midtown to see, wearing a new blue silk suit. (Guy preferred the French word, *costume*, since it was explicit about clothes as playacting.)

The lawyer, an old Hungarian whose fingers were yellow from nicotine and who had four original Magrittes on the wall, explained that Dalí's case was complicated, that nearly half the prints attributed to him were fake. "There are new prints that Dalí never made, then there are reprints that are adaptations of real Dalí paintings, then there are new fake prints added to authentic editions, then there facsimiles with forged signatures, and finally there are fake copies of real prints." The man smiled and made Guy an espresso on a machine he had next to his desk. He was a chain smoker. His office was on Fifth Avenue and had big windows that looked out across the street to the Forty-second Street library. "It's all a mess, especially because the master himself signed a hundred thousand blank sheets of paper. He was already gaga, but his greedy wife . . ." It was snowing, and Guy imagined the bronze library lions were shivering.

"Can we post bail for poor Andrés?"

"It might be very high because he's a foreigner who could flee."

"That's okay."

"Why would he do these forgeries?"

Guy thought the man was a sophisticated European and could deal with the truth. "Money. He's my . . . boyfriend and felt he had to keep up. I earn a lot. I'm a model." The man nodded his head in mock obeisance, which irritated Guy, who was quick to add, "It's a very brief career."

"Like a butterfly's," the man said politely. "All beauties have brief lives. Professional lives."

Guy wasn't sure if the man was flirting or just civilized. Guy had been in America too long, where real men were always gruff, might lunch but never dine with another man, and, seated even next to each other, conversed in loud voices as if they were miles apart. They didn't want to be seen conversing softly, confidingly. Nor would real men sit in adjoining chairs at a table for four, but were always seen facing each other. But in Europe even heterosexuals were refined, at least the educated ones. He'd had a very refined friend, a curator at the Louvre called Titus, and he'd asked him point-blank if he was gay. "*Non, je m'excuse, j'aime les filles*," he said after their twelfth intimate supper.

The lawyer, Lazlo, took down all Andrés's details and promised he'd get him out on bail in a day or two. "Does he speak English?"

"Perfectly," said Guy.

"I'll have to meet with him to put together our defense. I know a lot about the surrealists—Magritte was my friend, as was the photographer Kertész, another Hungarian in New York like me."

Guy nodded to show he recognized the names. He thanked Lazlo for taking on the case and the lawyer very politely accompanied him to the elevator. Guy handed him his card. "I'm just the right person for this job," Lazlo said. "A foreigner, an art expert, somewhat experienced as a lawyer." He smiled at his own modesty and patted Guy on the back. He was considerably shorter than Guy and his glasses, as Guy could see in the neon glare, were smudged. He was puffing away on his cigarette.

"What will happen to him?" Guy asked.

"He'll probably spend a few years in prison."

"Years?"

"Yes, it's a serious crime, you know. He must love you a lot.

We might get him out on parole with two hundred hours of community service."

Guy shook his head and stared at his own lustrous lace-up shoes below the knife-sharp crease of his trousers. "Yes," he said, "in love. Foolish boy."

That evening as Guy was eating unbuttered popcorn with Lucie and filling her in on the whole horror story, Lazlo phoned. "He'll be out tomorrow," he said.

"Thank you, thank you," Guy cried out. He never let himself show excitement (except in bed), but this time his gratitude burst forth. Lucie, puzzled by the astonishing enthusiasm, cocked her head and smiled quizzically, like a hard-of-hearing person listening to an explosion.

"And the . . . *caution*, the bail, was it very dear?"

"Not so bad, we'll talk about all that in the morning."

After Guy hung up he hugged Lucie and danced around the room with her in a sort of ecstasy-polka. Then he called Pierre-Georges with the good news.

Pierre-Georges said sourly, "That still doesn't mean he won't serve time."

Guy didn't want to think about that and said, "What are you watching? I can hear the TV."

"An old movie—horrible color."

"What movie?"

"*Seven Brides for Seven Brothers*."

"Oh, I like that one."

"It's idiotic." Then, after a pause, Pierre-Georges asked, "Do you think Andrés knew what kind of risk he was running?"

"Yes, I'm sure he did."

"He must love you very much." He was the second person to say that today.

Guy's instinct was to pass that off as a gibe or a joke, but he caught himself and said softly, "Yes. He must. It's crazy love, but it is love."

When Andrés was released the next morning at nine, Guy was there to greet him. It was from the federal prison down on Park Row and office workers were swarming around him. Guy had put on a black cashmere turtleneck and black slacks and was wearing his black cashmere peacoat. He thought all the black would highlight his pale face, and the touch of cashmere would be comforting. And it might suggest, as bright colors would not, how grave the situation was and that he was . . . in mourning (*en deuil*).

Andrés walked into his arms, though normally he was self-conscious in public. All that was behind them; they had so little time together left, Guy felt he was in an opera, the last tragic act. Andrés held Guy's head between his long hands and covered him with kisses. They were both crying.

"Wanna see my head shots?" Andrés asked with a grin, and showed him two mug shots the police had taken, one straight on and the other in profile. He was wearing a uniform in the pictures, though now he was back in yesterday's clothes. "My first modeling job," he said ruefully.

Guy said, "Good cheekbones, bad lighting."

Andrés said, "They actually call it a booking photo. Isn't that funny?"

Andrés smelled. They rushed home and went to bed. They made love twice in a row, and for once Guy didn't keep Andrés from kissing his nipples or his mouth. Guy licked Andrés's fluffy armpit, which smelled. Guy wanted to memorize his body, soon to be lost to him for years. Andrés had a few dark hairs between his nipples, but in the daylight Guy could see faint swirls of short, almost blond hair across his torso, the fuzz that would turn long and dark by the time he got out of prison. His uncircumcised penis tasted rank. Guy propped himself up and studied it. It was big and ugly, with such a long trunk and such a loose sack—it looked prehistoric but friendly, like some pet lizard relative known to the family alone. As Andrés bit into his nipple he looked up searchingly into Guy's face. "I guess you'll be doing this with other men now."

Guy said, "Hush." And then he added, "It depends on how many years . . . we're apart."

Andrés burst into tears and sobbed and sobbed on Guy's chest. Guy kept stroking his hair and wished he'd been more reassuring. The phone rang but Guy let the service pick up. Then it rang again. But Guy was trapped under a sobbing young man. What if it was poor blind Fred? Or a booking agent? He didn't want to crush this moment under the rolling juggernaut of his career, not now, when Andrés's life was going up in flames.

"I haven't even told my parents yet," Andrés said in a spookily quiet, solemn voice. It sounded like a whisper in a cavern. "It will break their hearts. They were living through me."

"Have you told Rutgers yet? Your adviser?" Guy asked.

"Of course not!" Andrés snapped. "When would I have told them?"

"I'm sorry. I forgot."

"And now with Interpol, this will follow me around the rest of my life. And I'll never get my degree. Who would hire a criminal anyway? In the past even a criminal could become a grade-school teacher in the Andes or Angola, but now everyplace is interconnected. Should I just kill myself?"

Guy was suddenly energized. "No, you should call this

brilliant lawyer who's an expert in art and immigration. He says maybe he'll get you out on parole."

"No, my contact at Drew Fine Arts got two years, and he's an American citizen—two years and a fine of three thousand dollars, and he wasn't forging fakes, just selling them."

"But Lazlo told me the whole Dalí estate is a mess because the master—"

"Yes, but Dalí's paper was watermarked with an infinity symbol and was from a particular factory that went belly-up in 1980. There are tons of Dalí products out there—shirts, cognac bottles, gilt oyster knives, ashtrays for Air India—but they're all authorized."

"How disgusting," Guy murmured.

Andrés took offense: "He's a great Catalan artist and I only worked on lithos of his best work. *The Great Masturbator*, the *Bullfight* series, *Cosmic Warrior*, *Caesar in Dalivision* . . ."

"Yes, of course," Guy said, trying to soothe him.

They went together to Lazlo's office the next morning at ten. And the lawyer seemed charmed by them both, two young men so handsome and appealingly happy, at least on a better day. Lazlo asked them lots of questions and both he and Andrés took copious notes. Guy looked out the window at the crowds surging down Fifth Avenue, and it seemed unreal to him that they were all free and soon Andrés would be behind bars. It seemed an utterly arbitrary thing, that society would care so much about its precious property that it would punish a young man in the flower of his youth for stealing some of it. "Stealing" was a big word, since he was only copying an inferior hack who endlessly plagiarized himself and invited everyone else to join in. Even the experts would trip all over themselves trying to pinpoint the exact crime Andrés had committed. Dalí himself was dead or dying, as waxy as his absurd mustaches, and there were no pockets in the shroud, but if the heirs and lawyers were all that greedy, then Guy could pay them off. Surely no one cared about the integrity of this artist who had made a career of selling himself out. Dalí would probably have even been flattered that such a clever, handsome guy had bothered to copy his images so industriously. A copy of a fake by a fraud was surely a negligible sort of offense.

Lazlo made them cups of espresso. The cups looked none too clean. He said something that suggested he, too, regarded Dalí as a charlatan, and Guy's passionate young Colombian took offense, predictably. And of course it was immaterial the absolute quality of the work he'd plagiarized. "Victimless crime" were the words stuck in Guy's head. The room smelled of coffee and Gitanes and Guy suspected the large panes of glass were slick with all these continental fumes.

They hurried home with a new urgency and fell on each other, famished and frightened. Guy could taste the coffee in Andrés's mouth. He admired his lean, muscled white ass as if he'd never seen it before, the play of muscles across it like summer lightning, except it was something humble and familiar, not cosmic but a companion, a friend, at once familiar and exciting. They were desperate and it occurred to Guy that the police could never come to arrest Andrés if Guy refused to answer the door, if they nailed it shut and fed only on each other, as white as lab mice. They were two solid men, each 150 or 160 pounds, over six feet tall, big beasts; they could afford to fast for days, weeks. Guy wanted to buy them just a month or two; when the police broke down the door they'd find them locked in each other's arms, forming a rotting crab on the beach of a bed rich in waves of linen. They might be dead.

"What if we just ran away?" Guy said. "There must be some drought-ridden farm near Cartagena where they'd never find us or some village in the Congo where the police would die of malaria. I don't want to live long—just a while longer with you. And then when the police closed in on our African shack we could set it on fire and go up in flames."

Andrés started to speak and then sobs overtook him and he cried for half an hour on Guy's chest. Something about his disarray, his vulnerability, excited Guy. The idea that this lithe, sinewy man was so wracked by sobs turned Guy on as Andrés thrashed from side to side. They wouldn't even have conjugal rights in prison.

Andrés couldn't bear not to be lodged inside Guy, sheathed inside Guy's body; it had nothing to do with being macho, it was just the need to hide, to merge, to infest.

Guy didn't dare refuse him. He didn't want to refuse him, but it was hard to get on with their ordinary lives with Andrés's finger hovering constantly over the pause button. They had to pretend at least they were living a normal life, didn't they, the unworried, unhurried rhythm of their average days, or else nothing was enjoyable. It was the dailiness of their existence that delighted them, especially when it was slashed through with passion, like burlap erupting into red velvet welts. They had to set the table, scramble the eggs, wash the dishes—they couldn't just devour each other, could they?

Guy had to visit poor blind Fred in St. Vincent's, the City of the Dead on the seventh floor of Spellman, small and dirty, all the single rooms converted into doubles. Surprisingly, it was a carnival atmosphere that afternoon—two drags were accompanying Rollerena, and she whizzed by, homely in her black glasses and dusty organdy, a fixed smile on her face, a wand in her hand. She looked like a nerdy high school girl with glasses and acne. Sister Patricia was silently patrolling the halls, her scrubbed face accented with her furry eyebrows, her white hands tucked into her full black sleeves. Fred was asleep. When Guy woke him, he smiled and said, "I wish you'd buy me a Walkman. It's so fuckin' boring being blind."

"A what?"

"You can listen to music with it," and he mimed earphones.

"*Ah! Un Baladeur!*"

"Do you people have your own names for everything? What's a computer?"

"*Ordinateur.*"

"See—and a hamburger?"

"*Merde.*"

Fred laughed and sobered up enough to say, "Come tomorrow at one. My lawyer will be able to transfer the deed."

"One? Is that within visiting hours? Most hospitals—"

"There are no hours up here. Sister Patricia accepts everything—hell, some of these guys even spend the night with their lovers. I've even heard they decorate their rooms with photos and blankets and balloons from home, not that that would do a blind man any good. No dogs so far, but that'll come."

Guy kissed Fred goodbye on his thin, sour-tasting lips. He worried that if he accepted the Fire Island house he'd get into a legal squabble with Fred's family. But, *merde*, if the Anglo Saxons had these crazy laws that allowed you to disinherit your own children, then he, Guy, would have to profit from their cruel, unreasonable rules. Anyway, the "children" were two middle-aged men well launched in their own careers, or so Fred said. Wasn't one of them a podiatrist? Sore feet surely must be lucrative. Anyway, they neglected Fred and had taken their mother's side in the divorce.

It was tempting to take the house—that way Guy would never have to worry again about money. He could rent it out every summer. And who knew how much Andrés's defense would set him back?

At twelve-thirty the next day when Guy was brushing his teeth and spraying his hair, Andrés seemed moody and childish about the prospect of even a half an hour's separation.

"The poor man's dying," Guy said. "He's already blind. You might as well be jealous of the parakeet."

Andrés said sullenly, "We don't have a parakeet." Then he laughed charmingly in spite of himself, the laugh cracking the marble of his face, and said, "And if you did, I'd be jealous of it."

Guy ruffled his hair and hurried out before Andrés could become desperate again. When Guy arrived on the seventh floor he could see Fred was propped up in bed. He looked shaved and washed for the occasion, his hair combed. That man Marty was sitting in the only chair, his little soft hands folded over his belly.

As he entered the room, Guy said hi. He didn't want to startle Fred by surprising him with a touch—Guy was good at imagining things from another person's point of view. Marty gave his hand to be shaken—he seemed to be unfamiliar with the custom of shaking hands. Guy felt Marty was disapproving—maybe he was friends with the seal. Or maybe it was Jewish tribal thing—why enrich the pretty goy? Or maybe Guy was just being paranoid.

"I brought you a Discman—and a dozen CDs. I'll bring you some more tomorrow—just tell me what you want."

"Bernard Herrmann. Dimitri Tiomkin. Classy music composers."

"What about Michel Legrand?"

"Who?"

"He did 'The Umbrellas of Cherbourg.'"

"French, right? Forget it. Well, let's get started."

Marty had drawn up the papers and now he sat beside Fred on the edge of the bed. "Do you want me to read it to you?"

"Just summarize it in ordinary language."

"Well, it leaves the Bel Air house to Ceil and twenty thousand to each of the boys and the Fire Island house to Guy. If anyone contests the will their bequest will be canceled. It's called the 'in terrorem' clause."

"Do you think that will stick?"

"I guess they could claim you were demented."

"I probably will be if the CMV goes into my head. That's why I want to get this over now."

"Only twenty thousand for each of the boys?" Guy asked, trying to sound fair.

"Fuck 'em! They stood by their mother. Anyway, that's all I have if I pay off the Fire Island house. I'm not made of money; I told you I am a very minor millionaire, unless I get my AIDS movie going. I live from film to film."

Marty had to guide Fred's hand for the will but also for the transfer of the deed to Guy. A nurse was called in as a witness.

"Ceil and the boys are going to be spittin' mad," Fred said with a big grin.

"You're right there," Marty muttered. "I can hear the schreiing already. So long, Fred."

"So long, Marty, don't be a stranger. Come back and see me."

"Will do. What about all your actors? They ever come to see you?"

"Those schwartzes? They're mostly ashamed to have been in all those *Super Fly* movies. They want to forget about it. That was a different period, Marty. Do you have Guy's address? For sending him the deed?"

"You wrote it down for me."

The minute Marty and the nurse were gone, Fred said, "Are we alone? Good. Kiss me."

Fred was chewing some of the gum Guy had brought him, so his lips were fresh and moist. But it all felt too much like a transaction to Guy—I'll give you the house if you give me a kiss. Of course the house was worth millions of kisses. It was just Fred's assumption he now had the right to a kiss that saddened Guy—everything in America was transactional!

Of course, Guy was the villain stealing the bread out of Fred's sons' well-fed jowls. There was more shrieking in the hallway—probably another surprise birthday complete with balloons and candles. But neither Guy nor Fred was curious.

Out of deference, since Fred was blind, Guy left the lights off as the night swept in; Guy felt he should share Fred's darkness.

It was strange how content they were just holding hands, after all the agony of his love-grappling with Andrés, the constant anguish of trying to get another millimeter inside each other's holes; it was kind, it was peaceful, it was companionable to just sit together like this. After all, Fred had come to the end and his last thought had been for Guy. He was a rough woodcut of a man, but the portrait was of a kind man even so.

Guy felt that his life was under assault and that Fred was doing something crucial to help him. Guy had a superstition that he could preserve his youth only so long as nothing touched him, so long as he remained immune to any intensity of feeling. But now his father's death, Andrés's looming plight, Fred's blindness and imminent death—all these events were threatening to engrave marks on Guy's face. Something (or maybe it was Nothing) had stunned him into eternal youth, into immobility and imperviousness, but now the ice was cracking, great glacier shelves were collapsing into the sea, a disaster was warming up—and soon he'd be just a shrinking iceberg, another weathered face, he would come to life only to die. He ran to the mirror to look at himself. Nothing had changed.

Another hour went by. By the last glimmer of daylight seeping down an airshaft and through the dirty window, Guy read a few articles out of *Variety* for Fred about the movie business. The slang and abbreviations were mostly unfamiliar to Guy. ("Is this English?" he asked, and Fred chuckled.)

Apropos of nothing, Fred said, "Remember that line: 'I grow old, I shall wear the bottom of my trousers rolled'? I always wondered what that meant. But now I know—you shrink as you get old and your pants are too long. And remember how gays are always supposed to be licking their eyebrows down, like this?" and he mimed licking his finger and pressing it down on his eyebrow. "That was always shorthand for saying someone was gay. But your eyebrows do grow long with age and a gay senior would worry about that."

Suddenly two men came into the room, wearing cream-colored masks and gloves and blue hospital gowns and shower caps. They switched the lights on and one of them said, "Dad?" and he came to sit beside his father, who touched him and said, "Howie? What are you wearing?"

"Who's this man, Dad?" To Guy he said, "Excuse me, but would you leave? This is a family moment."

"Stay right where you are, Guy. This putz is my son. Why are you wearing all that junk, Howie?"

"For self-protection, Dad. You're highly contagious, in case you forgot. A tear, a mosquito bite, a lick of saliva could infect us, then it's curtains. Guy, is that your name? Scram!"

"How dare you, Howie? Guy's my lover."

"Lover?" the other man said, and laughed. He was shorter and rounder than Howie. "Some lover! So you're the frog scumbag who infected our father, right? What's he doing here, Dad—how did he get permission to visit? Family only. Nurse! Nurse!"

Fred said, "Don't budge. These schmucks ignore me for months, then come rushing in for the money shot."

The one called Howie, his black eyes flashing with rage over his mask, said, "He has no right to be here. Lover? The law doesn't recognize same-sex lovers."

"Howie," Fred said, "we all know you're a shyster, but the usual laws don't apply here at St. Vincent's. Sister Patricia is running the AIDS wards and she knows we're all about to croak and she has the good sense to recognize real love as opposed to greedy so-called family love."

"But the law—"

"Law, schmaw," Fred said wearily. "I'm blind, so I can't see if you're all suited up, too, Buster, for your dad the hazmat."

"I've taken the normal precautions," Buster said primly.

"I suggest you reduce your risk pronto by getting the hell out."

"What about your estate, Dad? You're not leaving anything to this frog-slut, are you? We're the rightful heirs and we'll fight him tooth and nail."

"Nail?" Fred laughed. "I guess you know plenty about infected nails in the foot business. I'll give you ten to get out or I'll call two big interns to escort you out. Too bad our last meeting had to be so acrimonious."

"Dad!" Howie wailed indignantly. "We love you. Didn't we come in all the way from Scarsdale?"

"Big fuckin' deal. One, two, three—"

"We're going to fight this, Dad, poor old demented man. They call it the Stockholm syndrome, the victim bonds with his captor—"

"Shut the fuck up," Fred said. "You don't know anything bout this 'cause you haven't talked to me in two years. Five, six, seven—"

"He'll never get a dime," Buster said, "your scumbag so-called lover."

"Eight, nine, ten!" Fred pushed the emergency button and the nurse came running.

"Yes, Mr. Fred," a big Caribbean woman said. "What does my boyfriend want?"

"Helen, I want you to get these shmucks out of here. They're annoying the hell out of me."

"But darlin', they said they're your sons."

"No, they're just bill collectors."

Helen said, "Shame on you, bothering a nice man like my little sweetheart, Fred. Now git!"

"Ma'am, we really are his sons," Howie said.

"That's funny, I never sees you befo' and I been here the whole time."

"I can get a court order banning this Guy creep and—"

"You do that, hon, but visiting hours are up, now git before I call for help."

"And he can stay?" Howie pointed to Guy.

"He's Mr. Fred's special friend. Rules don't apply."

"We'll see about that. I'm going right now to the district judge."

Fred smiled. "I'd say, 'Over my dead body,' but I don't want to rush things."

"Dad," Buster said. "Don't you have any family feeling?"

"No more than you do," Fred said coolly. "No, don't touch me with your gloves and masks—just rush right back to your mother with horror stories of your demented dad."

"Do you admit you're demented?"

"Get out!" Fred bellowed.

"I've taped you saying that you're demented. It can be used in court."

The nurse, Helen, had gone off to fetch two orderlies in the meanwhile. "Would you boys escort these gen'men out? They're bothering my sweetie pie, Mr. Fred, and visiting hours are definitely over."

As the brothers were accompanied out, the lawyer shook a finger at Guy and said, "You'll be hearing from us!"

Fred was laughing. "How did I beget two such miserable specimens? Come sit here beside me." Guy complied and bent down to kiss Fred's puckered lips.

6

I N T H E C O U R T R O O M the lawyer for the prosecution had a
beautiful face, cruel blue eyes, and such a strong Scottish
brogue that neither Andrés nor Guy could understand anything
he said. Everything in the courtroom was dun-colored and
outmoded, starting with the short balding judge in his creased
black robe and with his grating Brooklyn accent, even his way
of sucking up his nasal phlegm after every halfhearted remark—
Guy agreed with Chanel that everything was fashion—the
weather, the room, the people.

Guy was so fearful of what was to become of Andrés, but it
was hard to think these common people would be deciding his
fate. Perhaps it was because of his privileged (even fairy-tale)
adulthood and his banal childhood and adolescence, but in
France, where everyone could be bought, Guy kept thinking if
he fucked or paid or befriended someone, he could make all
this go away. The idea that his beautiful lover's fate was in the
badly manicured hands of these slobs (okay, okay, the Scot
wasn't a slob) infuriated him. He knew he was just a poor kid
from Clermont-Ferrand, but suddenly he felt like a marquis by
contrast and this trial seemed to be the revenge of the vulgar on
the extraordinary. He was right to take Fred's house; never

again must he be poor or vulnerable. He must be armored against the assaults of the average with wealth and beauty and connections.

Lazlo was persuasive and showed reproductions of the blank paper Dalí had pre-signed, and he handed to the judge copies of papers on Dalí that Andrés had written for Rutgers. He argued that Andrés repented his misdemeanors now but that committing them had been so tempting because he was a desperately poor grad student who received nothing but free tuition and a $10,000 stipend in return for teaching three undergraduate sections of an art history lecture course.

The Scot took up each of Lazlo's arguments; Lazlo had to translate, in a whisper, his brogue into ordinary English. The Scot said that Andrés had lived perfectly well on his stipend for two years and hadn't even taken out a student loan. That he was a good student only made his forgery all the more reprehensible; he had diabolically used his Dalí expertise to facilitate his crimes. It was Dalí's choice to exploit his own name. If he wanted to sell his signature, that was his right and far from an argument in favor of legalizing the forgeries of a greedy, cynical interloper.

The judge found Andrés guilty and handed down a sentence of three years in prison without parole. He said that Andrés's crime was worse than that of his dealers (who'd been sent to prison for two years) precisely because of his skill and intelligence—and the training he'd received from a state-supported university. He'd learned how to forge works of art at the expense of the American taxpayer.

Guy noticed that the little judge seemed very jingoistic and Guy wished he hadn't engaged a lawyer with a foreign accent and name, and he wished he hadn't spoken to Lazlo in French. Americans could be very paranoid. They'd chosen a trial by

judge over a trial by jury because Lazlo had thought the tech-
nicalities of the case would baffle ordinary citizens, but then
again, maybe a jury would have pitied Andrés's obvious youth
and inexperience.

Andrés turned white when his sentence was read out, and he
was immediately handcuffed and taken off by two policemen.
Guy had foreseen a moment when they'd embrace, but that
didn't happen. Andrés was just led away. Guy turned to Lazlo
and said, "That's it? No more bail? He's gone for good?"

Lazlo smiled a sad little apologetic smile. "Of course we'll
appeal."

"On what grounds?"

"That the sentence is unreasonably harsh."

"Do you think the judge hated us because we're foreigners?"

Lazlo looked up through his bushy eyebrows and said, "No.
Because you're homosexuals. Handsome homosexuals. These
Jewish family men are like that sometimes."

Guy thought of Fred's vicious sons, but then he remembered
Lazlo himself was Jewish, and he seemed friendly enough.

Lazlo told him not to worry and hailed a taxi. Guy was
suddenly alone at eleven in the morning in an unfamiliar part
of town.

He took a cab home. This was the first warm day of April
after a long and difficult winter. The pear trees on his block
were budding, though they were the kind that never bore fruit.
Sterile trees. New York trees.

He picked up yogurt and fruit at a deli. Lucie was coming
over for lunch in an hour. The shopkeeper was friendly in a
routine way—today, dailiness seemed obscene, an outrage
when he thought of his poor Andrés in prison just for loving
him too much.

It felt empty, the day felt bruised, the light looked vacant and assaulted, his street felt at once familiar and strange, as if he were seeing it after a hundred-years' sleep. It was seldom he thought of himself as a single individual, whirling lonely through space, an unnoticed neural event pulsing somewhere in a minor, dimming universe, but today he felt alone and tiny and powerless.

He called his mother, which he did so seldom that he had to tell her right away that nothing was wrong, that he was just checking up on her, did she like her new Opel. He wanted to tell her about the terrible thing that had just happened to him but of course he couldn't, she'd never understand, he'd have to explain too many things going back too many years, so he ended up consoling her all over again for her husband's death. Because the telephone call and the renewed condolences were so unexpected, his mother sounded abashed and overly grateful, which left him feeling all the more empty when he hung up.

At least Lucie was warm and comforting. She held him as he told her about Andrés and they cried together. She was so fragrant and kind and gentle that he felt, guiltily, the shocking stirrings of desire. He never wanted to feel excited ever again, not over anyone. The very thought struck him as disloyal. Lucie sensed his discomfort and made popcorn and began to play with his hair, seriously considering if he'd look good with the wet look. She begged him to let her experiment. He could always just wash it out.

7.

WITH GREAT REGULARITY Guy intended to visit Andrés in prison and Fred in the hospital and felt perpetually guilty, as if he were responsible for their separate but horrible destinies. The first time he saw Andrés shorn and pale and skinny in his orange jumpsuit, he was thunderstruck. His arms looked so thin and helpless, his bald spot was gleaming, his face seemed to have sprouted five new moles, with the bad food he appeared to have grown a horrible little belly—not really! It was just a fold in his prison clothes. Guy could have slapped himself for the disparaging thought.

That afternoon, after he sat beside Fred and held his hand for fifteen minutes, Guy walked over to the Sheridan Square gym. All the rituals of his life had become so stale—and the perpetual guilt made him angry! He didn't want to feel like a bad person who brought disaster to everyone around him. He was listless with self-hatred and an irrational anger that could never find a rod to strike but idly played across the surface of his mind. As he trudged upstairs to the second floor and the gym's open door, he could smell the old sweat, hear the melancholy ring of dropped barbells, and he prepared himself to see those mastodons with their stained gym clothes, pockmarked faces, and neck veins about to pop.

But when he breached the entrance he saw identical blond twins, teenagers, maybe Finns like those models on the fold-out cover of *L'Uomo Vogue*. After Guy changed, he worked out near them so he could study them. They cheered him up. It was amusing to certify that they were identical down to the tiniest detail—the blond fuzz on their calves; the pointy nose that swerved to one side, thinned out, and turned red near the tip; the long eyetooth that gleamed with saliva; the bulging shoulder blades under identical crisp T-shirts with an unfamiliar logo—shoulder blades like unsprouted wings. They both touched their toes at the same moment and, as their T-shirts rose up, Guy could see identical black moles staining the intricately turned carpentry of their white, white waists. They were just as much mirror images in their behavior, murmuring to each other, exchanging fractional nods of encouragement, one bending to tie the laces of the other, but everything unemphatic. They were like gods posing as shepherds.

Their eyes lingered on Guy for an instant as if the camera, panning across his face and body, got stuck. It was such a slight hesitation as almost to go unremarked, but they both must have noticed Guy had intercepted their glance, because both boys blushed deeply, charmingly. A blush for them was nearly a cardiac arrest. Guy feared they'd faint due to the sudden concentration of blood. What did they see that instant when they looked at him? Compared to their freshness, he was wilted, lined, thick. Only in New York, where everyone was thirty-something, did he appear young. People had agreed he was young, as if by consensus. It was an article of faith. But these twins' skin was so fine-pored, so rosy; their arms were so firm, nothing was flabby, there was nothing ropy about their necks; they were dramatically thin but not starved-looking. They looked healthy. They hadn't been on diets. Their heads were too large for their bodies but their features were still small, neat, like entries written in a copperplate hand. The skin fit as neatly as a lady's glove on their long fingers, not a bit of sag or jiggle or looseness.

The twins must have been so embarrassed by the shared blush that they studiously ignored Guy for the rest of their workout and skipped their shower and hurried off still in their sweaty shorts. Guy thought they might be models, very young models, and he wished he'd seen them naked. They must live nearby.

That night he talked to Pierre-Georges. It was a relief to speak in French—he got all of Guy's allusions and shorthand and his muted sort of bitchiness. "Do you think Americans are vulgar? Like peasants?"

"Don't insult our poor peasants," Pierre-Georges said loftily.

"So you think French peasants are better than typical Americans?"

"You've been here too long to be able to say 'typical.' There are all kinds of Americans."

"But they're crude," Guy protested. "They talk so loud and sprawl. There's nothing tidy about them. They're materialists—nothing spiritual or cultured."

"Don't forget you're from Clermont-Ferrand, not Auteuil. People sprawl in your *département*. What's gotten into you?"

"Why are we here in this awful country?" Guy wailed. While Pierre-Georges paused for him to elaborate, Guy collapsed under the weight of everything, his life, this country. Finally Pierre-Georges said in a soft, consoling voice, "Put on your new cashmere blazer and I'll take you out to the Casa De Pré, you always liked that one."

"What will we talk about?" Guy asked plaintively.

"*Écoute*," Pierre-Georges said, vexed or pretending to be. "Listen—you're exaggerating. I'll see you there in thirty minutes. Don't keep me waiting."

"Forty-five?"

They ordered comfort food, a risotto with spring vegetables and a fruity bottle of Vouvray. Pierre-Georges sent the bread and butter back: too tempting. "Are you very sad about Andrés?"

Guy stared at Pierre-Georges and then just nodded gravely. Finally he said, "My life is such a mess. I thought it was supposed to be glamorous and enviable. That's what *Interview* said about me: glamorous, enviable. That's what *After Dark* said in its last issue in 1982: 'Gay, glittery, and glamorous.'"

"Only you remember that," Pierre-Georges said sourly.

"Yes, I'm sad. Crushed. I hate this country, with its puritanism and heartlessness and filthy diseases."

"And that's all Reagan's fault, I suppose?"

"Whose?" Guy asked, genuinely not recognizing the name.

"*Flute!*" Pierre-Georges lisped. It amused him to sound like a flustered French matron and to use out-of-date genteel swear words. "You honestly don't know who the president of the United States is?"

"Oh. *Her!*"

"They're going to revoke your green card."

"Good! I can't stand it here another day."

"Why?" Pierre-Georges asked. "People here think you're some sort of Norman aristocrat with a chateau. In France no one would be fooled. Just look at how you hold yourself at table."

Guy stopped slumping and sat upright. "Who cares about all that?" he asked.

"French people do. If you go back you'll have to deal with all that. Here you can reinvent yourself. And this is where the money is—important now that you're in your sunset years. How long have you been in the business?"

That night in bed Guy surprised himself because he was happy to be alone. He loved Andrés, he really did. No one had ever been so devoted to him. Guy realized that his way of measuring someone's devotion was a feminine aspect of his nature; only women wanted men who were devoted. Men wanted men and women who were hard to get. But he'd given himself entirely to Andrés; he'd never been so immersed in another man. But that night when he masturbated he didn't think of Andrés in his orange jumpsuit and bald spot. No, he imagined he was between the identical twins, that their bodies were as smooth as the alabaster lamps he'd seen once in Volterra. The boys were clambering over him in his fantasy like Sherpas on the slopes, everything coordinated between them. He fell asleep and dreamed they were all swimming together in some sort of low-ceilinged turbulent pool fed by hot springs. The boys were slippery as eels and in his dream one penis exploded in his anus and the identical penis flooded his mouth. Guy smiled in his sleep.

The fall menswear collections were being shown next week in Milan and Guy had a go-see with the new Armani representative in New York. It would be the usual cattle call. Guy could picture it all now, the way the boys, these angular giraffes, would be coiffed backstage with curlers and blow dryers, how makeup artists would swoop around them, highlighting their cheekbones (which already looked ready to explode through their skin), drawing bluish shadows under their heavily kohled eyes, retracing their lips with a vampirish color stick, and then the clothes, the sacred clothes, so much more important than the people wearing them, would be taken out of their sealed and numbered dry-cleaning bags. The boys would be lined up in their preposterous boots and leggings and velvet vests and jewelry, and the designer would fix each boy, spray a curl in place, unbutton a shirt one notch, turn up a collar, like an anxious chef standing at the kitchen door and arranging with greasy fingers the roast chicken to advantage before the grand presentation. They were all just chicken breasts under white sauce and bewigged with parsley.

The thought of trotting down the runway one more time as the buyers plied their paper fans against the stifling heat of the overhead lights and the bad but trendy rock music blared forth and the excited assistants applauded while the giraffes swarmed the runway for the finale and the modest couturier wore a shockingly conventional dark suit from Savile Row as he humbly took his bow, looking like a CEO or politician, a member of a different species from the models, and blew a kiss toward the buyer from Barneys—that prospect repelled Guy. He didn't want to go. Luckily the Armani representative didn't choose him; he told Pierre-Georges that Armani wanted more "ethnics" this year for his safari collection. Pierre-Georges was depressed, then frightened. "It's the beginning of the end. We're too old." Guy noticed the diplomatic "we."

Marty sent him the fully executed deed to the Fire Island house. That day, when Guy visited Fred, he thanked him again and offered him the chance again of leaving it to his sons.

"Why?" Fred asked. "They've never been out there and would be scared to go. That's where we were the happiest. It's sacred to us."

Fred's arms, torso, face, were covered with black spots—KS. Luckily, he couldn't see; he could nurse his illusions, with

Guy's help, that finally he was an A-list gay. Fred kept drifting off, but then he sat up with a sudden urgency: "There's a new test at last to see if you've got the virus. Guy, I want you to take it, pronto. I know you're very careful, whatever that means, but you've got to take care of yourself. I'd hate to think I'd given it to you. Promise you'll take the test."

"Can I do it right here in the hospital?"

"You bet."

"What'll I do if I'm positive? Who will take care of me?"

"Andrew?"

Guy reminded him that Andrés was in prison.

"Peter?" Fred said, meaning Pierre-Georges.

For a while Fred rambled on about Rock Hudson and how he'd "popularized" AIDS. "I wonder if those French doctors can help him. Imagine renting a private jet to take him to Paris—that must have set him back an arm and a leg." Guy didn't understand the reference to an arm and a leg—was he just raving? Amputation fantasies?

Suddenly Fred's attention concentrated and he asked almost slyly, "If you do have AIDS, have you thought who you'd leave the house to? My mother used to say, 'Never leave your jewelry to someone who doesn't have someone you know to leave it to—you don't want some distant cousin of your friend to end up with your stuff.'"

Guy said he was leaving everything to his own mother.

Fred smiled. "There's a good boy. She'd need it if you died."

Then Fred started talking disjointedly about his mother, long since dead.

When the neurologist came by, a German with an accent, a white beard, and a stomach, he made cheerful comments to his team and to Fred, who didn't exactly seem to know who he was. He was leading six neurology residents on rounds and he invited one young woman to examine the patient. She hammered Fred's elbows and knees with a mallet and looked at his eyes and tongue and poked him with her gloved hands. She asked him about his stool. She then said to her professor, "The patient shows signs of increased CMV infection, though reflexes remain stable. The liver is not hypertrophied. Patient's cognitive functions seem disoriented." The professor thanked Fred for cooperating—and suddenly they were all gone, leaving behind an audible silence.

"Sounds bad, huh?" Fred asked.

"About the same," Guy said with placid reassurance. "They were all so earnest."

"What was that about cognitive functions? Have I become dim-witted?"

"Not at all." Guy was angry that the resident had discussed Fred in front of him. He felt certain that would never happen in France—another example of American barbarism.

At the gym that evening he didn't see the twins, but the next day they were there. He was determined to speak to them, if only to ask something like when they'd be finished with the barbell. One of them left early, which seemed odd. The one who remained came right up to Guy and said, "You look familiar."

"I wish I could say the same," Guy replied with a smile.

The adolescent had a confused look in his eye but a brave, radiant smile on his lips as if he were determined to be in on the joke, mysterious as it might be. It was the same mixture of confusion and courage Guy had seen on the faces of the deaf.

They decided to spot each other while lifting a heavy barbell during a bench press. "Gee," Guy said, "you're much stronger than you look."

The twin smiled ruefully. "Do I look that out of shape?"

"Not at all." He looked him in the eye and said in a softer, sexier voice, "Not at all."

The twin had to adjust something in his jockstrap. He lowered his eyes and blushed a blood-red catastrophe, a total epidermal confession. And Guy felt a surge of power—what did people say, of agency?—once again. He felt triumphant that he could excite this boy. He was enthralled by his unique beauty. (He shouldn't say unique, since he knew it was twinned.)

Soon the other twin emerged from the locker room, showered and dressed, trailing a pine scent, unsmiling, one could almost say shy. He bade his brother farewell in a whispered mumble and was gone. He didn't look at Guy.

"I don't even know your name. I'm Guy."

"Is that spelled as in 'a guy'?"

"Maybe I should just say that."

"Never!" the boy exclaimed. "You're a foreigner?"

"French. Parisian."

"You don't meet many of those. Maybe you do in New York. We just moved here a week ago. We just moved here from Ely, Minnesota. I'm Kevin. My brother's Chris."

"I've never heard of Ely."

"It's just a small town in the north of Minnesota, near the Canadian border. It's where people get outfitted for canoe and camping trips into the Quetico-Superior country, which is on the Canadian side."

"Sounds cold."

"It is!" Kevin exclaimed excitedly, as if to encourage what might be a string of lucky guesses. When one of the other men working out looked up and frowned at the offending chitchat, Kevin blushed again, though pink, not red, this time. Social chatter not connected with working out was looked at askance, as in a library.

"Right now it's thirty-seven degrees in Ely. That's what my mom said. We're outfitters, right in the heart of town on Camp Street," he whispered, looking around nervously.

"Are you foreigners, too? You don't look American."

"Oh, we're Norwegian heritage. We went to Norwegian camp every summer. We can speak Norwegian, sort of. My sister married a real Norwegian ice hockey player and lives in Oslo now."

"You look Norwegian."

"You mean dumb?"

"Not at all, blond. Clean. Very clean."

Kevin got that confused look in his eye again, but he braved it out with a bigger smile, determined to be in on the joke, if that's what it was, at his own expense. "You mean clean as in boring?"

"Not at all," Guy protested. "Just because I'm French doesn't mean I'm nasty. I mean clean-handsome. Here, wanna do another set?"

"Okay." Kevin stretched out on the board and lifted the barbell and did ten more repetitions, though he slowed down for the last two and out of exhaustion let the bar drift to the left. Guy moved in tighter in case he needed to help him. Kevin looked up Guy's shorts.

After Guy did his set, Kevin whispered, "We're the only young guys in here, did you notice?"

So he thinks I'm young, Guy thought, relieved.

They sat in the sauna for five minutes and then took their showers. Kevin had a high, hairless butt of a lunar whiteness; there was no trace of hair, not even in the crack. His penis was small, nested in the merest excuse of a pubic bush. His torso was scarily childish, which prompted Guy to ask, "How old are you guys?"

"In June we'll be nineteen."

They decided to grab a cup of coffee together in the restaurant on the ground floor, where an old man was patiently mopping the linoleum, filling the air with the nostril-tickling smell of Lysol. The waitress, hair high and peroxided, asked with a steel-drilling accent, "What can I get you boys?" and Guy liked her for including him as one of the boys and absolving him of being a child molester.

"So what do you do, Guy?"

"I'm a model."

"Like in a fashion model?"

"Exactly."

"Cool. Somebody wanted to photograph Chris and me for some fashion shoot, but in the nude, which Chris didn't want to do. I'm gay but he's not."

"How strange. I thought you'd both be straight or both gay."

"Well, we've both experimented with boys and girls, and *yes*, we have slept together, but only a few times, twice, actually, but Chris has decided he's really straight and I think I'm really gay."

American straightforwardness still astounded Guy. A European could take years to get there, but it just popped out of this Minnesota mouth with the lips like Froot Loops and the teeth like Chiclets. It was all so simple, so innocent, but Guy didn't despise it, he could see Kevin was very pure.

"Don't you know for sure if you're gay? Haven't you tried it with lots of fellows?"

Again the bloodbath blush. "I'm a virgin," Kevin said, in a small, strangled voice, and Guy thought, irrationally, *Of course, that's why his dick is so small and his ass so rubbery*, but that stupid theory evaporated in the first warmth of reflection. "Except fooling around with my brother those two times."

"I see," Guy said, stalling for time, wondering what he could say that would be appropriate and maybe consoling, though perhaps consolation wasn't what was called for. "You were right not to do any nude shots."

"Why?"

"Real models, professional models, don't pose in the nude." And Guy remembered how his own nude photos had ended in *Blueboy* all those years ago.

"Oh, really? Why not?"

"Swimsuit ads, possibly, maybe underwear, but not total nudity. It just lowers your prestige, I guess, your mystery."

"Do you think I have some model potential?"

"It's no fun. It's not a good career for men. Maybe twelve men in the whole United States make as much as one hundred sixty thousand a year."

"Do you think I'm handsome enough?"

"It doesn't really have to do with looks. It's whether you're photogenic."

"Am I photogenic?"

"We won't know till you put together your portfolio." Guy had found young guys were more hypnotized by an authority if he wasn't entirely "supportive"; his reluctance to enthuse paralleled his own self-doubts. "But everyone treats models like you're beef, like meat, interchangeable. They try to pay you with clothes, not money. It's the girls who count, because it's women who buy clothes and beauty products. They're paid ten times more than us. And most of the population thinks we're all gay, though most male models are straight." Guy sighed.

"It's endless." He cocked his head to one side. "You're a little short. You have to be at least six feet tall, a size-forty jacket, a fifteen-inch neck. You have to fit into the clothes. Maybe for catalogue work they can pin the clothes here and there to fit, but for runway or fashion or editorial work you have to be a perfect size. The models are hired because the clothes fit them. You can't be five-foot-eleven."

"Do you think I have a good face?"

Guy whispered, "Angelic. Your jaw is a little strong, but that could be your trademark. I'd draw a little cleft into your chin to emphasize it."

"You can do whatever you like to me."

Guy hadn't been openly flirting and was taken aback by the kid's sudden flying of a white flag. "But you've really got to want it," Guy warned. "You've got to pound the pavement for six months and accept rejection. It's hard to be rejected. New York is all about rejection. They're so fucking rude, photographers, art directors, casting agents. The client is the worst of all. Secretly they resent us for doing nothing and getting rich. That's what they think. We don't do anything in their eyes."

Kevin scanned Guy's face. "With those cheekbones I could get rich, I'll bet."

They made a date to work out together the same time the next day. Kevin's brother, Chris, could barely look Guy in the eye, and he quickly absented himself to exercise on the other side of the gym.

"Did I say something wrong?" Guy asked.

"Naw, he's doing legs and squats today."

"Does he need us to spot him? Squats can be dangerous."

"He's wearing a belt." After reflecting a moment, Kevin said, "He wants to give us a little space." After another pause he said, "He might be jealous." Another set, and Kevin added, "He's probably worried you might want to have a three-way. You'd be surprised how many men have that fantasy, to be Lucky Pierre between identical twins."

"Gross," Guy said, ashamed that he'd had that fantasy himself.

"Guys are freaky. And like I said, Chris thinks he's more straight."

Over coffee downstairs, Guy said, "It must be strange to be identical twins. If you have to make a big decision in your life, is he the one you call automatically?"

"He's my best friend. Our mother used to dress us alike. We had a private language till we were eight and then a school psychologist told our mom that she must stop us from doing that, otherwise we'd never socialize with the other kids."

"Was the psychologist right?"

"Yep. Now we can't even remember it—it just evaporated, except 'weepie' was our word for 'basketball.' That's all we can remember. And I called him 'old cock' and he called me 'big cock,' though our cocks of course are identical and small."

Guy said, "If you slept with your brother, you're not really a virgin." Embarrassed by his own coarse remark, he asked, "Do you have shared experiences, nonverbal ones?"

Kevin said, "Oh, yeah! Like once he got socked in the stomach and I was miles away and doubled over with pain. We don't need more than a word to make the other one crack up over some remembered joke. Or if someone says something asinine, Chris will just poke his cheek with his tongue and we're both weeping with laughter."

When they were about to pay at the cash register, Kevin said, "Don't look now, but that old guy in the corner bugs the shit out of me. He's always cruising me, and I'm sorry, but I hate old trolls."

Guy glanced rapidly at the troll and said, "But Kevin, that man's not old. He couldn't be more than thirty."

"He gives me the creeps. I guess I'm weird, but I've never even kissed anyone over twenty-five. By the way, Chris thinks you're older than we are."

Guy said, "I'm certainly older than you. I'm twenty-five. Too old to kiss?"

"Gee, I'm surprised," Kevin said. "I told Chris I thought you were more like twenty-two."

Guy became worried that Kevin might ask around the fashion world and find out he was nearly forty, so he said, "By the way, I haven't been working much as a model, so I'm looking for a job as a waiter or a sales clerk." Guy wasn't sure a *vendeur* was called a "sales clerk." He didn't want Kevin to think of him as a rich forty-year-old model with two houses, but rather as a poor kid like himself just starting out.

"That really surprises me. I'm sure I've seen you in ads and commercials."

"Nope," Guy said. "Just one peanuts commercial two years ago."

"Excellent," Kevin said, using the new vogue word.

Kevin began almost instantly to treat Guy with a suggestion of tenderness and less admiration. For him, perhaps, Guy was no longer a successful grown-up but another beginner struggling to survive. He was easier for Kevin to care about—and Kevin insisted they split the check for coffee and cherry pie right down the middle.

For the first time, as they left the coffee shop Kevin put his arm around Guy's waist. It occurred to Guy that Kevin might be active in bed. He was startled by the boy's friendly gesture. He must be lonely, Guy thought.

The next morning when Guy swung by to see Fred, he wasn't there and his plants and flowers and get-well cards had all been cleared out and the bed was freshly made. The room was in a sort of twilight, lit only by the hall light coming through the door. Had they taken him to the emergency room? Stripped of its colorful ornaments, the room looked smaller, like a cell, and the narrow bed with its crisp sheets and hospital corners looked like one of those restraining cots used for lethal injections.

Blinded by tears and confused, Guy stumbled out into the hallway and saw one of his favorite nurses, the Seventh-Day Adventist with her carefully braided hair. "Oh, honey," she said, opening her arms. He let her hold him, though she was so much shorter and stouter. "Your poor Mr. Fred passed during the night about three A.M. I was the one who discovered him. He may have had a heart attack. He looked startled and was almost sitting up. He eyes buggin' out and his mouth open. Those vulture sons were here by eight and put all his belongings in a big black plastic garbage bag. They were gone by eight-thirty after they made sure there were no checked valuables."

"Valuables?"

"Watch, ring, that sort of thing. They did cry a little. And then they were squabblin' with each other. You were his real son."

That thought made Guy cry again, and the nurse, who smelled of vanilla extract dabbed right out of the bottle, held him again in her short arms. "You're skinny, boy," she said.

Fred had been such a strong personality, so full of noise and vulgarity and longing, that his abrupt absence left a roaring vacuum behind, the sort you see in a movie when the villain punctures the shell of the airplane and the passengers are all sucked out into the freezing stratosphere. Guy kept thinking he should do something for Fred, that there was some ritual he was neglecting or some form to fill out. But there was nothing to do. No duties.

He went to the Elephant and Castle downstairs, though it was too early to eat and the waiters were just tying on aprons, and the grill, he was told, would take twenty minutes to heat up. There were no other customers. The windows were sparkling clean. The waiter brought him a cup of coffee as an act of mercy.

Suddenly the day seemed so vacant, great empty lots of time laid out before him like fields planted in the same crop. He didn't know what to do with himself and went to the gym to work out halfheartedly. For some reason he looked at everyone yearningly, including the least likely men, even the owner's brother, that big straight blowhard who drank a pint of bull's blood a day and, crippled with gout, had to be handed up the stairs. Grief made Guy masochistic and he could imagine shrinking and living in that brute's crotch, his only exercise crossing from one small ball to the other. (He'd seen them, and steroids had made them pea-sized.) He felt so lonely. With Fred gone and Andrés in prison. Nothing was as lonely as the gym, with its averted glances, its surround of reproachful mirrors, its weights cast aside like broken manacles.

He took the Greyhound bus ninety minutes to Otisville, the minimum-security federal prison. It looked like a junior high in the middle of a lot. He was shocked by how small and peaceful it looked—small and without walls. A dozen passengers from New York had gotten off with him; they were all women, mostly black and Hispanic—some the mothers or elderly wives of prisoners, others possibly their adult children or younger wives, two with Muslim headscarves, all with packages in their hands. He wished he'd talked to the forty-something woman sitting next to him, with her mobcap of shiny black hair, straightened and varnished, and her pretty dress and clear lip gloss. He might have received some clues from her as to what to expect. He'd called ahead and his name was on the list, which the fat female guard in her bulging trousers pronounced *Guy* as in "gigh" to rhyme with "sigh."

He sat on an orange sectional sofa marooned in the visitors' lounge. He'd had to pass through three checkpoints and metal detectors. He'd been patted down twice. And yet this room was casual in a studied way—no partitions "protecting" the visitors from the prisoners, two floor lamps to soften the neon glare from the ceiling, three dispensers loaded with soft drinks and sweets, bright acrylic colors swirled on the walls as on an empty lot in Harlem. But he did spot two cameras monitoring the room—*I guess you couldn't slip someone a knife or diet pills in here.*

At last Andrés was brought in, with one wrist handcuffed. He darted a glance at Guy and muttered something to the guard, who accompanied him to the couch, unlocked their handcuffs, and walked over to another guard, who was sipping a cardboard container of coffee.

Guy smiled sheepishly at Andrés. After all, Andrés was here for years more to come because of a misguided desire to keep up with his rich model lover. *I refuse to feel guilty!* he thought guiltily. "How's it going?" Guy asked.

"I wish I could make love to you," Andrés said. "Can you see the outline of my erection?" and Andrés scooted down on the sofa so his uniform stretched tight. *Already?* Guy thought. The petit bourgeois in Guy wanted to stop him, make him sit up straight, not get in trouble, but his own cock stiffened automatically, like a new mother lactating when her baby cries in another room. "I miss you so much," Andrés said. "I guess you've already found someone else."

"No," Guy said, "but have you?"

"That's all bullshit about sex in prison, at least the rape part," Andrés said angrily. "Maybe the high-security prisoners, the lifers, maybe they team up with some swishy long-haired bitch. Here the guys—but let's not waste time," and Andrés fell into a brown study, staring at some point in space so hard that Guy turned to see what it was. "So you've already found someone?" Andrés said angrily.

"No, I haven't," Guy said simply. "No one could ever replace you in my heart." He wondered if that sounded sincere.

"Oh, really?" Andrés asked bitterly. "Why is that? Even if there was a nice Parisian town house in the deal or a penthouse overlooking the Champs de Mars?"

"I never schemed to get a house. Anyway, I have enough real estate."

"But you have a weakness for rich old men."

"I only have a weakness for a young Colombian who gets an erection the minute he sees me."

Andrés at first scowled and looked grumpy, as if he were going to object to something, but then in spite of himself he burst into a big grin and lost ten years. He shook his head as if in disbelief and said, "I love you. So much. It hurts."

"I love you, too, Andrés."

He asked Guy to put $500 in his account so that he could buy junk food at the canteen.

"What's your day like?" Guy asked.

"Always the same. I'm awake by five. Which is early, since on the weekends we're allowed to watch TV well after midnight, and reveille's at six. Then there's exercise in the yard. I've been doing pull-ups—look." He made a muscle, and the sudden movement caused both guards' eyes to swivel in their direction, then drift away.

"We have hours and hours alone. Some guys are studying the law, trying to get a retrial." Andrés looked at his hands and said in a softer voice, "I've been reading the Bible."

"Why?"

Andrés ruffled his feathers and said, "Why not?" Then he added, "But I can't understand that fuckin' old-ass English. Maybe you could bring me a Spanish Bible. What's wrong with these muthafuckers, why ain't their English up-to-date?"

Andrés had never sworn before, not in English, though in Spanish it had always been *puta*, and *coño*, as with all young South Americans. He must be learning a new way to speak English from his cellmates.

He looked at Guy and said, "If you don't love me I'll kill you."

Suddenly all Guy's alarms went off. "But I do love you," in a little voice he'd never heard before out of his own mouth, shallow and childish. "I've never loved anyone so much," and Guy couldn't help noticing Andrés's thick cock flexing again inside his taut orange trousers, an autonomic response to the desire tormenting his features.

"Sure?"

"I'm absolutely sure."

"I saw you checking out that hairy-chested gorilla over there. Would you like some of that?"

"Andrés, don't drive us both crazy. I haven't touched anyone since you went away."

"But you'd like to. I know you," Andrés said, and Guy thought guiltily of Kevin, his hairless torso and little pink cock and tiny untried nipples.

"Is the food here edible?"

"It's okay. On weekends we even have barbecue. Too many starches. I don't want to get fat. Are there some dynamite new men in your gym? Probably Pierre-Georges is fixing you up with some studs—he must be happy I'm behind bars. No class, no money, no connections—that's me. Does he say that or just think it? He must be happy to distract you with some young stallion in his stable. Is that how you stay so fresh and young, drinking the sperm of teenage males?"

"Come on, Andrés. Let's say kind things to each other, loving things—"

"Or what? You won't come back?" Andrés looked at the tip of his shoe, which he flexed. "You hold all the cards here."

"Is it boring here? Dangerous? Infuriating?"

"Check, check, and check." For some reason Andrés suddenly inspected the nails on his right hand. "It's okay here, once they break your spirit. God, you're beautiful when you smile like that!"

"Th-thanks."

"Has everyone always been in love with you? Of course they have, who am I kidding? What did they say about Helen of Troy? That her face launched a thousand ships? That's you, you're that beautiful. A thousand ships. There's no one even close to you around here. Maybe in Manhattan there are two or three."

"I'm no longer young," Guy said.

He thought how boring this visit was. The truth was he and Andrés had nothing in common except their life together. ("Don't forget to buy the wine! Oh, and some bread.") Just as they spoke an imperfect English together, which wasn't the mother tongue of either of them, in the same way sex and the dailiness of daily life were what they had in common, though it wasn't what either of them was most proficient at. Maybe sex was Andrés's strong suit. Yes, he was good at that.

Andrés had once accused him of liking him only for sex. At the time, Guy had thought that wasn't fair; it was Andrés who always nudged him when they were watching a game show in the afternoon and indicated with a toss of his head that they should repair to the bedroom for sex. It was Andrés who wanted to fuck first thing in the morning (he'd show his morning wood, which to be funny he'd call in Spanish his *madera*): Guy had started getting up half an hour early so he'd be clean and his teeth brushed, which made him feel like a woman, not an altogether unpleasant fantasy. Andrés was the one with the constant erection that had to be addressed several times a day; his hard-on was their metronome, sometimes their tyrant. Guy thought he was always accommodating it, but he liked the feeling of being that desired (a womanly feeling, too, he supposed). Now they couldn't touch, though they could drink each other in with their eyes, and Andrés could slouch in his chair so that his erection was big and visible. Guy would just have to stretch his hand out—but that was no more permissible than Orpheus looking back at Eurydice. Strictly forbidden.

Guy could remember Andrés's back so clearly—the broad

shoulders straining to be broader, the ass-cheeks just unmolded from the curved baking pan, indented at the sides, the crack looking so innocent and boyish—and, most glorious of all, the silky indentation of his spine, slicing his back in two, luminous as a prayer, an infolding of light.

Their time was up! Oh, it was so heartbreaking leaving Andrés there, so unfair, with his unsatisfied *madera* and his aristocratic hands, so pale next to the brutal orange of his uniform, and on his face a lost, devastated look.

Guy made an appointment to take the AIDS test as he'd promised Fred. He went back to St. Vincent's at the right time, sat with some other glum single men with expensive haircuts and tight jeans. His name was called, he went into the male nurse's cubicle, and rolled up his sleeve. The nurse smelled of cigarettes and the new cologne by Perry Ellis, the only good American scent. Poor Perry, everyone said he had AIDS, half his face was paralyzed during his last runway show and he nearly swooned. His partner was also about to go, both of them under fifty.

The nurse put a red rubber tourniquet around his bicep and looked at the form he'd filled out. "There's a mistake here, it says you were born in 1945, but that should be 1965."

"No," Guy said, smiling, "'45 is right."

"What is your secret, girl? Surgery?"

"Good genes, I guess. Moisturizer."

"I use Indigo Body Butter, but I don't look like you, darlin'."

"Try Retin-A," Guy said.

"Retinal?"

Guy picked up a pencil and scribbled with it in the air. The nurse slipped a prescription pad under his hand and Guy wrote a word.

"Retin-A? I never heard of that. Is that some Swiss monkey gland or sheep bladder? Do you also sleep twelve hours a night in a walk-in refrigerator?"

"Yes. I do," Guy said, and the nurse hummed an emphatic, "Un-hum." Suddenly serious, he said gravely, "Make a fist." He then tapped Guy's arm and the back of his hand in several places. "It's good you're no heroin addict; I can't find no good veins." Suddenly he stabbed Guy, who looked away.

The results were available a day later. That night Guy meditated (which he never did, which he didn't believe in, which he scarcely knew how to do), and he asked his body if it was infected and if it was going to die right away. It said (but this didn't make any sense), *No. I'm not infected and I'm going to live a long time*. Guy couldn't tell anyone about this, it was too superstitious and silly, but for some reason he felt reassured, though he didn't believe in it and he wasn't even sure what had happened.

Nevertheless, he went to St. Vincent's with a mixture of confidence and fatalism. He wished he'd never entered into all of this. There was nothing to do anyway if you were ill. He recognized that everyone liked him because he was handsome. Would they all go away if he was dying (and it was a fatal disease)? If he was Auschwitz-thin and covered with black spots? Pierre-Georges would drop him slowly but surely, if he could no longer work. The baron might send him a basket of fruit, Kevin would be horrified. Fred was gone and Andrés locked up. Only Lucie would stay faithful. Women were the loyal ones, he thought wearily.

An intern in a blue uniform and expensive shoes and a Swatch made a fuss about setting Guy down in his cubicle. He glanced at the report and then he looked Guy in the eye and said with a slow smile, "I have good news. You're negative. I'm not supposed to blurt it out; I'm supposed to talk first about safe sex and condom use, but hey, we're both grown-ups, right? But for God's sake, keep up the good work." And then, looking flirtatiously up through his eyelashes, the intern said, "You must be one of the few tops in the Village."

"Not always, I'm more versatile," Guy said. The intern's smile evaporated.

"Are you new at this?"

"At what?" Guy asked.

"Same-sex practices?"

"Not particularly," Guy said, a bit shocked at the man's impertinence, although he admitted to himself he'd find the situation intriguing if the nurse was better-looking.

Guy said, "No, I must be just very lucky."

The man said, "We recommend you know the name of everyone you sleep with and limit the number of your partners." That made sense to Guy, kind of.

He was vastly relieved and he remembered his stupid "meditation" when his body had made its own prognostication. *Ridiculous!* he thought, though he had a new respect for the augury.

In the bright, fragile spring day, all blue and crystal, which felt as if it might shatter at any moment in the rising warmth like ice gloving a branch, each evergreen needle inside vivid and distinct, he sauntered forth, walking all the way over to the Hudson. He never took a walk without a destination but now he was powered by his relief at being negative.

He thought, *I must settle down with and be faithful to a virgin boy*, and he thought immediately of Kevin. He thought of Kevin's pure white body, tinged with pink, like new snow at dawn. He could hear the ice melting above Ely, Minnesota, with its loud gunshot reports as it broke loose and cracked in the sunlight. He thought of that little penis like a cherub on its cloudlet of pubic hair, those lips the color of raspberry sherbet, that white butt, perched high and inviolate.

8

"ARE YOU SINGLE?" Kevin asked in his clear high choir-boy voice as soon as he'd finished another set.

"Yes," Guy said, knowing he'd betrayed Andrés with a monosyllable, poor Andrés languishing in that junior high school of a prison, a silly place denuded of thick sweating walls, tiny barred fragments of light, unoiled dungeon doors. No, it didn't have the dignity of imprisonment, it was a ludicrous space for warehousing tax evaders and corporate scoundrels.

He wondered if Andrés jerked off seven times a day or ten, thinking about him. Or did he already have a warmer bruder, someone who'd give him a helping hand? Why couldn't the Colombian government get him extradited? Guy thought he should be bankrolling an appeals process, though the lawyer had said to him, "This isn't a banana republic. You can't pull strings in America, pay off an official, lean on your cousin. It's not like France or Spain—those banana republics. You just have to wait your turn like everyone else. It will only work against you if you try to jump the queue."

Guy repeated this to Pierre-Georges, who said loftily, "We don't have bananas in France."

"No, I'm single," Guy repeated, "which sounds funny to say to an identical twin. You're never single."

"Yes, I am," Kevin protested. "Chris weighs five more pounds than me—guess that's his straight side. He met a girl on the stoop outside our building and he's spending nights with her. I guess I should be all jealous and possessive, but I'm not. I'm relieved."

"Would you spend the night with me?" Guy asked.

Again the bucket of blood immersed in the pint of milk: a blush.

"Sure." Pause. "When do you want me?"

"Tonight? Are you free tonight? We could grab a bite and watch some TV and go to bed."

"I don't know if I should eat something before we fuck—wouldn't it get messy down there?"

Guy laughed and said, "Shit is the best lubricant."

"Eww-w-w."

"Anyway, who knows, you might be the pitcher and I the catcher."

"Huh?"

"You might be the plus and I the minus."

"You'd permit that?" Kevin asked, wide-eyed.

"You sure like to get down to basics. In France we prefer the unsaid, the *non-dit*. More romantic, we think."

"I guess you got me typed as a Norwegian oaf."

"We'll just play it by ear."

The idea of improvisation seemed to make Kevin even more anxious. They agreed to meet at seven-thirty. Feeling traitorous, Guy set about hiding all the pictures of Andrés. He just wanted one happy night with this perfect boy. His lies would surface eventually: his age; his commitment to Andrés; even his success as a model and his relative wealth. But he was desperate to make this happen, one rapturous night with Kevin. He could already hear the boy's tearful accusations. Guy thought this was the moment to pluck the pear, when it was still streaked with green and was woody, before it turned to brown mush, all sweet and runny. Somehow it seemed less reprehensible to be a connoisseur of the *fruit vert* than simply a traitor to his imprisoned lover. Guy saw himself as a horny man who felt that every moment of his improbable youth might be his last.

When he looked back over his life he realized his twenty-sixth birthday had been the hardest because he thought he was no longer young, could no longer pass for a student, not even a grad student. So many of his classmates were getting married, starting businesses, buying houses, fathering children. Then at thirty he'd blown a farewell kiss to his years as a desirable man—but still his extraordinary looks had lingered on.

Not that he'd done anything unusual or disciplined to stay young. Well, maybe a little, but no surgery. He'd cut out bread and desserts, though he couldn't forgo a daily glass of fattening orange juice. He had a facial every weekday from a very unglamorous Korean woman who worked on Twenty-sixth and Broadway. He used Retin-A on the nights he was alone. He worked out, but only three times a week and only for an hour. He preferred low weights and high reps because he was aiming for definition and didn't want to bulk up. He'd had electrolysis on his torso. He did facial isometrics after he shaved. He didn't tan and he applied sunscreen every morning. His hair was expensively styled and feathered and lightened and he held it in place with Tenax. He thinned his eyebrows. If he watched TV alone he made himself do fifty sit-ups every half hour.

He'd stopped smoking and only drank two glasses of wine at dinner. People said white wine gave you headaches but he preferred it because it didn't discolor your teeth. He had his teeth cleaned once a month. Now that he was nearly forty he had to yank out nose and ear hairs and shave his neck since gray hair might grow there. His clothes were always dark and thinning and unnoticeable. No jewelry. No facial hair. If he gained five pounds he'd make a big pot of vegetable soup and eat nothing else for a week. He applied Rogaine regularly to his scalp, though his hair was still thick.

More importantly, he'd trained himself not to be nostalgic, not to recognize pop songs or movies or TV series from other decades, to greet names (even French names) from the sixties or seventies with a look of incomprehension, even bewilderment. For him the threshold of the recognizable was years later, 1980. Whereas other people relaxed into squalid orgies of smiling over their memories, a warm self-indulgence of conjuring up the past not in all its dullness or pain but in a sentimental form, he remained aloof, untouched, strategically uncomprehending. They were all false anyway, these memories, protecting people against the harsh truth. He hated the past. He had suffered as an adolescent from frustration, in his twenties from insecurities (how long could this career of his go on?), and in his thirties from disillusionment (how long must this career of his go on?). Now at nearly forty he could start up all over again. He'd been handed this miracle, eternal youth.

In a world of shiny consumer goods, he was the shiniest one of all. If someone else would have said that to him, it would have enraged him, but he had to admit it was true. He was a product, artfully wrapped, refrigerated like expensive chocolates; he'd been in stock, however, way past his shelf life.

They'd have to slash the price in half in order to get the item to move.

Was he being predatory and deceitful to Kevin? Certainly deceitful; he'd said he was twenty-five. Predatory, not really. He hadn't seduced the boy except by the cool distance he'd maintained and by the natural appeal of his looks and accent and profession. And his barely perceptible friendliness. He wasn't really a catch—soiled goods, maybe a bit vapid, no longer fresh—but a provincial of nineteen might think he was a rare find, confuse the cleverness he'd picked up from his milieu with a personal acuity.

Kevin rang his bell precisely at seven-thirty and Guy buzzed him up.

"Wow! This place is a palace," Kevin exclaimed, looking around. He appeared absurdly young, a mere tot, with his freshly pressed shirt and perfect sparkling smile. With his gelled hair and his minty, toothpaste mouth when Guy kissed him, a mere peck, and his cheap straight-boy cologne (was it Mennen's?), he looked so incorrigibly young that Guy feared going out with him—bad for business, he'd look worn by contrast, *faux jeune*.

"Yes, isn't it great?" Guy said. "My aunt left it to me in her will. It's too fancy for a guy like me and might give people the wrong idea . . ."

"Was your aunt American? I'm sorry she died," and Kevin lowered his eyes in routine respect. *So Minnesota!* Guy thought, though he knew next to nothing about Midwesterners and was only now slowly modeling a wax effigy of the type in his imagination, but he was sure it was a region of pure streams, big skies, and artless boys with good manners and odorless crotches.

"Yes, she was French but married a rich American, *enfin*, he was a soldier when they met, black—"

"Black? Cool!"

"But he made money later—"

"Doing what?"

"Barbecue," Guy improvised wildly.

"Cool."

"And they had no children. First he died—"

"From what?"

"Cholesterol." Guy wasn't sure that was fatal, but it sounded like something a black cook might get.

"Poor man. And what did she die from?"

"Malnourishment. Anorexia." He felt on sure ground with this disease.

"How ironic!"

"Why ironic?"

"Her husband made barbecue."

A shadowy image of a fat, sweating black man in a starched white chef's toque crossed his imagination. "She was a vegetarian," Guy blurted.

"This doesn't look like an old person's apartment. I mean, the brass lamps and chocolate-brown walls look so up-to-date."

"Thanks," Guy said weakly, "I've made a few improvements. Should we go out for dinner?"

They strolled over to Duff's on Christopher Street and were seated in a booth under a big industrial lamp. They ordered a cheap bottle of white wine and two rare steaks with green beans, hold the potatoes. "A real model's meal, right?"

"I guess," Guy said.

"Can I be honest with you?"

Guy's stomach clenched with fear. "Of course."

"My brother thinks I'm too boring for a sharp guy like you."

"You're not boring—not as boring as I am. At least you're doing advanced studies."

"Just college. Everybody does college, and most college kids are dumb."

"I didn't go to college."

"Why not?"

"My parents are aristocrats, a count and countess, and they wanted me to manage the family estates." Guy resolved that he should write down all his lies in a locked diary and draw a timeline of this life he was inventing for himself.

"It's never too late to go to school," Kevin said. Guy smiled frostily.

He took off his own clothes as soon as they got in the door of his apartment. (He thought that would bypass any fumbling or the suggestion of seduction.) He went bare-assed into the kitchen to fetch them two glasses of water. When he came back, Kevin was stepping out of his jeans. He'd already untied his blue Top-Siders and now he was frowning slightly as he unbuttoned his shirt. He stood there in all his boyish beauty. He was wearing traditional Hanes underpants, which his mom had probably bought, six to a pack. Guy took the little erection slanting off to the right as a tribute. Did Kevin, inexperienced as he was, imagine that all gay men shed their clothes the minute they crossed the threshold?

He walked slowly over to Kevin, put their glasses on the coffee table, and folded him into his arms. Guy believed everything in sex should be done slowly so as not to scare the wildlife and to ensure his own natural grace and poise.

Kevin shuddered in his arms. Guy tried to re-create in his mind the delights and repulsions of a virgin's first time, but he decided to be bold, firm, not a sensitive reed bending in the gusts of the boy's desire and dismay. If they were both hesitant the whole thing would prove a fiasco.

Kevin's skin was so cool it was almost clammy, especially the high, rubbery buttocks. They probed each other's mouths with big, slippery tongues, eels flowing into and out of deep-sea grottoes, shrinking to enter, bloating once inside.

When he knelt to suck Kevin, he glanced up and caught him grimacing. "Are you okay?"

"You mean my wincing? I always do that when I'm jerking off. It's pleasure—too painful. Is that too weird for you?" His way of submitting his behavior so innocently to Guy's judgment was so guileless.

Guy thought, *Pain as pleasure.* He understood that. He licked the boy's balls, raised high and taut in their hairless sac, and Kevin groaned a bit stagily. Then he shook all over, flinching like a splashed horse. The flinching seemed real, involuntary. Guy thought of a Thoroughbred, how his curried coat drank the light. Guy touched the boy's fragile pink nipples—no reaction. His body hadn't been thoroughly eroticized yet, which made Guy think of that Chinese model he'd slept with once, a guy he'd met in São Paulo, someone who wore his body like armor, which had made Guy irrationally conclude the Chinese weren't sensual, weren't good sex. They didn't inhabit their bodies, Guy had decided on the basis of his sample of one.

Kevin fucked him. Guy guided the little hard penis into his body; Guy was lying on his stomach in order to afford Kevin the full plush glamour of his muscular buttocks. The boy didn't seem to know how to thrust. He just lay couched on Guy's bigger sleek body, this million-dollar body soaked for decades in costly unguents, and more or less wobbled in there for a very short time until he exploded.

"Oh, I'm sorry," Kevin said. "I came in you. I wasn't expecting it."

"That's fine," Guy said, kissing him and then running toward the shower. "I wanted it. That was great," he lied. He didn't know if Kevin might be feeling guilty after his orgasm. (So many men did at first.) That's why he didn't linger in bed. But then again, he didn't want to seem cold, so he called back, "Come take a shower with me," and the boy almost ran to join him. They rotated in the narrow tub under the showerhead; whoever wasn't under the water soaped up, stood with legs ajar to wash his own crack, took the blast full in the face, lifted his arms to clean his hairless pits. Kevin was already spotlessly clean except for the lubricant greasing the length of his little cock; he washed it. Then, their bodies warm from the water, they waltzed around so neither of them would get cold. In a few seconds Kevin was hard again and Guy filled his mouth with hot water and knelt to engulf him. The boy let out a groan and tried to lift Guy to his feet. "We should take turns. It's only fair."

"Only Princeton boys care about fairness," Guy said. "That's why they rub against each other. The Princeton rub." He whispered, "You're my stud, my mister," and filled his mouth again and dipped back to his chore.

"How can I be your stud?" Even the word seemed to embarrass him.

Guy looked up, the water splashing on his face, his wet hair dripping over his eyes. "Bet you can come three times."

"I came five times once. But it was jerking off. And it was pretty limp and watery at the end."

Guy looked up admiringly.

After Kevin came, Guy rubbed him dry with a hotel-sized towel and wanted to say, "My little stud," but censored himself. The "little" might not be appreciated. And post coitum the "stud" might rankle.

Guy put Kevin to bed and gave him the TV remote. Then he went back to the toilet, closed the door, and was oddly proud of how much semen Kevin had squirted into him. Of course, Kevin wasn't Andrés, with all his barbaric beauty and gypsy passion, as thin and tortured as a Spanish Christ who'd climbed down from the cross, banished the god within, and resurrected the outer man.

Before dawn Guy woke up to an exquisite pain, an inner plundering that his dream tried to make sense of (a hand was reaching for his heart), then he woke up and realized the boy was fucking him again and simultaneously reaching around and jerking Guy off. They both came at the same moment.

Guy's strategy was to make the boy into the active partner based on the notion that with his small dick and youth he would seldom be cast in that role and that it would build up his confidence. He knew most experienced gays would find such a policy counterintuitive; they all said the way to a man's heart was through his asshole. But Pierre-Georges had told him otherwise, that men might style themselves as passive at first because it was easier to take it than give it, but that as a young man became self-assured in a relationship he became more assertive—the return of the repressed. So that both male partners in a couple end up as tops and look for the occasional bottom to fuck.

Perhaps it wasn't that systematic, but Guy trusted his instincts, and after a week together Kevin was walking with a new swagger and even swatting Guy on the butt the minute they turned a corner. Because Kevin thought of Guy as more sophisticated and five or six years older, more the New Yorker, he let Guy decide when they'd go to the gym or what movie they'd see. They usually ate at a diner because it was quick and cheap and Kevin, if left to his own devices, could live on cheeseburgers and fries. He wanted, however, to have cheekbones like Guy, those knuckles about to burst through the taut sheet, and so he docilely ordered the salad and Diet Coke but then rewarded himself with a slice of cherry cheesecake, a taste for which was a New York acquisition, just as he could order now a poppy-seed bagel with lox and a "schmear" (salmon and cream cheese)—and he never gained an ounce.

His legs were meaty enough to remind Guy he was a man, but each segment of his six-pack when he sat up was the width of a beer can and he was so thin his stomach almost touched his backbone, and he had three muscles on his side under his armpit, "obliques" (the gym teacher had called them) that looked like finger-paint daubs or streaked commas or fingers holding his core as if it were a glass of milk. When he turned on his stomach, his spine and ribs looked like a trilobite fossil.

Kevin had bought a Walkman and was obsessed with Madonna and U2 and New Order. He spoke often about his "music" and defended it as if Guy were challenging it. His music was his one article of faith, the sole fatherland he pledged allegiance to. He'd sit there with his black earphones on and nod his head rhythmically, mouthing the words. He knew all the words and for him they were canonical. He would often cite them to Guy as if they expressed superior wisdom. Guy never doubted their gravity or timelessness and that seemed to pacify Kevin, who would tense up in advance, spoiling for a fight. Otherwise he was docility itself, always good-humored and smiling, almost too affectionate. Guy found his affection oppressive, as if he were a joyful lapdog circling around his feet and yipping and biting excitedly, impeding his progress. Indifference and mystery were more appealing. A little distance let your partner's imagination and tenderness expand to fill the space between you and him, give your mind and emotions permission to work, to *yearn*. Hankering might constitute an attachment in Buddhism, but in love it was a virtue, one that was constructive, that allowed you to build and articulate the very object of your affection. Whether the Buddhists were right or wrong—that love itself was always disappointing—was a matter of indifference to Guy. Love was his vocation, though he'd inspired more love than he'd experienced. He was like one of those legendary Hollywood actresses who drove men mad with desire and yet felt nothing themselves, who became old, fat, gap-toothed, and right-wing after years of being synonymous with the bikini and Saint-Tropez, say. Guy knew that the baron and Fred and Andrés had all loved him and that even now Andrés might be beating off in his lonely cell and whispering, "Guy," as he came, afraid that he'd rock the bunk bed and wake the brute below.

Thoughts of Andrés made him sick with guilt but also glowed beckoningly like the idea of a Liberty Bond that was accruing interest and that someday he'd be able to cash in.

When he went out walking in the evening with Kevin, the boy wrapped his arm around Guy's waist, the way Latin men did with their women. They'd stroll very slowly. Guy wondered what people were thinking as they passed. That Guy was a child molester who'd hypnotized his victim? That Kevin was mentally ill and the only person he trusted was his uncle, and that the patient was lavishing on Guy all the affection he should be distributing over several people? Guy had once seen an overgrown, amorous, curly-haired bar mitzvah boy kissing his little balding father in the same way, as if all the youngster's budding sexual energy and affection were centered on this one unlikely person whom he cherished like a lover. Kevin was like that—a bar mitzvah boy utterly enraptured with his father.

One day, whether by design or accident, they ran into Kevin's twin, Chris, who was with the gum-snapping girl he was dating. Kevin seemed all the leaner beside his twin. And prouder—*his* date was more beautiful than his brother's. They all filed into the corner bar, which was strangely dark. The girl, Betty, was surprisingly quick and clever. She was a native New Yorker, she said, "conceived in the Village and born in Queens," and she had the disabused savviness to prove it. She paused for a second and let her eyes roam before launching into an "original" observation, like an opera singer who composes herself before starting the famous coloratura aria. She seemed acutely conscious that Guy and Kevin were a couple, and she was at pains to show she was so familiar with homos as to be bored by them, even while she was faintly satirical at their expense. "What are you *boys* up to?" she said, giving an audible wink. "Out for a cruise?"

Guy, with all the generosity of the beautiful, found Betty amusing and turned his killer smile on her. Impertinently she asked, "Do you dye your eyelashes black, or have you tattooed them black? It's rare to see eyelashes that black —but I must say it does wonders for your eyes."

"Nothing like that," Guy said, unoffended. "They're just that way. Girls tattoo their eyebrows but not their eyelashes— that would be too dangerous." Betty winked at Chris, as if this were a little lie they'd dissect and relish later.

Two minutes after they'd finished their beers, Kevin hustled

Guy out of there. Chris seemed surprised by the decisiveness on his brother's part.

On the street Kevin said, "I'm sick of staying home every night. Let's go to the Roxy and dance."

"Great idea," Guy said, pleased by Kevin's assertiveness but vexed by the prospect of disco dancing. They couldn't arrive there before two in the morning. They'd have to snort a little blow to get their energy up, though Kevin was too budget-conscious to do it all night, thank God.

"I want to show you off," Kevin said.

Two days later Guy took the bus again to Andrés's prison. He lied to Kevin that he was posing at LaGuardia for a German skiwear catalogue all day.

Andrés was in a dark mood and it took Guy a minute to realize he was consumed with jealousy. Suddenly he said, "I have an idea."

"What is it?"

"I think we should get identical tattoos."

"Really?"

"Facial tattoos."

"But I have to work," Guy said.

"Don't worry, I'm not going to spoil your precious asset." Guy thought Andrés's English was much more idiomatic than in his pre-prison past; he must be sitting around gabbing all day with his American cellmate. Even his accent was more ghetto.

"How could a facial tattoo go unnoticed?" Guy asked.

"Behind your earlobe. Just a small number eight."

Guy thought immediately of Kevin, who'd be sure to notice and descend into a paroxysm of rage. Maybe that was Andrés's idea—to mark his property with his brand. "What does the eight stand for?"

Andrés touched his fly, for all the world like a rapper. "Don't you remember? It's when we met—February eighth? But it's also the symbol for infinity if it's turned on its side. That's how long our love will last—infinitely. At least mine for you."

Guy smiled and said, "Okay, okay."

Andrés suddenly seemed more alert. "You'll do it?"

"Sure," Guy said, thinking he could always think up an excuse later. "But how will you get a tattoo in prison?"

"Not a problem, my man," he muttered. "It's cool." Andrés sounded more and more like a very low-class thug, and that alarmed and excited Guy. He'd always been passionate—would he be more so now? Would his dick be even bigger and blacker? Would he smell even more like saffron and olive oil in which chopped shallots were sizzling? "Oh, baby," Andrés said, "would you do that for me?" And Guy thought he had that mellow, late-night romantic voice of a black disc jockey talking about his "African queen." "Would you really do that for me, baby?"

Guy realized Andrés had never called him "baby" before, nor had he ever spoken in this crooning baritone. Suddenly Guy was jealous thinking about his Afro-American rival, and he said, "You never talk about your cellmate. Is he here now? Can you point him out? Subtly."

"Why?"

"Because you sound different. Is he your lover?"

Andrés shut down. His anger (or was it his embarrassment?) became such a heavy charge that it shorted him out, with only a few bright noisy sparks to express his total outage. "You're the one with the lover!" Andrés shouted, getting up out of his chair and causing the guards to come striding quickly toward them.

"Is everything cool, here?" a thick-chested black guard asked. "Are you boys playing nicely? Staying cool, Andy?"

Guy thought the intonation sounded familiar. "We're cool," Andrés said sullenly, and sat back down. His chin dropped to his chest.

Of course, Guy thought. *The black guard got the Colombian beauty. He won't let anyone else near that prime beef. That's the voice Andrés is imitating.*

But then Andrés was telling him he had joined a Puerto Rican gang in prison. "It's so good to be speaking Spanish again, even if it's their funny kind of Spanish. Here you have to choose the black gang or the P.R. gang. I feel sorry for these Wall Street cats. They don't have no gang."

"Are you sure the eight isn't just the name of your Spanish gang? Ocho? And you want to make it sound like our symbol so I won't get jealous?"

"*Baby* . . ." Andrés said with such a hurt, reproachful look that Guy immediately backed off. He leaned in to kiss Andrés on the cheek, but Andrés shrank away and looked around nervously. "I told them you be my cousin."

"I've seen other people in here kissing."

"Not guys."

"Not even cousins?"

Andrés smiled and said, "Get outta here."

Guy noticed the stretched orange fabric crotch: no hard-on this time. Maybe only a crooning black voice excited him now.

Kevin insisted they go up to the hot-tarred roof of their brown-stone to "lay out," as he put it. While there, they fraternized with a friendly young couple of chubs, Mr. and Mrs. Something

Polish to whom Guy had rented out the top floor. They were newlyweds and so much in love they couldn't keep their paws off each other. He was in pest control, he said, and she was a baker, which meant she had to get up at four in the morning. She worked for the French baker down the street and brought home very American carrot cupcakes onto which she had piped orange and green frosting.

They were always leaving a baguette on Guy's doorstep or a cherry cheesecake, once she'd discovered that was Kevin's favorite. With the coldhearted discipline of a farmer drowning kittens, Guy systematically sprayed the baked goods with detergent so they'd be inedible. "You're incredibly sweet, Dorothy," Guy overheard Kevin say on the landing, "but we're models and we can't indulge," he wailed. Guy would never have said anything: He didn't want people to think of them as Martians.

Pierre-Georges came by and treated Kevin frostily. He kept speaking to Guy in French, using the most difficult argot (*pieu* for "bed" and *tignasse* for "hair") just in case Kevin had picked up ordinary French in school.

"Speak in English," Guy said.

"Honestly, I don't mind, you guys can knock yourselves out with your French. Honestly. I'll just read a magazine."

Guy knew that Pierre-Georges would take Kevin's politeness as a form of wimpiness (*mièverie*). Pierre-Georges had been warned not to say anything that would give away Guy's real age.

That night in bed Kevin confessed that when he was twelve he'd gotten his hands on a copy of *Blueboy*. And he'd jerked off to a guy named Ralph. "And he looked just like you, but of course he couldn't have been, because that was seven years ago. But I swear he looked just like you! It's weird! Same little jug ears,

same eyes exactly the same shape, same small hands, same . . ."—
here he lowered his voice—"dick."

Oh, no, Guy thought, *of all the pictures that might have surfaced
and imprinted him, it had to be mine, the one that sneaky American
photographer talked me into and swore never to show anyone.*

"But it looks just the way you do now," and Kevin sheepishly brought out from under the mattress a dog-eared copy of
Blueboy, the pages limp from use and stiff with semen. "Doesn't
it?" And he held the picture up and thrust it into Guy's face.
"Or am I crazy or what?"

"There is a resemblance."

"If you only knew how much cum that photo cost me!
Gallons and gallons."

Kevin blushed, not one of his deep, cranberry blushes, but a
hawthorn-pink one. "I used to fantasize I'd call up the *Blueboy*
offices in Miami and I'd ask for the art director, his name is
printed here, Gabriel Sanchez, and I'd say I was calling on
behalf of Ralph's mother who was dying, and I had to have
Ralph's telephone number immediately. But then I thought
that probably wasn't even his real name. And maybe *Blueboy*
didn't even deal with him directly. The photo is credited to Big
One Studio. They probably just sold it to *Blueboy*."

Kevin lay back on the pillow and closed his eyes. In the
slanting evening light coming through the window and against
the crisp white pillowcase he looked even more tanned.
Suddenly his eyes snapped open. "And go figure, now I have a
Ralph all of my own, my very own Ralph."

Guy smiled. "You make me sound like a Ralph Doll."

Kevin laughed. "You're my little Ralph Doll." He unbuttoned
Guy's shirt. "And I can dress you in any outfit I like or
undress you completely." His small fingers undid the buttons

of Guy's 501s and he tugged his jeans down. "And I can bend my Ralph Doll in any position I like." He rolled Guy over onto his side, folded the upper knee up, and straightened the lower leg, pushed his upper shoulder to the mattress, and then wriggled out of his own underpants, releasing his hard cock. A moment later he was fucking Guy, holding him by the sharp pelvis bones and pulling him back onto his dick. "Do you like that, Ralph?"

"Yes. I. Do," Guy said in a robot voice. "Very. Much," he said in staccato bursts.

"This is too weird, but I like it," Kevin said. The heat of the afternoon made him sweat, which matted his hair down on his forehead, as Guy noticed when he looked back. Guy wondered if he could tell Kevin to thrust a bit more, but no, that would sap his confidence. Better show him how it was done when it was Guy's turn. The boy just rocked like a Roto-Rooter and came with a terrible war whoop.

"My little Ralph," Kevin whispered into Guy's ear. It was the first time he was amorous after he came, and Guy took that as progress. Nor did Kevin go, "Ew-w," when he pulled his penis out and it was brown and smelly, and that, too, Guy considered a *rite de passage*.

Guy invited Kevin to the Spanish restaurant on the corner. The baron was there with a big muscular German named Hans whose head was shaved and who had a silver stud through his right eyebrow. He was wearing black Doc Martens and skinny jeans and a bicycle chain instead of a belt. "I thought I might see you here, Guy, in our old neighborhood. What a lovely companion you have—Kevin? So honored to meet you. This is Hans—he's East German, so his English isn't very good. But he's good at lots of other things."

Guy felt intensely uncomfortable standing there. He thought, *If I shouted "Fire!" and pulled Kevin away, I might save the day, but that won't happen.* Guy felt he was walking toward a fatal accident.

"I hear our old friend died and left you yet another house." He looked at Guy from head to toe. "How do you do it? You don't look a day older than you did all those years ago. Gene therapy? The sperm of infant lads?" (And his glance took in Kevin.) "And don't tell me you got rid of that virile Colombian."

"He's in prison—for forgery."

"Poor thing." Édouard didn't want to know any more about what was unpleasant. Once more a complete survey of Guy's person. "They really should exhibit you at the Smithsonian as one of the wonders of the age. How many years ago did I meet you?"

"I rarely think about the past," Guy said coldly.

"Quite right, too, when you have such a promising present," and this with another head-to-toe look at Kevin. "Guy, you look just as fresh as the day I met you."

"Thank you," Guy said. Guy was looking at Hans's big, lumpy crotch; everything about him—his wide stance, his direct stare, his bald, missile-shaped head—spelled Big Cock.

"And how is our house? Comfortable?"

"Yes. As always. You and Hans must come by someday for drinks."

"Definitely," piped Kevin politely. "You're always welcome."

"What a dear child," the baron said with a mocking smile, and he actually patted Kevin on the cheek with his gem-studded, age-spotted hand. "Don't let him lead you astray, my child. He's such a wicked man, woof!" and the baron pretended to shiver with delight.

After they sat down they both studied their menus, and finally Guy said, "You don't even want to know."

"I feel I don't know you at all."

"Don't you think what we have is real and solid?"

Kevin looked at him with tears in his eyes. "I want to believe that. Jesus, I want to. But how can I trust you? I don't know what to think now."

This was the first time Guy had heard Kevin say "Jesus" and the way he said it sounded like a genuine cry from the heart. Guy thought that if he lost Kevin, at least he'd have had one perfect month from him, and what did you ever have with another person anyway? Certainly not much more. And breaking up with him would simplify his life. He wouldn't have to lie anymore to Andrés.

But he'd miss the little guy, his sweetness, his good humor, his devotion to his silly music, his warm perfect body, his amateur lovemaking, the sperm of an infant lad.

"Do you think it's worth it, working through all this mess?" Guy asked.

Kevin looked startled. "What! You're breaking up with me? I love you, Guy. You're my sweetheart. I'd marry you if I could. You don't doubt that?"

Guy reached across the table and squeezed Kevin's hand, which felt feverish.

"First of all," Kevin said, "who was that man?"

"He's a Belgian baron. He's called Édouard and he's the one who gave me the house."

"So there was no aunt, no black GI?"

"No."

"Were you the baron's lover?"

"I slept with him once. He was in love with me."

"How old are you really?"

"Going on forty. That photo of Ralph you have—that's me when I was twenty."

"Really? It is? How do you do it?"

"I don't do anything."

"Seriously, how do you stay so young? You look the same as Ralph did. You haven't changed at all."

"I have. I have hair now in my ears. The flesh around my fingers is loose, wobbly—see, yours fits tight, like a good glove, mine is creased and shiny and baggy. And my elbows are dry and scaly. My nose is too big—a nose keeps growing with the years. Luckily I was born with small ears. You are just a bit shorter than me but weigh twenty pounds less without looking cadaverous. Only real young people can do that. You have *duvet*—fuzz—on your cheeks that lights up in the cross light."

"So you're really Ralph?"

Guy told him the whole story of how the American photographer back in Paris had tricked him into posing nude and then sold the picture to *Blueboy*.

"And so you're a much bigger supermodel than you let on? And not an aristocrat?"

Guy gave him a rundown on his entire career, from meeting Pierre-Georges at the Café Flore to doing runway work for Pierre Cardin to coming to the States and meeting Bruce Weber in 1980 ("He changed my life") and eventually posing for Calvin Klein and Abercrombie & Fitch.

"And who is the virile Colombian he mentioned?"

Guy said, "He's called Andrés and he's in prison." Guy explained that he'd been arrested for forgery.

"Do you mean that if he weren't in prison you'd still be with him and not with me? Am I his temporary replacement?"

"Don't talk like that," Guy said. "Don't even think like that."

"And who was that man who died that the baron mentioned? Where is the house he gave you?"

"His name was Fred. He died of AIDS. He left me his house on Fire Island."

"Did you lie about that, too? Are you infected by AIDS? And me? Am I going to get it and die?"

"No, no," Guy said, and he explained that he had just tested negative and he could show Kevin the results. "There's no reason for you to believe me, I know. My word is worthless. But I do have the document. If you're really as inexperienced as you say, then there's no reason to worry."

"*I've* always told you the truth," Kevin blurted out. A second later they both realized what a heavy condemnation lay in those spontaneous words.

"Unlike me," Guy said. "I'm a terrible person." He expected Kevin to contradict him, but when he didn't, Guy sank another foot into the mud.

It must have been eight-thirty on a July night but it was still light out, warm and windless. Neither of them was hungry, so they stirred their green paella around on their plates, paid, and left. On the way out Guy nodded to the baron.

As if by a prearranged agreement, they sat on the stoop to their building and looked out on the uninteresting street. At last Kevin said, as if responding to a question, "Were you ever going to come clean with me?"

"About what?" Guy wasn't sure what "come clean" meant.

"About how you came to own this house, about how you have a Latin lover, about your unemployed father, about how you're fifteen years older than you said—oh, forget it."

"I don't know," Guy said, "I don't know when I would have told you. I was afraid of losing you."

A moment went by, and a mother and her preteen daughter walked past. When they were out of earshot Kevin said, "At least that sounded honest."

That night they made love for a long time and for the first time Guy fucked Kevin. Guy spent a long time rimming him and then put a lubricated finger up there.

"I've wanted this for such a long time," Kevin said.

"Me, too."

"I'm not sure it's clean."

"So what?" Guy asked. "You must tell me if it hurts. I don't have to use a condom, do I?"

"Of course not," Kevin murmured, and perhaps thought better of it. Could he trust Guy? "No," he said. "We're married. We're faithful."

Kevin's words were like a vote of confidence. Guy inched his way into the boy's ass while studying his face (pain as pleasure). It was the most wonderful feeling, muscular velvet, an intimacy only a virgin could grant, or so he said to himself for the moment, just to make it all the more exciting. He was taking Kevin's cherry! The words made him harder and made him feel privileged, masterful, married. He thought how many men would pay unlimited amounts to have this inaugurating experience with this boy. He didn't want to feel like a middle-aged pedophile, he didn't even want to think all this would make a good porn film. He wanted every thrust, every second, to be laden with tenderness, a salute from him to Kevin, a deep recognition. He wanted Kevin to like what was being done to him, to push back for another joyous millimeter of penetration. He didn't want him to label it Guy's First Fuck or Kevin's First Time. He didn't want the idea and the label to crowd out the sensation or to sharpen it; he wanted it to be pure sex, undramatized.

Guy took a long time. He thought that way Kevin would get used to it, stop fearing it, realize how pleasurable it was. Guy reached around and stroked his hard cock: Good, he was still erect. He'd lose his erection if he was in pain, wouldn't he? Guy whispered in his ear, "I love you." How many times he'd wanted to say that. The words thrilled both of them and Kevin trembled all over as he had the very first time they'd kissed, and again Guy thought of him as a skittish colt. He strummed his ribs as if he were playing a harp. "Am I hurting you?" Guy asked.

"It feels really neat!" Kevin said, which prompted Guy to lie on top of him, pull out, balance his weight on his outstretched hands, then plunge deeper and faster into him. Kevin seemed to give in to him, to stop acting and to start uttering a high-pitched little call Guy had never heard before. Kevin experimented with spreading his legs, pulling his buttocks wider open, nibbling Guy's hands, clenching his rectum. "Just lie still," Guy murmured, and Kevin did. Guy felt the last locks opening. He couldn't resist glancing up at their reflection in the mirror. They looked good. Now the light coming through the windows was rich and grainy with shadow and discretion. Their individuality had been airbrushed out and they were just two charcoal smudges, one covering the other. Suddenly nothing in the world seemed to Guy more glamorous than homosexuality, as romantic as heady white gardenias nested in polished green leaves. "Can I come in you?"

"What?" Kevin asked, arching his back and looking over his nacreous shoulder.

"Can I come in you?"

"God, yes!" and Guy pressed his whole body into Kevin and shuddered.

Kevin was breathing heavily. When his breath evened out, Guy pulled out and wiped himself with a tissue from a box on the night table.

Kevin propped himself up on one elbow and looked at Guy intently, seriously, with those dark circles of weariness under his eyes, so touching in a kid. He started to cry and Guy kissed away his tears. At last Kevin said, "That's dangerous, fucking me. Are you ready for me to fall in love with you forevermore?"

A little fatuously, Guy said, "So you liked that?" and Kevin nodded solemnly, which sobered Guy enough to say, "Yes, I'm ready for your love. Give me all you've got."

They kissed each other languorously again and, suddenly rousing himself, Guy slapped him on the ass and said, "Okay, okay. Your turn."

For a second bewildered, Kevin said, "You want me to fuck you?"

"Yes, dummy."

Kevin lubricated Guy with a sticky finger, then entered him; they were both lying on their sides. Guy advanced his upper knee and crooked it and rotated it upward, the Ralph position. Kevin had learned through imitation how to thrust; he already knew that Guy's G-spots were his ears and nipples, though he'd been warned to go easy on the nipples lest they become enlarged. Guy liked the idea that Kevin's ass was full of his come and that tribal physics would make it seep through his loins and spurt through his little cock.

Afterward, Kevin balanced his head on his open hand, lying on his side, and beamed into Guy's face, smiled and smiled, wondering. Guy could feel and smell his warm breath, smelling like coffee, a fine stream of air on his cheek.

"What am I going to do with you?" Kevin said, shaking his head. "My little Ralph."

Bright and early the next day, Fred's lawyer, Marty, phoned. He said that Fred's sons, the attorney and the podiatrist, had been driving him crazy. (Guy noticed that lawyers called each other "attorneys," just as doctors referred to each other as "physicians," as if the normal word weren't sufficiently reverential.) "So, those little schnorrers are indignant their dad gave you the house, the lion's share of the estate, and they want to contest it in court. I told them they'd lose the fifty thousand Fred willed them if they contested—and they might get nothing. I told them they didn't have a very strong case, that I'd been there and could testify they hadn't bothered to visit their father more than once, that they'd taken Ceil's side in the divorce, that they'd treated their father's new lifestyle with contempt, that you'd been there every day. Of course, they started howling that you'd infected Fred and killed him."

"I had the test last week," Guy said, "and I was negative."

"That's great news! Would you be willing to show that report in court, if it came to that?"

"Why not?"

"Could you xerox it and send me a copy?"

"Sure."

"I told them I was their father's oldest friend from Brooklyn days, grade school days, good ol' Theodore Herschl days, and that I knew Fred was fed up with Ceil and the boys and that he'd known real happiness with you, and I'd say as much to the presiding magistrate, who's another ol' Herschl boy. Now, if I have a copy of your health report, their whole case will fall apart, though that Howie is an underemployed lawyer and could keep this thing going on for years. I hate to think of that house on Fire Island sitting empty and you missing out on those big summer rentals. The bastards . . . you better be prepared for a long, drawn-out fight we may lose. The courts have been favoring the relatives over the lovers, the gay lovers, the *fegalas*. You might as well be going out there to use the house yourself. Sort of establish a presence. And enjoy!"

Pierre-Georges came by for Guy's signature on a contract. "It's for a horrible American fragrance. Why can't Americans come up with something that smells good, that has woodsy notes or lemon? Don't they have noses?"

"Noses?" Kevin asked. "What's a nose, sir?"

Guy saw Pierre-Georges bridle at the word "sir" and its suggestion of an age difference. Of course there was a considerable age difference, but fashionistas didn't want to acknowledge it. They were young forever, and that's what the all-night dancing and cocaine was all about, though in the long run the drugs and the late nights only made them look older, more desiccated.

Pierre-Georges was just back from Paris. He'd flown on the Concorde that very morning and sat next to an old German baroness who owned her own bank and smelled bad; he'd left at ten and arrived in New York two hours earlier. He was full of Paris gossip and was wearing a new floaty black jacket by Yamamoto and baggy gray trousers by Kenzo, more culottes than trousers. He looked silly. Guy thought he must warn Kevin not to call people in fashion "sir." His faux pas wasn't as serious as Guy's had been when he'd called Édouard "Monsieur le Baron" when Édouard had been posing as an unruly dog in need of discipline; nevertheless, fashion people worried about losing their looks. Kenzo's clothes looked ageless because he'd brought his whole team of Japanese seamstresses and *stylistes* to

Paris and they had their own way of assembling clothes. And Pierre-Georges, in wearing Kenzo, was obviously up to date, though Kenzo had been around for a decade already and his women's wear was much more adventurous than his boxy, conservative men's line.

"You look very chic," Guy said. "Is that Kenzo?" That was as meaningless in their world as saying hello.

"Of course it is," Pierre-Georges snapped, pouring himself a glass of Perrier from the fridge. "I'm through with all those Hugo Boss suits, with their silk pochettes and solid silk ties and lace-up polished shoes. I'm sick of the rich banker look. I'm going geisha."

"Well, it's very chic," Guy said.

"Which is more than I can say for you, with your dull Ralph Lauren slacks and tassel loafers and baggy Brooks button-down shirts. I mean, *please*, this isn't 1950! We're almost through the eighties and men are falling so far behind women. Women are in their Arlésienne Christian Lacroix, so gay, so cheerful, and bright, and their beautiful Paloma jewelry, and here we are in Brooks Brothers. You say you're a fashion model, but look at you! So boring! Since you're so old and you've been around so long, you've accumulated all these clothes, but you're not running a museum. I know, let's clean out your whole closet and give it to Good Volunté—Goodwill, that's what they call it.

"And then you should develop a new look all your own. With attention to detail. You must have exquisite detail. Refined detail. Look at your heels. Run-down. And you're going out like that! You must inspire designers, not just cover your back against the sun or rain. You are a *fashion* model. That means you yourself must be inspirational to couturiers. I know there aren't any good ones over here. But what if you ran into Karl Lagerfeld dressed as you are now? He comes over here a lot. Everyone in Paris is dressing now! The jewels: Now that they see Mitterrand isn't going to ruin them, that he's the capitalists' best friend, they've brought all their jewels out of hiding. Marie-Hélène tried New York but she hated it, all those dull businessmen, no amusing actors or writers, and all those CEOs in bed by ten o'clock? Karl has decided *accessories* are the important things. I saw him and a boy from his entourage at Le Palace, so chic, I danced with Jimmy Sommerville, and Roland Barthes wrote an essay about it before he was run over, poor dear, though he had the most extraordinary *hair* growing out of his nose! It must have been four inches long. He never recovered from his mother's death. Anyway, Karl's boy had on the most miraculous silver belt with interlocking eighteenth century heads complete with wigs, he said he got them off his andirons, you know he has that chateau now and lives as if he were in a Mozart opera. Karl himself I thought was carrying a purse, but, my dear, it was a book! *Les Liaison Dangereuses*, in a first edition. Oh, so chic, reading at a disco! And of course he had his fan and monocle and his hair in a ponytail, but he should lose weight. He's wearing a sort of blouson by Yamamoto, but all his boys are wonderfully thin and they're all wearing silver, long, heavy necklaces with the head of Medusa, such bad luck, or ravishing gypsy bracelets all up one arm, very thin jingly bracelets. Keiser Karl had on a silver brooch, art moderne, I'd say, his mother's, I think, with an emerald the size of a quail egg, of course not art deco, he auctioned off all that, including the Ruhlmann desks and the things from Jeanne Lanvin's house, he can't abide that now, such a restless spirit, such a genius! I told one of his *mignons* that I liked his silk vest and he said, can you believe it, 'I'm so glad you like it. I've ordered it in twelve colors.'"

"Excuse me, what's a nose?" Kevin repeated with a big smile. Guy winced. He'd never seen Pierre-Georges so revved up, virtually hysterical. Maybe it was the excitement of Paris or the Concorde, but it seemed like cocaine.

"A nose!" Pierre-Georges shouted. "*Un Nez*. The man who creates new perfumes."

"Oh, I get it, like he's a nose because he smells—"

"Are you *retarded*?" Pierre-Georges said, staring the boy down. "He's a little retarded, no?" he said, addressing Guy.

"I guess when it comes to fashion," Kevin said, smiling again, imagining he could conquer this Parisian viper with homegrown charm, "I am sort of retarded."

"Obviously," Pierre-Georges snarled without a moment's hesitation, giving a sweeping glance at Kevin's jeans and checked shirt and sneakers. "Who made your clothes—FAO Schwarz?" naming the children's toy store.

Kevin laughed at that one, interpreting it incorrectly as a friendly if deadpan jibe. "That's a good one, Pierre," he said, imagining that was his given name and that Georges must be his last name. "You've been in the business for years and years." Pierre-Georges cast his eyes to heaven. "Would you say I have any potential as a model?" Kevin had boldly put himself in the line of fire, something American parents taught their children to do.

"My dear, you have a certain *naïf fraicheur*, most appealing in bed, I'm sure, especially in the satanic embrace of an *old* master like this one"—and he jerked his head toward Guy—"but you're too short for the runway, and for print you don't have that *je ne sais* what that makes us dream, fantasize, that evokes the opera or silent movie stars or impossibly decadent aristocrats, *enfin*, you look like an American farmer, an uncultured pig farmer"—Pierre-Georges actually shuddered—"but lacking, how do I say? The necessary virility. Guy has told me you and your twin have very small *verges*, penises, which seems tragic for nature to have made the same mistake twice, I mention that only—"

"I never said that!" Guy sputtered. "I would never say that."

"*Enfin*, you said his sex is touching, which means small, no?"

"It means large," Guy said.

Now Pierre-Georges looked directly at Kevin. "You and your brother are identical? Maybe I could find something, Italians love blonds, they love wholesome, maybe because they themselves are so devious, so oily."

Looking shattered by the discussion of his penis size but still resolutely smiling, unshaken in his belief in affability, Kevin said, "My brother isn't really gay and he doesn't want to be a model."

"That's all that was missing. But I'm not really concerned with these taxonomic distinctions," Pierre-Georges said loftily. "I just thought *L'Uomo Vogue* might be amused by blond twins, but if you're not interested . . ."

"Oh, *I'm* very interested, but Chris doesn't even look that much like me now. He's put on weight—"

Pierre-Georges shrank back in horror. "Another retarded," he said, "destroying his youth." And with that, he was out the door without so much as a peck on Guy's cheek.

"Now, that's what you call a vicious French queen. I never discussed your penis size—"

"Bet you did," Kevin said, "at the beginning. I've heard the way gay guys talk at the gym. Nothing's sacred. Not even my poor little penis."

"Your penis is fine, I worship it." And Guy fell to his knees and started nuzzling his crotch until Kevin pulled him to his feet.

"Chris told me I shouldn't trust you, and he was right, but I love you anyway."

Kevin brooded about his modeling prospects and all Guy's lies, and more than once Guy overheard him talking on the phone with Chris in their strange shorthand punctuated with giggles. Guy gathered from Kevin's end of the conversation that it must not be too flattering, since he lowered his voice whenever Guy entered the room. Yet Kevin, whenever he walked past Guy, couldn't resist kissing him on the neck. It excited Guy that Kevin, when he wanted to make love, would perch beside him, say sweet things, and begin to touch him amorously; Guy figured that must be what girls expected, to be "warmed up," and that Kevin's experience must be entirely with girls.

They went out to Fire Island for a long weekend, as the lawyer had suggested. Kevin had never been there before and was impressed by everything—the ferryboat traversing the bay, all these suntanned, muscled men in baseball caps, pastel shorts, and silver necklaces carrying boxloads of red geraniums, the distant sound of the surf pounding on the Atlantic beach invisible just over the dunes, all these grown-ups pulling little red wagons over the raised wooden walkways, the tranquil regard of an unfrightened deer and her fawn in the sandy brush just a hand's breadth away from the main path, the fantastical torqued shapes of the stylish houses mounted on unpainted stilts ("There's Calvin Klein's house, there's Tommy Tune's"), the absence of cars, and the sudden burst of cackling from unseen men already hard at drinks around a pool just behind that weathered wood fence, the extraordinary friendliness of every-one saying hello. At first Kevin suspected Guy must have slept with half these guys, but then he figured out everyone must be stoned or mellow—and that the walkways here were far more friendly than the streets of Manhattan.

At last they reached Guy's house. He felt a bit like an intruder putting the key in the gate to the outer wall. Inside, the pool, filled and glittering, awaited them. Someone must be main-taining it, it looked clean, and water was bubbling at one end. It smelled of chlorine.

Inside, the house reeked of mildew and garbage. Flimsy aluminum beach chairs were stacked in the living room. Guy flung open the sliding glass doors after first lifting the obstruct-ing one-by-twos in the metal floor doorframes.

Kevin was flabbergasted by how big and sunny and baronial the house was. Guy was checking that the lights worked and that the water could be turned on in the bathroom. Everything was functioning, and Guy wondered how the house had weathered the harsh winter without the pipes bursting. Was there a caretaker? Who was paying for the utilities? Could it be an automatic monthly deduction?

Guy took their bag into the bedroom and opened those sliding glass doors, too, and verified that there were sheets on the bed and towels in the bathroom. Everything felt slightly damp. He could hear Kevin in the living room, carrying the folding chairs out to the pool and setting them up. A cool breath was sluicing now all through the house and the smell of brine had replaced the odor of rot.

Kevin came into the bedroom with an astonished smile and said, "This place is palatial. I can't believe it all belongs to you."

"Not yet, exactly. Fred's sons are contesting the will."

"But didn't this Fred leave it to you?"

"Poor boy, you're so new to gay life, you don't realize we don't have any rights. The family almost always wins, no matter how shitty they were to their relative."

Kevin came up to Guy and took him in his arms. "Does it make you sad"—he nodded at an old jockstrap and sneakers in the open closet on the floor—"to see Fred's things? Stuff he left behind because he was sure he'd be coming back?"

Guy kissed him, then stepped away and held him at arm's length. "You do have an old soul. You're so kind. So sweet. So emotionally intelligent. How did you guess what I was feeling?"

"I could see the stuff on the floor and it was too old and stained to be yours and I could imagine what you must be thinking,"

A moment later they were naked and lying on the bed. Guy couldn't get enough of Kevin and kept kissing him as if he wanted to drink his blood. "I want you in me," Guy said. A moment later Kevin had entered him, and Guy could smell the tuna fish sandwiches they'd eaten on the ferry over. This time Guy didn't want to take his turn. Nor did he want Kevin to pull out of him. They spooned, although the sea wind was almost too cold. They kept snuggling closer and closer to stay warm; Kevin ran his hands over Guy's body.

"Do you know anyone out here?"

"Not that I could call at ten in the morning to chat. But you'll see. It's very tribal. Everyone dancing all night and eventually at dawn heading out to the dunes to have sex. But it's so beautiful here, with the surf and the houses on the shore—"

"Will we go out there for sex?"

"I only want to be with you," Guy said. "But if you're bored with me . . ."

"What?"

"Well, you're so inexperienced I don't want to deprive you, just so you come back to Daddy. But to insure our health, maybe it would be best if we were faithful for the duration. I'm sure AIDS will be over next year."

The word "daddy" made Kevin hard. Or maybe it was the idea of a fidelity pact.

"I want to fuck my daddy again," Kevin said, and did.

They showered—the water came out at first in dirty cold bursts but then ran clear and hot—and put on shorts and T's and sneakers and pulled a red wagon to the grocery. On the way everyone said hello, and one group of five stopped in their tracks and watched Guy and Kevin go by. Kevin looked back, but Guy sauntered on, pulling his noisy wagon over the bumpy boards. Kevin could hear the words "models" and "stuck-up" and he was pleased they had said "models" plural.

"Is everyone always so friendly and in such a good mood?" Kevin asked. He felt strange being so pale, but he'd dutifully applied sunscreen all over.

"They're drunk now," Guy said, "and optimistic, but they will soon be squabbling over household expenses and hoping they'll find love later in the Meat Rack. They'll be arguing. 'Why did you buy that expensive leg of lamb?' And they become especially cross at the beginning of September when they realize the season is over and they've danced their tushes off and fucked a lot in the bushes, but, hey, they haven't bagged a beau for the winter and they've maxed out their credit cards."

Kevin laughed and put an arm around Guy and said, "I didn't know you knew all those words."

"Out here I've heard them often enough," Guy said. Because of oncoming traffic on the boardwalk, Kevin had to fall back and follow Guy, which allowed him to take a long look at Guy's ass pistoning away inside his clinging Speedo. Kevin felt his dick getting hard and he looked away, embarrassed.

They encountered a sunburned man of fifty in cargo shorts, with a red belly and hairless torso and Play-Doh features, thick lips and a bulbous nose and one eye permanently half closed. He was with three sleek youngsters, each more muscular and handsome than the next.

"Hey, Jim," Guy said, stopping to kiss the man on just one cheek as they did out here. "Jim, Kevin," he said, and the man shook Kevin's hand and introduced his "bravos," as Kevin thought of them because he saw them as a Renaissance escort of tough guys.

"Guy," Jim said. "You and—Kevin, is it?—should come to dinner tonight."

Guy looked at Kevin, who nodded. "Great," Guy said. "What time?"

"Oh, anytime. Nine? Ten? You remember where the house is? And Guy, I was so sorry to hear about Fred. This AIDS, it's not funny anymore. Fred was such a sweetheart!" And they all went their separate ways, but one dark bravo, who must have been French, murmured to Guy, "*À ce soir.*"

A moment later Jim had doubled back and said, "You're not vegetarians, are you?"

Guy laughed and said, "No, we're French." And Kevin liked that and said in his best Minnesota accent, "Yeah, we're French as hell." And they all three laughed.

"Are all these guys out here hustlers or porn stars?" Kevin asked. "They're so gorgeous."

"No, they only look that way. They're all lawyers or surgeons but as beautiful as gigolos."

Kevin swept out the house and washed down the counters, then went nude for a late afternoon swim in the pool. They walked to the Botel for tea dance and Kevin was amazed there were so many men dancing in swimsuits, "all gorgeous," he said. They drank big blue cocktails called Blue Whales. "What makes them blue?" Kevin asked. "Are my questions too dumb?"

"Not at all, sweetheart. Blue curaçao, whatever that is."

All eyes were on them as they leaned against the railing around the deck or danced nonchalantly to the deafening music—or rather, everyone looked away the instant Kevin glanced at them, but if he caught their eye by surprise they were staring at them as if they were movie stars or royalty. Guy's cheekbones were more prominent than everyone else's, his hair more expertly cut, his muscles more compact and defined, his waist more dramatically sinewy, his toenails more beautifully buffed; if you studied the others, they had leathery tans or coarse features or they had bulked up grotesquely from the waist up but their legs were skinny or their smiles were tarnished or their torsos were thick. Only Guy was perfect, Kevin thought. Only he looked both masculine and refined.

Jim's house was eccentrically modern. As they walked up to it at nine-thirty that night, it looked like an old-fashioned view camera—just one small window, the lens, in the center of the facade framed by receding slatted squares, the bellows. Inside, it was all two steps up, one step down, track lighting, Memphis modular furniture, a small outdoor pool lit from within like a sapphire, big, gaudy, unframed abstractions on the wall, all seemingly by the same hand. Or were they just silk-screened batik fabric posing as paintings? The rooms flowed into one another. The guys had drinks on an orange molded plastic couch and pink beanbag chairs, then went to the long, narrow dining room table, with its tall black crystal helix candlesticks, glazed turquoise plates, and twelve matching chairs that looked made out of plasticized cobwebs or molded lace. The food was exotic but light, a salad of kiwis, orange sections, and fresh thyme, and two giant sea bass cooked in salt shells, served with black pasta made from squid ink. A few raspberries and crystallized mint leaves for dessert. Lots of cheap wine, both colors. Fat joints were passed and everyone spoke at once in strangulated voices. They were laughing uproariously at nothing. The handsome Frenchman felt, under the table, Guy's knee bared by the navy blue perfectly tailored linen shorts, and even tried to wedge a hand up his pant leg toward his crotch, though Guy discreetly lifted the man's hand and put it back in his lap, but patted it to be polite. They talked about Madonna, whom the others were bored with but whom Kevin hotly defended, though he worried he was talking too much.

When they got home Guy was so stoned he didn't even stop to think what Kevin might want but just pulled off his trousers and raped him, assuming he'd like that, and he was right, by some miracle, Kevin did like it. They didn't even shower afterward, but fell asleep in each other's arms, smelling of sex—or like horses, Kevin thought, smiling into the dark.

The next day in the afternoon a uniformed chauffeur, for an event organized by Pierre-Georges, carried Guy's luggage to a waiting speedboat, which conveyed him to a waiting limousine, which took him to the airport, where he boarded a waiting plane bound for Milan and runway shows for Versace and Armani. Kevin was at loose ends and already missed Guy, though he'd be back in a week. On the ferryboat to Sayville, Kevin looked at all these hung-over men in their bright pastel patterned clothes. Several of them had expensive-looking dogs and most of them looked much older and lined in the cold light of day than before. They weren't all so young and intimidating as he'd thought, but they were tanned. One of the men from dinner last night sat beside him and asked how long he and Guy had been dating. Kevin was proud to be half of a couple, though he knew he shouldn't trust Guy, such a liar. He could still feel his cock in his ass and took comfort in that. He and his twin had burritos together that evening, took a long walk, and had a thorough debriefing. He told Chris all about Fire Island, Guy's beach house, all the spaceship houses on stilts, and how you couldn't tell the brokers from the houseboys, how friendly everyone was, and how they all said hi just like the folks back in Ely. Kevin had already filled Chris in on all Guy's lies, how he was really almost forty and had a crooked lover in the clink and how rich old men kept giving him houses, but Kevin didn't like it that Chris was bringing this up now. That night, he jerked off twice in their bed and whispered, "Guy," and molded his phantom back with his free hand. He sprayed himself with Guy's toilet water and slept with his perfumed hand next to his nose.

The next morning he slept in, and then around eleven-thirty the doorbell rang. It was the baron and Hans. Kevin was in just his underpants but immediately put on a long white dress shirt that belonged to Guy, far too big for him.

"Oh, forgive us," the baron said. "You were sleeping. You sleep a lot—like a dog when his master is away. I know it's unforgivable in New York to just drop in, but we were walking by and I wanted Hans to see the house because we're looking at one like it."

"Not at all," Kevin said, which was something Guy said. "Guy's in Milan."

"Still at it, is he, even at his age?" the baron said. "Though he looks the same."

"Come in," Kevin said, worried about how you received a baron. "Please sit down. Would you like a glass of orange juice?"

"Orange juice at noon? But go ahead, pour yourself one, you're obviously longing for one," and Kevin wondered how the baron knew.

Hans perched on the edge of the couch, his hands hanging down between his spread legs. He had on a tight green short-sleeved shirt with its golden Brooks Brothers sheep insignia, incongruous, really, for such a tough guy, though it did flatter his biceps. The baron sat beside him and put a possessive hand on Hans's knee.

"Glass of water? Or I can make some coffee," Kevin piped.

"You're most gracious," the baron said. "We'll be gone in a second, we'll fly like the Dutchman so you can finish your toilette." And Kevin ran a hand through his hair, wondering if it was sticking up. He realized his legs with their fine hair like glints of gold looked good under the voluminous shirt, as did his small shapely feet, which he'd drawn up under his body to one side as if he were the White Rock girl. He was very aware of Hans's eyes scanning him, assessing him; Hans was probably wondering what he could do to him.

The baron turned to Hans and said in a professional, consulting voice, as if they were alone, "Notice the high ceilings and the moldings and the fireplace and the harmonious proportions. And all the sunlight. I'm sure our place is the same, these houses were all built at the same time."

Hans was too masculine, too imposing and sadistic for these domestic details, and it was beneath his dignity to do anything but nod curtly. His woodenness suited the baron just fine, who smiled contentedly.

Since Hans didn't want to engage in talking real estate, the baron turned malicious out of ennui and addressed Kevin. "Perhaps I shouldn't ask, but do you and Guy indulge in sado-masochism? I ask because he liked to inflict pain on me, however ineptly. I introduced him to these exquisite pleasures, but I wondered if the seeds I'd planted had sprouted. I'm sort of the Johnny Appleseed of pain. Has he hurt you?"

"I'm not sure I want to talk about my private life," Kevin said; then, realizing that sounded feminine and middle-class, and feeling reckless, he added, "No, but I like to hurt him."

Suddenly Hans looked up now, thoroughly interested and appraising Kevin with an insider's eye. "Oh-hoh!" the baron crowed. "I see. No wonder Guy is so attached to you. Nothing is more *attachant* than sadism," and the baron smiled with courteous complicity at Hans and then, generously, took in little Kevin as an honorary sadist. Smiling back, Kevin felt stupid and on the wrong foot. After his surprise guests left, Kevin called his twin. He told him everything, how the baron really was a decadent European noble and how he, Kevin, had lied and pretended to be a sort of mini-sadist because he disliked the baron's assumption that he was the passive one. For the first time he felt uneasy about confiding so much in Chris. He'd thought there never would be a day when he'd want to keep a secret from Chris.

Talking long-distance to Italy the next day at noon, Kevin told Guy about the baron's and Hans's visit. "Are you really a sadist?" Kevin asked.

"That's just his sick fantasy," Guy said. "He hires skinny, balding guys with big dicks to beat him up." Guy told Kevin of his unforgivable faux pas in asking Édouard, "*Ça va, Monsieur le Baron?*" And how that had terminated their relationship. "I guess the antique dealer has already been replaced."

"So what are you doing over there?" Kevin asked, introducing a less controversial topic.

"For work? I guess they think I could be Italian, so I've been doing a commercial for pasta, but of course my dialogue has to be dubbed, though I mouth the words. But people like working with me, why not? I'm a friendly guy," he said with a laugh. "On the runway I've had to model these really tacky clothes, all black lace and gold lamé and thigh-high boots, they look so cheap, but Versace likes me and next year he wants an exclusive, that means I don't work for anyone else but he pays me five, no, six times my current rate. He had me open the show and close it. You'd think I'd be indifferent, but it gave me a huge adrenaline rush. Coming out, all those people looking up at you, all those cameras flashing, knowing that the whole world will be watching. It all seemed like a dream. It must be like being in war, you don't remember what you did or how you did it. You're all alone on the runway, then backstage, three or four people are pulling at you getting you dressed in your next ensemble. Then I've done some print work where I'm just atmosphere."

"Atmosphere?"

"That's what we call it when you're just the guy in the background, helping the girl out of the car or pouring her wine, one of the crowd, soft-focus."

"And you still get paid a lot for that?"

"I do, because my agent over here is Élite, not a lot, but I work every day, I'm not complaining."

"Are you partying every night?"

"No, that's where I feel my age, and I don't have fun if I don't do some coke. If I do coke I'm depressed the next day." Guy thought it was such a relief now to be able to talk with Kevin about his age.

"Daddy no do blow," Kevin said in baby talk, and they both laughed. Thousands of miles apart, and Kevin started to get hard. Maybe it was the word "daddy," even tossed off as a joke, or maybe it was just imagining laughing in his arms. Kevin had a perfectly nice father back in Minnesota who'd always been affectionate enough, but still Kevin liked fucking Daddy-Guy, how perverted was that?

"Hope you're not fucking too many cute guys," Kevin said, then added, "Daddy," to indicate he was just playacting and not really jealous.

"No, I'm just thinking of my baby boy," Guy said, and now Kevin really did have an erection. Kevin had heard of men who kept their boys in diapers and playpens and showed them cartoons all day and fed them Gerber's—but that was sick, he didn't want to go that far, yet it was exciting, maybe just the thought of regressing or giving up or being held in Daddy's arms.

9.

G UY FLEW IN early, since the client had paid for a ticket on the Concorde. (You could get a deal for a first-class seat on a jet going over and a Concorde seat coming back.) When he let himself in at nine in the morning, he did so silently and discovered Kevin and Chris asleep. They were together, entwined, those two identical faces, both of them in matching Jockey shorts and nothing else, identical small erections, morning wood, their hands and feet so small, elegant, matching, their blond Norwegian heads pressed together, both of them with open mouths and ruby lips.

Kevin was the first to wake up. "You're back early. Concorde?"

"Yes. You two look so great together." Guy felt torn between lust and jealousy.

"We went out last night dancing at the Roxy and didn't get home till dawn. If I'd known you were flying the Concorde . . ."

"It was all very last-minute. You know fashion people— hurry up and wait." If Guy were cheekier he would lie down in the midst of this flowery bower.

Their voices had awakened Chris, who smiled weakly and waved, looked grumpy, adjusted himself, ran into the bathroom, and dressed quickly. A moment later he was gone, his hair all scrunched to one side.

"Why does he have a burr up his ass?"

"He's just jealous," Kevin said. Guy wondered why jealous if Chris was so straight, and why was he dancing in a gay club? Chris was barely out the door before Kevin clawed off Guy's clothes. Afterward, he said to Kevin, while holding him in his arms, what he'd rehearsed so many times, "Baby?"

"Yes, Daddy?" Kevin was holding him and hadn't yet pulled out.

"What if we each got a discreet tattoo?"

Kevin thought for a moment about this proposal, more jarring than anything he'd anticipated: A model with a tattoo? Weren't tattoos forever? Did people like them ever get them? Weren't they something white trash had? "Pardon?" he said.

Guy pulled free, sat up on the towel he'd spread out, and looked Kevin in the eye. Guy worried that he looked strange with his sprayed-on tan just on his face and hands from his last job for sunglasses. (Didn't they say they wanted an exclusive? How much would that pay? For how many days? Would Élite work all that out with Pierre-Georges? Would the client shoot in New York? Did that young Italian photographer, Giorgio, ever work in New York?) "I'm sorry, I'm still half in Milan, worrying about work."

"Poor guy," Kevin said, stroking his face and worrying about Guy's unrelieved erection now shrinking to half-mast.

"I thought we could get tiny number eights behind our earlobes."

"Why that number?"

"If it's on its side, it's the symbol for infinity and could stand for our eternal love."

"Aw, that's so sweet," Kevin said, and pecked him on the lips. Quite the commitment, Kevin thought, smiling. "How did you even know that?" he asked, astonished that Guy knew so many things he didn't; must be his French background.

And indeed Guy explained he'd read about it in a story but he couldn't remember whose. It probably was a French author's, a man was in love with a nun and managed to have the infinity symbol projected on the convent lawn just outside her window.

"That's so romantic," Kevin said with a frown. "Wouldn't it be dangerous? I mean, if it got infected?"

Guy made a clucking sound of dismissal and Kevin felt about as daring as a grandmother. "Yeah," Guy said, "they might have to amputate our heads."

Kevin said, "That wouldn't affect me in the least," though secretly he thought he and Chris were smarter than Guy. They both did well in trig, whereas Guy could barely add. He felt startled, even offended, when Guy knew things he didn't. Though superior knowledge was only natural in a sophisticated man who'd traveled the world's capitals for two decades and who liked to read, Guy's occasional pockets of esoteric knowledge were still disturbing to Kevin, who didn't want to think of all those years before they'd met or all the conversations Guy might be having now without Kevin, some shared laugh of camaraderie with another runway model backstage as they both wore protective cloth coats over their white alpaca suits, so easy to soil, so likely to shed.

"I guess that would mean we really were married," Kevin said. "It would be a statement of some sort, that this time it's for keeps."

"Of course it's for keeps," Guy said. What if Kevin ever met Andrés and saw that he had the same tattoo? Guy could foresee a disaster like that, but the one thing he counted on was that, even if his whole world exploded, he'd always be able to attract new people, maybe of not the same caliber, but good enough. He'd once gotten drunk with a handsome flight attendant who'd said, "The good thing and the bad thing about being a steward is that you never have to make anything work with a guy, because you're always flying off and meeting new guys." Being an international model was like that; even in Milan he'd met two other models who'd fancied him. He liked models—they were so clean. Everyone said they were shallow, but he thought it depended. He knew one, that black guy with the Afro he'd met in Chicago, who'd gotten a Ph.D. in something.

"But won't a facial tattoo be a problem for a model?" Kevin asked.

"Pierre-Georges was right. I need a new look. Anyway, I'm going to grow my hair long to cover my ears—and I have such dumb ears."

"Aw, they're cute!"

"And I'm going to stop shaving every day. I'll have some stubble. I saw a model in Milan with stubble and it was very chic. Everyone was fascinated." He thought for a moment, picturing his new look. "Ultra-masculine. I'll start wearing punk, masculine clothes to go-sees. Lots of leather. Safety pins. If that works I'll push my hair back on one side and show my tattoo. Enough with the *Gentleman's Quarterly* look. Models are so square."

"Who will tattoo us? Does it hurt? It will be so strange to have something . . . permanent . . . making me different from Chris. I mean, a mustache, okay, or five pounds, a haircut, but a brand on your flesh?"

"A brand? Let's not be melodramatic. I think they give you

an anesthetic. I'll find a clean, artistic tattoo artist. It's becoming far more common."

"Really? I don't want to look like a scumbag. We used to say you should never have anything on your body that you couldn't cover up with long sleeves before a judge."

"Did you, now? In Ely?" Guy said with just the right combination, he hoped, of ridicule and condescension.

Not wishing to be vexed with Guy, Kevin kissed him and said, "I don't want to look like a convict."

Guy had an attack of vertigo at the mention of the word "convict." He went pale and said, "It must be late for me. Eleven. Let's go eat something."

"I'm going to cook something. A mushroom risotto."

Where on earth did he learn to make that? Guy wondered. Rice sounded fattening, but he thought he'd eat only two spoonfuls. He was disciplined enough to do that, and if he ate three he'd vomit his entire lunch. That was a promise he made himself.

Lucie knew the name of an aesthetic tattoo artist. They made an appointment and went to a dirty little parlor in Chinatown, a third-floor walk-up, smelling of roach spray and Kools. The man, a wizened ex-sailor with sleeves of faded tattoos on both arms, looked like Popeye. All he lacked were a corncob pipe and a can of spinach. It took a hastily drawn sketch to convince him they wanted matching eights behind their left ears, tiny and no colors, visible only behind the lobe.

"I might just as well make them in lemon juice," the man said mournfully. "But I get it. I've had timid gentlemen like you two before. Sure, I can do it. Guess you guys are special pals?" and he set to work on Guy first. His needles looked dirty, and Guy worried he might get the AIDS or hepatitis from them, but he didn't dare show any qualms, lest Kevin back down.

That night neither of them could sleep from the pain behind their earlobes. The man had said the tattoos would scab over in a day, and the whole thing had taken less than an hour. It was the last burst of warm weather and they strolled over to a café on MacDougal that was open all night. As they were coming home, they ran into Pierre-Georges, who was with one of his older tough guys.

"Thanks for calling to say you were back," Pierre-Georges said snidely, after the cursory introductions in which he mentioned only Guy's and Kevin's names.

"So where are you coming from?" Kevin asked brightly. "Boots & Saddle, or, as we say, Bras & Girdle?"

"Ha-ha," Pierre-Georges said as words, not a laugh; he was clearly irritated. The overweight trick, pockmarked and reeking of beer, put his arm around Pierre-Georges's waist as if Pierre-Georges might go off with his friends—or maybe to steady himself. "We were at Ty's, if you must know." Then to Guy: "What's with the stubble? The long hair? The bandage?"

"I just got back today. As you suggested, I'm trying for a new image. Stubble—something hypermasculine. Pietro Whatsit in Milano was all stubble in the Armani *défilé* and all the photographers went crazy over him."

"You might have consulted me before you took such a drastic step—and the bandage?"

"Oh, it's nothing. I nicked myself. *Je me suis blessé en rasant.*"

"You were shaving behind your ear? Both of you?" because he'd registered that Kevin had a bandage in the same place. "You don't shave at all, I suspect," he said to Kevin as a reproach.

The trick looked startled by the few words Guy had said in French. New Yorkers were used to Spanish, at least the Puerto Rican kind, which sounded normal if substandard to them, rapid-fire and familiar, especially when English words were constantly dropped in. French, however, startled New Yorkers. It was a serious grown-up language, and New Yorkers suspected Parisians considered themselves their equals if not their superiors. Pierre-Georges didn't want to lose his trick, who just as easily might have lurched off into the night, heading back to the bar for a second strike, though Ty's had looked pretty much fished out.

"They're tattoos," Guy said. "Tiny ones behind the ear."

"Chic," Pierre-Georges whispered with awe instead of exploding. "Come along," he said to the trick; he obviously didn't know his name. Pierre-Georges lurched forward for air-kisses on both of Guy's cheeks.

When they were out of earshot, Kevin said, "He's weird."

"You mean rude? Don't imagine he ever approves of my boyfriends. French, Spanish, American—he's rude to all of them."

Kevin found being one of many was troubling, not reassuring as Guy had probably intended. "Does he have any other clients?"

"Two. Both French. But since everyone knows me and likes me, he doesn't book them often. Poor guys."

"How does he survive?"

"He's signed some very lucrative contracts for me, and my commercials keep bringing in big residuals for months. And remember a manager gets a bigger slice of the pie than an agent."

"So you're really his cash cow. Is that why he's so possessive? Or is he in love with you?"

"You saw the kind of brute he goes for. No, let's just say he's my Chris, not in love but jealous anyway."

They were sitting on their stoop, speaking in low voices, watching these huge behemoth American cars lurch by. (There was a stop sign on their corner.) A tall, prissy young man strode by, belting out show tunes to himself at midnight. Oh, he was wearing earphones, Guy noticed, and probably had no idea how loud he was singing. It was an old one, "New York, New York, it's a wonderful town, the Bronx is up and the Battery's down." The man's voice was operatic, his diction was as fruity as an old diva's, and his pitch was wobbly. Guy thought, *These absurd showbiz queens are as much a part of New York street life as sirens, steam from manholes, or ghostly Asian deliverymen ferrying chop-suey-to-go on unlit bikes going the wrong way.*

The next morning Guy and Kevin pulled off their bandages and Guy applied antibiotic cream to their tattoos. Lucie came by for coffee.

"I like your new look," she said to Guy. "Stubble, jeans, and a wife-beater."

"Is that what you call a *débardeur*?"

"Yes, or a Guinea T-shirt."

"That's a riot," Guy said. "A wife-beater."

"And you, sweetheart?" she said to Kevin. "Is it true you're going to try modeling?"

"No, Pierre-Georges said I was too short and not virile enough and not a perfect size-forty."

Lucie said, "I guess compared to the thugs he goes for, big smelly guys with guts. So what are you going to do?"

Guy listened attentively to Kevin's answer. So often the unspoken etiquette of the couple forbade direct questions and clear answers and an outsider's chance inquiry was more likely to flush out plans than any discussion (or silence) between lovers.

"I'm going to get my B.A. in poli-sci at Columbia and then a master's at Georgetown or wherever and take the civil service exam and hopefully become a career diplomat. Chris wants to go back to Ely and take over Dad's business and become an outfitter, though he'll have to wait, because Dad's just forty-five now."

Five years older than me, Guy thought.

"A diplomat, huh?" Lucie said.

"Yeah," Kevin said. "I've always wanted to travel. And I've always liked history and politics. And I'm polite and diplomatic, people say."

"You'd be a very handsome ambassador."

"Thanks, but ambassadors are used car salesmen who made big contributions to the party coffers. I want to be a cultural attaché or something—that's why you two guys have to teach me French! Let's speak French at least one hour a day. Well, after I've had a semester. Right now it'd be useless. You'll see, I'm good at languages, at least we were stars at Norwegian camp back in Minnesota." Kevin realized instantly he'd said "we" and hoped that Guy wouldn't be jealous or even notice.

When they were alone, Kevin said, "That Lucie is so sweet. Finally a friend of yours I can reach out to."

"You would have liked Fred, too. Very down-to-earth." Guy was proud of that expression, "down-to-earth." Americans used it all the time, though he wasn't quite sure what it meant—*terre-à-terre*?

"What kind of movies did he make?"

Guy stumbled over the unfamiliar word: "Blaxploitation."

"Oh, dear."

"What? I think it was kind of him to make movies for Africans. Well, let's not argue. So you want to be a diplomat?"

"My adviser at Colombia thinks I'd make a good one."

"But wouldn't that take you far away—to Peru?"

"It'll be years from now," Kevin said, smiling, "if ever. Maybe you'll be . . . tired of modeling and can come with me."

"Tired or fired or retired."

"I want to support you, for once. It'll be my turn. I'll try to get us a French-speaking country."

"The Côte d'Ivoire? They have nice beaches. I was there once for a swimsuit commercial."

"I want to see your reel sometime!"

"We'll get it from Pierre-Georges. He keeps it up-to-date."

And so the charms of their lives, their futures, were changed in a casual conversation led by a third person. Would he and Kevin stay together? How many years? Guy felt he should provide for his old age, but he was hooked on the present. With any luck he'd die ten years from now or twenty and leave a beautiful corpse. He had his two houses and his apartment in Paris. Some models were making exercise films or even getting into the business as agents. Others were buying real estate unless all their money was going up their noses. Guy had heard of one Bruce Weber star who'd bought a prewar apartment near Borough Hall and rented it out to visiting models, male and female, four units, cheaper than a midtown hotel, and they could share the kitchen, and no ordinary person was around to complain about the sound of hair dryers blowing all day or the sound of the phone ringing off the hook. Not too convenient for Manhattan clubbing, but usually there was a limo someone had sent for one of the girls.

Guy didn't like the idea of moving to Peru. That sounded lonely. Bad for the skin. And by then he'd be too old to learn another language. Everyone said Spanish was easy if you knew

French. But "fear" was *miedo* in Spanish and *peur* in French, a wave was *ola* not *vague*—nothing like! And what would they make of two adult men living together in South America, one of them the American cultural attaché?

"All we have is the present," Guy said, settling into one of his favorite themes, one he'd worked out already back in Clermont-Ferrand. "There is no past and no future, only the present." He'd argued that position with one of the priests at school, who was torn because he was besotted with Guy but of course wanted him to think of his ultimate reward in heaven.

"That's interesting." Kevin said, bored.

Guy was sorry that Kevin didn't argue with him. Most people did, at least other models did. "No future? You've got to be kidding! What about my next job in Saint-Tropez?" they'd say indignantly, and then he'd take them to a higher if paradoxical level. But Kevin didn't like to philosophize. All he wanted to do when they were together was chitchat or have sex. He wasn't very intellectual. Or maybe it was just American practicality, whereas the French like to soar on the wings of speculation.

Guy loved the feeling he got when he was tiptoeing into the cobwebs of the stratosphere. He'd smile benignly at his own familiarity with these difficult subjects, his calm, mature mastery of these paradoxes. He didn't want to be down-to-earth all the time. Being earthbound didn't do much for him.

Kevin turned off the minute Guy got that contented smile on his face and launched into one of his idiotic rants, what he considered philosophizing. Kevin had studied real philosophy at Columbia and had received an A on his term paper about the difference between ideology and ideas. (Ideology was a false view promoted by the ruling class in order to hoodwink the proletariat.) He was sickened by Guy's rambling on about time, and wondered how much longer he'd be able to stomach it.

Three days later Guy took the bus to see Andrés. This time he told Kevin where he was going and Kevin said, "I admire you for that. You're a very loyal person."

Guy agreed. He was very loyal. He still sent his mother a thousand dollars a month, which wasn't so much, given the downgrading of the dollar, but it was something. It allowed her to live correctly, now that she had a car in good running order and all paid for. She owned her home. And she got a welfare check from the government. She'd had to hide the allowance she got from Guy in order to qualify for the government stipend. He mailed a money order to his brother, who handed her the cash. So far they hadn't been caught. From time to time Lucie helped Guy fill a big box of shawls, sweaters, dresses— everything she could pick up in his mother's size after a collection was shown. His mother complained that the clothes were too stylish or flashy or daring for their neighborhood, and he was certain she was still shopping in her old raincoat and paisley scarf she'd bought from the Arabs in the market in the shadow of the cathedral.

Guy had been loyal to Fred, more than anyone else had, and he would have stayed on good terms with the baron if he hadn't been exiled. He was *fidel* to Andrés and took the long, boring bus ride out there every week. He'd even become friendly with one of the other "wives," a delicate young black woman who bathed herself in a sweet candied perfume she said was invented by Elizabeth Taylor. She really smelled like cotton candy. Yes, he was a loyal friend—he'd stuck with Pierre-Georges even though bigger agents had tried to lure him away. Of course, he knew Pierre-Georges was watching out for him 24/7, and he doubted another agent could wrangle him bigger contracts. Guy had been around too long; everyone knew what he was worth.

"What if Andrés notices the tattoo? Won't you have some explaining to do?" Kevin asked, lifting an eyebrow.

"Oh, he won't. He's pretty—how do you say? Narcisse?"

"Narcissistic. That's a tough one." Kevin thought it advisable to comment on the word rather than the character flaw.

"He never notices anything," Guy said.

Of course, he did, and to make sure he did, as soon as they were seated opposite each other in the visiting room, Guy pushed his hair back and flipped his earlobe forward. "See what I did for you? Just as I promised."

Andrés, rather than being delighted, looked around nervously at the guard, the same handsome thick one as before, who was studying them carefully. He strode over to them and pulled back his ear; the tattoo of the number eight was bigger than Guy's and harder to distinguish on black skin. And then he grabbed Andrés, wrenched his head around, and revealed his tattoo, the same number eight. At that point he grunted and walked away, back to the other guard he'd been chatting with.

"That wasn't cool," Andrés said to Guy.

"You got the tattoo to please your new love or master or whatever he is, and to cover yourself around me you convinced me to do it, too—for you. You pretended—" And Guy couldn't help but laugh when he realized he'd played the same trick on Kevin. Guy thought that he and Andrés were both wily, always plotting, and Kevin and the black man were typical Yankee dopes. "What's your lover's name, anyway?"

"Lester," Andrés said in a surly tone. "He's not my lover." He lowered his eyes and said in a small voice, "He's my protector. You're my lover."

"Did you choose him to be your protector? Or did he choose you as his protégé?"

Andrés exploded, "You don't know what it's like to live in here all day, every day. I need someone to protect me."

Guy could see that Andrés had been working out hard. His arms and shoulders looked twice as big as before. How dangerous really was this junior high of a prison? Knowing that he'd duped Kevin in the same way Andrés had duped him made Guy forgive him, though with an edge of exasperation. He hoped Lester wouldn't punish Andrés—beat him or put him in solitary. Lester might have hit Andrés now if it weren't for the surveillance cameras and so many witnesses from the outside world. "I'm sorry—I had no idea."

So unexpected was Guy's apology that Andrés broke into a sweet boyish smile: That sweetness had almost been extinguished in this new tough, hardened Andrés here in prison where anger seemed to be the default mode, but Guy's kindness called to the boy hidden within, who slowly emerged from the darkest cave of Andrés's heart, where the child had been declared dead. He wasn't dead, just weakened and frightened. "I should be the one begging your forgiveness," Andrés said softly.

"Let's forget the whole thing."

They smiled long and hard at each other, shook hands warmly, and Andrés even got tears in his eyes. Guy wondered what Andrés would do with this sweet-feeling child at the entrance of the cave now that the tide was rushing in around his knees.

What Andrés had done, apparently, was start a major fight between the Puerto Rican gang to which he belonged and the black gang—with the result he was put in lockdown and his sentence was increased by two years. The next time Guy saw him, he still had a bump on his head and a black eye and his lip was torn. He was still indignant, and plagued Guy with a long "he said, I said" narrative Guy couldn't follow. Then he simmered down and looked morose, probably at the prospect of the addition to his sentence. He talked about his new interest in the Catholic Church and his pious reading of the lives of the saints: "Those were some far-out cats," Andrés exclaimed with his torn-lipped smile.

Then, on a new, obviously rehearsed confidential note, Andrés said, with care and solemnity, "I have a great favor to ask of you."

"Anything," Guy said, hoping it wasn't for a metal file in a cake.

"My sister, the one who moved from Bogotá to Murcia, has been diagnosed with cancer. Her husband vanished years ago. She's been raising her son, Vicente, all on her own. He's fifteen now. She can't take care of him anymore, she's too sick and poor. You remember my sister Concepción?"

"Poor girl. I had no idea. Does she write you in prison?"

"All the time. Anyway, Vicente is staying with a distant cousin in Lackawanna. She, that cousin, we call her King Kong because she's so black, is married to an Arab, I think he's a terrorist but he says he's in air-conditioning repair, anyway he's fed up with Vicente, not because he's a bad boy but because he's poor, Mohammed isn't earning anything, they're on welfare, and they can't get an allowance for Vicente, he's an illegal, he overstayed his three-month tourist visa."

"We only have five more minutes. What do you want me to do—send them a check?"

"No, I want you to take Vicente in."

Guy immediately wondered what Kevin would think. Then he thought about what the boy would mean to his own life. Guy liked crazy, unforeseen twists in fate, maybe because his life had become so predictable, so narrow—regular jaunts to Europe, an hour three times a week at the gym, life's long diet and only occasional prudent lapses, sex with Kevin, visits to Andrés, every two weeks a phone call to his mother, strategy sessions with Pierre-Georges. ("She said you were rude to her," Pierre-Georges said of a stylist from Saks. "She also said the suit was wearing you rather than you were wearing the suit."

"Whatever that means," Guy muttered. "And she was the rude one, stabbing me with pins, trying to smooth out a cheap shirt that was born wrinkled.") Life had become confining and routine; even their Saturday night drug vacations dancing at the Roxy were always the same, with MDA, cocaine, and grass, staggering home at dawn with grins on their famous faces. At least Guy's would be famous if it weren't so generic—now even his trademark jug ears would soon be invisible under wings of dark hair covering them, carefully arranged in "un brushing."

A kid would serve the same function as a bad love affair to introduce a note of chaos into our overly organized lives. He's not going to sit around doing nothing or reading. He'll need a part-time job. I'm sure he could do mimeographing for Pierre-Georges. "Is he cute?"

Andrés made a face, as he did when people told a dirty joke. "He's fifteen. Cute enough, I guess. Keep your mitts off him, okay?"

"Fifteen is safe with me." He thought guiltily of Kevin, who was nineteen. "Is he black, too, like your sister King Kong?"

"King Kong is my cousin, my sister is Concepción."

"I forgot. Will I get in trouble with my own green card if I'm caught hosting an illegal?"

Andrés looked bored, or maybe turned off by Guy's self-centeredness. "Ask your lawyer. That's why we have lawyers, though yours didn't do much good for me."

Guy chose to ignore the reproach, and said brightly, like a violinist launching into a gigue after the tedious largo, "Okay. I'll do it. At least I'll look into it. Anything for you."

Guy felt he was marching out to the end of a diving board and, without a pause, going into a double somersault before making sure there was water in the pool. Would Vicente double his expenses? Quadruple them? What if he was a juvenile delinquent, or worse, a terrorist? What if he and Kevin fought all the time and Kevin said, "It's either him or me"? What if he was a hostile heterosexual who scorned his gay uncles and imitated them with a limp wrist to his cigarette-smoking buddies from high school?

He memorized King Kong's phone number. "What's her real name? I can't call her Signora Kong."

"Pilar."

"What?"

"Pilar, like the virgin of the pillar."

A bell was ringing, indicating an end to the visiting hour. Guy shook Andrés's hand distractedly but was preoccupied with repeating Pilar's number until he found a pencil and a scrap of paper, maybe from one of the prison wives.

Guy waited till Kevin had had two glasses of sake over dinner at the Japanese restaurant on Thirteenth Street before he brought up Vicente. Pierre-Georges had told Guy to go down another ten pounds—thin was in, he said. Maybe the weight loss would wreak havoc on his arms and chest and deflate his ass, but the new clients like Guess all demanded gaunt faces and cheekbones like flying buttresses. Guy ordered nothing but miso soup and sashimi and he left the cubes of tofu in the bowl. And he permitted himself just one cup of sake; otherwise he was living on a diet of espressos and cocaine.

They were sitting outside behind a metal railing and noisy people kept going by—oh, it was Friday! That's why people were out. For Guy, every day was the same. Across the street were the dim lights of a holistic medicine shop-cum-ashram, closed for the weekend.

Initially, Kevin took it well because he assumed Vicente must be a polite, shy boy from some provincial town in Spain, a good Catholic boy who let himself be buggered in stoic silence once a week by Padre Jesús and then assisted at the mass, a bum full of jizz, handing the priest the silver cup of wine. But when Kevin found out Vicente had been living in Lackawanna with King Kong and a terrorist named Mohammed, he shrank back in distaste. "But what if he tries to make a bomb and blows up your brownstone by mistake?" Kevin asked. "I'm serious. What if he's wearing gold chains around his neck and a backwards baseball cap?"

They decided to invite Vicente down for a week, all expenses paid, and look him over. Guy called King Kong, but she was too nervous speaking on the phone and apparently couldn't understand Guy's French accent, so she handed the receiver to Mohammed, who sounded very ghetto and suspicious. Guy explained he was Andrés's friend.

"That loser?" Mohammed asked.

"Yes, the very one. He said that Vicente was living with you."

"You got the wrong number."

Guy repeated the boy's name. Maybe he was saying it the wrong way.

"Oh, Vince," Mohammed shouted. "Why didn't you say so?" When he understood that this dude with the weird accent was inviting Vince the Freeloader to New York for a week, he suddenly became more cooperative and friendly. Guy noticed that Vicente himself was never consulted.

Guy sent a limo from his regular service to Lackawanna to pick up the boy. Explaining train or bus schedules and how to pick up prepaid tickets seemed insurmountable with these poor foreigners and their approximate English. Explaining a car service was problematic enough. When Vicente arrived, sitting up front with the Israeli driver, who was sweating and gabbling and was obviously on speed, Guy looked the boy over and said to himself, *Un pauvre type, mauvais genre*, which meant he was hopeless.

Vicente was dressed in a sleazy blue tracksuit and high-tops that might have been stolen. He was short and dark and had a scar on his right cheek. He couldn't look Guy in the eye and his handshake was boneless. He then pressed his hand to his heart with some sort of salaam he might have picked up from Mohammed. He smelled funny, like warmed-over sweat.

The boy seemed determined not to be impressed by anything as Guy showed him around. He trudged about in his unlaced shoes; he seemed exhausted, and the smile he'd been wearing as he listened to the excited Israeli had long since faded. "Now, this is your room," Guy said, opening the door onto the guest room, with a white candlewick bedspread over a single bed, its captain's chest, its armless chair upholstered in pale chintz, and its wall ornament, a nineteenth century brass compass Kevin had found in an antique store on Bleecker. "That some kind of clock?" Vince said, nodding toward the compass.

"More or less," Guy said, not wanting to discourage him.

Vicente slept around the clock in a dirty, smelly pile on the immaculate bedspread. Guy insisted they leave him alone. The boy didn't even take his shoes off; maybe he couldn't be sure they wouldn't in turn be stolen.

"Does he look like Andrés?" Kevin asked, genuinely curious.

"Not in the least," Guy snapped. "Andrés is tall and handsome and a real hidalgo. This boy's father is Ecuadorian or something and he looks like a statue you might find in the jungle, flat nose, wide forehead, dirty skin, almost Asian eyes, certainly padded cheeks. No expressions, like some cruel Incan god. And he's short."

"You certainly have your standards! I've noticed that about both you and Pierre-Georges. Are all French people like that?"

"Like what?" Guy asked, not happy about being linked to his bitchy agent.

"So sure of your opinions? Americans are never that sure about what we think."

"Yes, we have definite standards and we're very confident about our taste. We learn at an early age what's good and what's bad."

That sounded a little narrow-minded even to Guy's ears and he hoped Kevin wouldn't pursue the matter.

This sort of cultural tyranny joined with the fragile convictions nourished by cocaine made Guy argumentative. Kevin had learned to end every dispute with a smile and a kiss. The rhetorical kiss had also begun to irritate Guy.

"Why are you snorting cocaine all the time?" Kevin dared to ask. "Do you like it so much? Enough to jeopardize our happy home?"

Kevin wrapped "our happy home" in ironic quotation marks to indicate he wasn't all that serious, which only worsened Guy's mood; he thought irony was cowardly.

"I'm doing it because I'm hungry," Guy nearly shouted, with a full stop between each word. Then he said in a normal voice and rhythm, "Everyone wants the heroin look now and I hate heroin, but you've seen the ads with skinny green-skinned guys with asymmetrical haircuts sitting around and staring in shabby retro living rooms, all acid greens and duck-turd browns, wearing jeans that look sprayed on and gaudy shirts and tiny German sunglasses, looking stunned. In French we say when people are silent, 'an angel is passing,' but here the angel must be Satan. And I'm doing it to keep our happy home afloat. You've got to understand that fashion means change, even for the worse, and right now healthy, wholesome Americans with their teeth and muscles and tans are out, finished, kaput, whereas sickly Scottish boys with their bed-sit pallor and druggie anorexia are in. I've kept ahead of the curve for two decades now. Scruff and hair over my ears and a tattoo—that's a beginning, but I'm going toward a total Lou Reed look. Maybe I'll shave my skull. Or get a lip piercing."

Kevin thought Guy was raving and had no idea what Lou Reed looked like. Anyway, Reed was so seventies! He'd never heard Guy talk so much and attributed it to the coke. It was coke-fueled talk. All because Pierre-Georges had said yesterday over the phone to Guy, "Stylists are looking for a Harley-Davidson

these days and you're a Rolls-Royce, the male counterpart to
Catherine Deneuve."

The comment had kept Guy awake, and at three in the
morning Kevin discovered him in the kitchen contemplating a
piece of toast.

"What are you doing?"

"I dare not eat it."

"Come back to bed," Kevin said, wrapping his arm around
Guy's waist.

When they got up later that morning at ten, Vicente was
already slumped in a kitchen table chair but wide awake. He
said, "Yo!" and made his funny little salaam gesture. Kevin
didn't know if it was ghetto for "hi" or Spanish for "me." He
was still wearing the same clothes, though he'd added a round
woven beige beanie that looked Muslim.

"Poor Vicente," Guy said. "You must be starving and wondering, 'Where the hell am I?'"

"Vince!" the boy said. "It's Vince, man. You got any food in
this crib?"

"Toast? Cereal? Banana? Do you drink coffee? We'll go out
to lunch soon."

"Coffee and banana," the boy said. He still hadn't looked
them in the eye.

Kevin moved closer to him and put a hand on his
shoulder, which Vicente inspected with fear in his eyes as
though it were something foreign and dangerous, a scorpion.
"We don't have to do anything," Kevin said. "There's a little
TV in your room. Did you find it in that cabinet at the foot of
the bed?"

Vicente said, "No. Thanks," in a meek little voice and with
a nearly amorous smile.

Kevin smiled back. Vicente's smile was a shocking momentary break of spontaneity and friendliness in an otherwise uniform sullenness, and suggested there was someone sweet and scared and nice living inside there. That was the one way he was like Andrés, Guy thought.

"How did you learn English so well?" Kevin asked.

"The truth? From trying to pick up English and Dutch girls on the beach near Valencia. And in Lackawanna. Mohammed had the TV on all the time and didn't want us to talk. Man, he'd watch soap operas, commercials, reruns of *Kojak*, infomercials, all that shit!"

"Would you two shut up?" Guy shouted, fidgeting from his coke hangover; then, to cover his rudeness, "But it's lovely outside!" he said, throwing his arms wide open and going to the window. "Indian summer. Isn't that what you call it in English?" Kevin and Vicente exchanged a glance. It was so fruity and big-city to talk about the loveliness of the weather. Kevin provided a banana and made some espresso for them all. Latins drink espresso, right? "Milk? Sugar?"

"Sugar," Vicente said, "if you got it. You guys don't work? You're like Mohammed—he sleeps till noon, though Pilar is usually up early," Vicente said. It was the longest sentence he'd ventured yet, and Guy, still at the window, was tempted to turn around and smile approvingly, but he was afraid of jinxing the moment. He thought Kevin had established a beachhead and should be encouraged to press on. When the bitter coffee was ready, Guy tossed a boiling cup down his throat but without sitting down. Sitting down was fatal; it might lead him to eat something, a green, seedless grape, say. He needed to jog, to head for the gym and do his crunches and lunges, but he felt light-headed. He needed to do a line.

"I'm a student," Kevin said. "School starts next week. Guy is a model."

When Vicente looked blank, Kevin said, "*Fotomodello*," in what he hoped might be Spanish, but the kid still looked quizzical. Meanwhile, Kevin had finally found the packet of sugar he'd stolen from a diner for just such an emergency.

"Got another one?" Vicente asked. "I like a little coffee with my sugar," and he smiled at his own witticism.

"I'm going for a run," Guy announced impulsively, and scurried off to the bedroom for a little "blush-on," as he called his lines of cocaine. Kevin's heart sank, thinking the hamster was about to start on the treadmill. *I'm living with a hamster and a zombie*, Kevin said to himself. *Guy will be running all day and well into the night.* Somewhere, a fly, caught between window and screen, was shaking its autumn death rattle. Kevin could hear it only because the room was so silent, though the fridge was humming and the house was creaking, as old houses will.

"You found everything? The guest bathroom? The air conditioner? The shower?" Kevin asked with a suspicion of emphasis on "shower." "By the way, if you ever want to wash your clothes, we've got a washer and a dryer."

"Here? Inside? Inside the house?"

Kevin nodded. "Let's go out and get some lunch." He wasn't sure he liked being saddled with the responsibility of squiring this kid around, and the kid looked fearful at the prospect of a sortie.

He took him to the restaurant downstairs from the gym, thinking that a cheeseburger and fries would be less intimidating than goat cheese on focaccia and a beetroot and pear salad, the sort of thing you'd get in most of the neighborhood restaurants.

"Where's Uncle Guy?" Vicente said, pronouncing the name as in *Guys and Dolls*. They were seated in a booth and Vicente had already slumped forward across the Formica table, exhausted, and was monotonously rearranging the salt and pepper shakers, the sugar dispenser, salt pepper sugar ketchup.

"Oh, he's trying to make weight."

"Is he a wrestler?"

"Like that. A model. He's up for a big jeans commercial and needs to come in at a hundred and forty pounds. How much do you weigh?"

"Fifty-five kilos. I only know kilos. You?"

"I'm not sure," Kevin said. Suddenly he had an idea. "Maybe you could teach me Spanish." He thought that might also be a way of improving Vicente's English. Kevin was always improving himself, more so than his twin. Each time he'd sat on the toilet back in Ely he'd read an entry in *The Oxford Companion to English Literature*. He'd never read novels. Too frivolous. But he was always deep into the history of ancient Rome or a pop science account of the giant molecule. He was determined to make his airhead boyfriend, Guy, teach him French. These days he was reading a secondhand volume of Edmund Burke, which on the spine read *On the Sublime French Revolution*, and it took him a while to realize that these were two different titles. He read labels for the contents and calorie counts and he comparison-shopped. Because of his family background, he had strong ecological views, and if he'd owned a car, the bumper sticker would have read "Save the Wilderness."

He admired Ralph Nader. He was appalled by capitalism. In class, he wrote down all the names of the books and authors the professor mentioned in passing and checked them out of Butler Library. His twin was much more of a goof-off and Kevin would have attributed his insouciance to his lack of a "gay gene," but they had identical genes and their differences must be due to nurture, not nature, although it was hard to pinpoint any differences there. They'd been raised together, dressed identically, and had exactly the same health history. Their grandmother couldn't tell them apart, though their mother could. It was obvious, she insisted. Chris was meaner and ran in circles.

Even with several attempts, Kevin couldn't get Vicente to teach him any Spanish. ("What's 'table' in Spanish? *Tavola?*" But the boy looked confused and bored.)

Upstairs in the gym, Guy was doing lunges and sit-ups fueled by cocaine, gabbling and laughing to himself—until he fainted. He was only out for a second; when he came to, the gym instructor was kneeling over him. "Are you okay?"

"Yeah. Fine."

"How come you passed out?"

"I guess I forgot to eat this morning."

The instructor frowned. "Man, you're too skinny! Better just go home now and rest."

"Good idea."

"Take your shower at home. Do you need anyone to go with you? Scoot. Get outta here!" Guy thought he'd take some Ex-lax and shed the pounds that way if he couldn't exercise any more today. When he got home, he called the nearest Chinese restaurant and ordered four bowls of soup to be delivered. Soup was not very fattening. He'd do another line and another espresso before he tackled the soup. That way he might only drink half a bowl.

Pierre-Georges dropped by and was very pleased. "You've never looked more ethereal. Just another five pounds and you'll be perfect. The go-see is Friday—if you're named the Cavalier flagship it's a million-dollar campaign."

"What's Cavalier?"

"Oh, come on. Earth calling Planet Guy."

"I thought it was Guess."

"Guess was decided a month ago. Frederick Ross got that. Hello-o-o."

By Friday, Guy could barely cross the room, and if he went for a walk, he had to lean on Kevin, or Vicente, who didn't like the contact with another man. But Guy did seem to have landed the job and to have beaten out some of his seventeen- or eighteen-year-old rivals—that's what counted to him. As a Buddhist, he didn't think of himself as competitive, that was all samsara, but he did like to win. He hated the idea that some of these guys, just mere kids, with no experience in the business, could beat him out. They were just skinny *beaufres* (clods) and didn't know how to give angles. They brought nothing to the creative process, no input, no sense of style! They didn't know how to work with photographers. They just drooped around. One night after another horrible dinner in El Faro, a Spanish restaurant where Vicente didn't talk except to the waiter in Spanish and Guy babbled and played with his food, Kevin was smoldering, and when he was alone in the apartment with Guy, he said, "This has got to stop. Today I was with him all day! He's your boyfriend's nephew, not mine. We spent three hours looking at track shoes and he still couldn't make up his mind which ones to buy. New York is horrible in August. Everything smells like sauerkraut and garbage. And look at you. You're a bag of bones! Where'd that nice ass go, the one I liked to fuck?"

"I'll grow you a big fat new one," Guy said, smiling. "Can I help it if Vicente's bonded with you and not with me? You're nicer than me."

Kevin slapped his hand in playful reproach.

"You never want to have sex now. I can see why monks fast—it keeps them celibate. You whimper in your sleep—must be the body protesting. You spend a lot of time in the bathroom at dinner. Were you throwing up your meal?" Guy hung his head. "Anyway, you're my boyfriend."

They decided to keep Vicente just out of kindness and because King Kong said she didn't want him back in Lackawanna and the boy's mother in Murcia was now bedridden.

Each time Guy took the bus over to see Andrés, the prisoner was happy to hear Vicente's news and grateful to Guy. Andrés suggested that Guy send Vicente up to visit him one week in his place.

Guy agreed, but he thought he had to instruct Vicente not to mention Kevin. Vicente seemed astonished to discover his blood uncle, Andrés, from Columbia was a *maricón*, too. He hadn't understood that before. A French maricón, normal. An American maricón, why not? To be expected. But a Columbian maricón, his mother's brother—oh, *coño*, that wasn't cool. American prisoner, yes, that was cool, but Latin maricón, no way. The boy seemed utterly lost and slept all the time, though Guy insisted he look for a job. He thought a job was important for the boy's self-esteem. There was talk of his xeroxing and mailing and manning phones for Pierre-Georges—talk that came to nothing, partly because Pierre-Georges couldn't be bothered. And Vicente was an eyesore. Guy bought him some new jeans and two cowboy shirts he liked for some reason, some underthings and a peacoat for the cold weather that was just around the corner. Vicente liked Kevin's brother, Chris, because he was young and not all groomed and was out of shape and had a girl, he was not a maricón but normal, but Chris didn't like him, he couldn't be bothered, either. Vicente was vastly amused by the resemblance between the twins, but they thought his delight was boring and predictable, and neither Kevin nor Chris liked to have their interchangeability emphasized, since they were rapidly individuating, or so they hoped.

It was so odd being identical twins entering an urban maturity, which gave them so many opportunities for evolving independently. They each longed to be individuals, and yet they knew they shared a genetic fate, that they would have heart attacks during the same months twenty years from now and die the same year, but more subtly find the same weird jokes funny and unaccountably get depressed at the same time, even if they were separated by a thousand miles. It was odd, because one of them had decided he was straight and one gay, and these different orientations would lead them to have entirely different fates—and yet each would evaluate his experiences with the same lifted eyebrow or the same chuckle or stab of compassion. Chris, for all his much-vaunted heterosexuality, would cruise the same hot guy who'd catch Kevin's eye, and the same girl would charm both brothers. Both brothers were turned on by Lucie. Perhaps because he was more "normal," Chris would dress more eccentrically; he even entered a long period of Santa Fe excess, everything weighted down with turquoise, whereas Kevin, despite (or because of) the marginality of his sexuality, hewed close to the norm. It was kind of neat, almost as if they were leading two lives at once, a laboratory case of controlled variance, Manhattan variations on a theme by Ely. All Kevin had to do was observe Chris with his girl, see him holding her hand or protecting her head as he opened her umbrella, to have the same experience himself, to feel it, to feel it in his bones, in his solar plexus, to register it along his nerves. And if Kevin touched Guy's shoulder and even kissed his neck, then Chris would smile, even pucker sympathetically, though he'd raise a hand instantly to wipe away the abominable sign of affection. Because they saw the point of the other's actions and attractions, each felt he was playacting in producing and pursuing his own. How authentic could any impulse be if it also contained its opposite? And how resolute could any lifestyle choice be if it was based on neither nature nor nurture, just a whim? If Chris acted the macho too fiercely, they'd both crack up, just as Kevin's efforts to primp, or act the proper hostess, reduced them both to tears of laughter. True, Chris had been born first, and during the first three months gurgled more and smiled less than his brother and had broken more toys. At two years, Chris had walked a week before Kevin and had hit him angrily over the head with a toy car, though he'd instantly looked bewildered and wailed. Kevin talked first. When they were allowed in grade school to dress differently, Kevin wore brighter colors— did that make him gay? Anyway, that was all family legend invented by parents who out of idle curiosity wanted to find differences between the boys while marveling at the way they mirrored each other. As in many families, the antics of the children were a constant floor show, a distraction from television, as absorbing as a fire in the fireplace, somewhere slim and darting for adult eyes immured in fat to go.

Exactly at the moment Kevin started losing patience with Guy, Chris was tiring of his girlfriend, and both accepted the coincidence as natural. Were they both following the same trajectory, or did the ambivalent feelings of one permit the other to voice his own doubts? Or were they being drawn irresistibly back to each other? Were they fated to end up together? These parallel developments, no matter how mysteriously related, had never surprised them, just as when one of them had a sore throat he automatically handed a lozenge to the other.

"Guy is so predictable," Kevin complained.

"Dumb, just go ahead and say it. Most people are dumber than we are but—treats you nice—gives you money."

"That kid—Vince—annoying."

"Back off," Chris said. "Not your responsibility."

"Guy—whatta flake."

Soon their out-loud shorthand comments were exhausted and the dialogue went underground as they each arrived at subterranean insights together. They were sitting next to each other on a stoop and their silent conversation erupted in half smiles, a shared widening of the eyes, a shoulder bump, a gasp of understanding.

"Really?" one of them said after five minutes of apparent silence. The other nodded.

Their father's brother, a dapper man they scarcely knew because he lived in far-off Minneapolis, where he was a florist, came to New York for the first time in his life. He stayed in a drab, expensive hotel for businessmen across from Penn Station. He was traveling alone (he'd never married, for some reason), but he had a long list of Broadway shows he intended to see. He seemed disappointed that his attractive nephews knew nothing about the stars, the directors, or even the names of all these musicals, some of which had already been playing for two or three years. Back in Minnesota, he'd pictured them as taking in a show nightly and then dining at Sardi's or sipping a cocktail at the Rainbow Room, but they drew a blank at the mention of these eateries, just as they'd never heard of Mama Leone's or the Carnegie Deli. Chris explained he got a nosebleed if he went north of Fourteenth Street, and Kevin, who seemed marginally more sophisticated, said he thought most Broadway shows were tacky and overmiked, or so he'd heard.

Uncle Phil had obviously come to town with thousands of dollars and wanted to live it up every night—steakhouses but also charming, out-of-the-way Greenwich Village bistros that only insiders knew about. The twins only dimly remembered him from family reunions and a cousin's wedding, where Uncle Phil had done the flowers, all glads, baby's breath, and birds-of-paradise, with lots of eucalyptus leaves, which made their mother sneeze. He wore an unusual amount of cologne for a Midwestern man of his generation and his breath was always sweetened with Sen-Sen. He was talkative and upbeat, which the boys found preferable to their parents' dourness, though tiring.

One night Kevin had gone with Phil to see *Cats*, which was impressive for its special effects if not for its imperceptible plot and generic music; afterward, Phil, exhilarated by the show, wanted to go to what he'd read was a trendy show-business restaurant, Joe Allen's, where the walls were lined with posters of shows that had flopped.

"I really, really like your friend Guy. So handsome!" Uncle Phil said. "I saw him years ago in a Pepsi commercial. It was a yard party, looked so typically American, I had no idea he was French. He looked like just one more cute college kid—gee, that must have been twenty years ago. I'd just moved to the Twin Cities—yeah, twenty years ago."

"It's remarkable how young he still looks, isn't it?" Kevin said. He found talk about Guy's eternal youth as boring as talk about how closely he resembled Chris; those were the two great "tropes" of their lives, as he'd learned to say at Columbia.

"Yeah, but your parents don't like the idea that you're living with a rich, older man and he's paying all the bills. That's not my view. I'm a little more sophisticated, but they're worried about exploitation."

"Who's exploiting whom? Am I because I'm the gold digger, or is he because I'm half his age and he's made me his sex slave?"

"Why, he is, of course. Your parents wish you'd find a nice guy your own age, white, possibly, a college student, someone who pays his own way, an American, I mean. Guy is a perfectly nice guy, if a bit irritable—"

"That's the cocaine talking," Kevin said, tucking into his pecan pie. Around Guy he didn't order dessert; it was as though he were gobbling in front of Muslims during Ramadan.

"Cocaine? Oh, dear—it's worse than I thought."

"Cocaine's not dangerous!" Kevin said too loud, eliciting smiles of agreement from neighboring tables. He added in a softer but more pedantic voice, "All the studies show it's not addictive. It just sharpens your mind and makes you want to work more—that's why it's called the yuppie's drug of choice. It's not really a drug, it's related to Novocain. It numbs you." He thought he'd add a shocking gay note for his uncle's benefit: "That's why guys who have trouble getting fucked sprinkle it on their assholes. It numbs the pain."

Uncle Phil looked both amused and troubled by this confidence and said with a little smile, "That may well be. I guess I'm just being too Lutheran about it."

"My parents would be even happier if I moved back to Ely and married a girl."

"As a matter of fact, your mom says you used to be sweet on a girl in your class back home—Sally Gunn. The school beauty. Blue eyes, the straight nose of a Greek goddess, big tits, skinny hips like a boy. As you know, her dad is the other big outfitter in Ely—"

"And if we got married it would be a dynastic consolidation," Kevin added grimly.

"Well . . ."

"There's only one little problem. I'm gay. I like men."

"You know, your mother has kept up with Sally and they get together for drinks at the Log Cabin."

"That smelly old bar? Smells like kerosene and old beer. I didn't think women went in there."

"Anyway, it turns out they've discussed your being gay."

"Wait—my mother and my old girlfriend have discussed my sexuality?"

"I didn't know it was a secret."

Kevin sipped his decaf. "Well, it's not," he mumbled. "But still!"

"So Sally said she'd always known you were gay and that didn't bother her, in fact she preferred it because she hates sex and she always thought you were a perfect gentleman because you didn't want to feel up her tits all the time like the other guys and you were a good dancer, as good as her, and you let her drive you both around in her little MG."

"So we're to have an arranged, sexless marriage, consolidating our family businesses? Nifty."

Phil smiled brightly. "Do you really think so?"

"No, I don't think so. I'm in love with Guy."

"No wonder," Phil was quick to chime in. "He's a historic beauty."

"What's your type?" Kevin asked bluntly, tired of pretending Phil was safely in the closet and not liking the sound of "historic."

Uncle Phil blushed their famous Norwegian blush and said, "All kinds."

"Very ecumenical, " Kevin said, dubious. "Younger?"

"Yes."

"Much younger?"

"Yes, strangely enough."

"It's not that strange. Blond?"

"Yes."

"Butch? Aggressive?"

Phil whispered, "Yes."

Kevin thought he should stop his interrogation before Phil made an awkward declaration of love.

After a moment's silence, Phil said, "So what should I tell your parents?"

"That Guy is an upstanding, mature, responsible man who fucks me good."

Phil exclaimed, "I can't say that!"

"No, you can't. Just tell them you liked Guy and that we're both negative and faithful. That's what parents worry about. Really worry about. AIDS. And I understand it."

Kevin turned out to be a brilliant student—imaginative, punctual with his assignments, analytical and skeptical, a nonstop reader, endlessly curious and diplomatic with his fellow students—and especially with his professors. He picked up right away that he might have the right looks (Nordic) to be a career diplomat; a standard Midwestern accent that needed to be placed farther back in the throat and made softer and less nasal; an unexceptionable pedigree (no Nazis or criminals or rabble-rousers hanging from the family tree and no controversial tycoons or scientists, either); ambitious but not pushy, earnest at the right serious moments but otherwise a mild American joker, always laughing. His was an obliging politeness that never shaded off into obsequiousness, a mental precision that never turned pedantic. He had all the virtues and, because of his generic, small-town family background, no entangling alliances with politicians, lobbyists, plutocrats, or radicals. On the other hand, he was a bit too far out of the closet, untraveled, a mono-glot, naïvely trusting, as friendly as a family pet. And he had the usual defect of a twin: excessive unguarded loyalty and transpar-ence to his brother. Would he be able to keep a secret from Chris?

His adviser, Dr. Blumenstein, warned him that these were some of the questions the Foreign Service and the FBI would be eventually asking about him and his suitability to serve. Blumenstein hoped Kevin would eventually apply to Columbia's School of International and Public Affairs if he did well in his courses and Graduate Record Exams. He hoped Kevin as an undergrad would take a broad range of courses from political geography to Arabic to Asian studies in the next few years. Any interest in learning to speak Hmong? Urdu? Pity. Of the usual languages, Spanish was crucial. Kevin realized, didn't he, that the Foreign Service could be extremely dangerous and that his first postings would be in Third World countries deprived of creature comforts? He really should consider Urdu, if for no other reason than to be able to read Hafez in the original.

Would Kevin be looking for a wife with social graces, endless patience, and few prejudices, preferably a private income? That was the sort of wife/hostess an ambassador needed.

Kevin smiled and took his courage in his hands. He said, "There aren't any young ladies in my future."

"Are you a Minorite? An Athenian? A Uranian?"

Kevin had never heard these euphemisms before, but he could guess at their meaning from the leer in Blumenstein's eye and his unusually wet, prolonged smile. The boy said, "Yes." He figured his adviser wouldn't know these strange words unless he himself was an initiate.

"You'll find," Blumenstein said, lighting his pipe, "that the Foreign Service is full of Friends of Dorothy, though most of them are, as the Italians say, *insospettabile*."

Kevin, despite his sunny nature, made few friends at school. He didn't want any classmates dropping in unexpectedly. Guy wouldn't like that. Guy didn't really approve of casual American ways. One time Chris had gone uninvited into the kitchen and stared into the fridge. "I'm hungry! Looks like you guys never snack." Eventually he found an unopened package of prosciutto, which he gobbled down, cursing that he had to peel off the individual pieces of paper. Guy was outraged and said, "What if that had been an essential ingredient of our dinner? How dare he ransack our refrigerator like that?"

"Come on, Guy, he's my brother. Whatever is mine is his."

"We don't think that way in France. No French person would behave like that. He's not well educated." (Guy always made that mistake in English, "educated" for "brought up.")

The other students at Columbia, after an initial show of friendliness, didn't warm up to Kevin. When a shaggy guy with a Brooklyn accent asked him to join him and some other guys for a beer, Kevin said he had to hurry home. "Where's home?"

"The Village."

"Lucky guy. Where?"

"West Eleventh and West Fourth."

"Wow, best address in New York. Your folks live there? Rent control?"

"No. A friend lives there. He owns the house." Kevin started to pull away, not wanting to be interrogated further. He was proud to be living on that prime, leafy street with a man-in-a-million but it made him uncomfortable to be envied. He'd never gloried in his fate to a stranger and, unperceived, it was only the shadow of a reality. It scarcely existed. But if examined in depth he could easily be taken for a leech, a kept boy, a pariah with a secret. That could end up on his FBI record. Living a double life was possible in New York. Columbia was far from the Village, and other students rarely strayed south of Ninety-sixth Street. He never ran into anyone he knew from school. Manhattan was perfect for anonymity.

Isolated from his classmates, he spent many an evening with Guy and Vicente, sometimes with Chris or Chris and his spiky sarcastic girl. Guy would get a huge take-out platter of sashimi, though Betty said she wasn't into slimy raw fish and she cooked up a package of ramen noodles in the kitchen. They all sniffed the microwaved beef broth covetously. "Look at you all, like bloodhounds pursuing a rabbit in heat," she said, rat-a-tatting her mirthless laugh.

Guy said, "Studies show ramen noodles can cause heart attacks, especially in women."

"Bullshit!" Betty shot back without a pause. "But go ahead, choking on your mercury-rich raw fish. Hey, Guy, studies also show deli-style roast beef is as low in calories as chicken or fish, that the fibers in beans and whole-grain rice cause people to absorb 6 percent fewer calories, and that microwaved potatoes stuffed with cottage cheese shrink fat cells, but far be it from me to suggest edible food to you hunger artists."

Wearing his backward New York cap, Vicente smiled and touched his balls like a rapper. "This chick is *fly*," he said with stoned approval and an open mouth that wouldn't close. With the allowance Guy gave him he indulged in family-sized pizzas for himself alone at Famous Ray's—and never gained an ounce. He was attending a local Catholic high school and working for two dollars an hour running errands for Pierre-Georges. He spent his entire salary on weed, which Betty obtained for him. He was a wake-and-bake guy who seldom let reality abrade him through his haze of cushioning smoke. He didn't understand fully half of the things people said to him in English, but that was cool. He was content to have a roof over his head, and the weird maricóns didn't molest him. The only thing he missed was pussy. Back in Murcia and again in Lackawanna he'd had enough pussy, but not here in New York. He figured with all the maricóns in New York there must be a lot of frustrated bitches with cobwebs in their cunts, but chicks here were kinda stuck-up. Maybe because he lived with two maricóns, girls thought he was one. He thought of his baggy jeans, baseball cap, gold necklaces, and unlaced shoes as fashionable, but he didn't see many other dudes dressed like him. Maybe it made him look too young or poor. Bitches liked dudes with scratch. Best to smoke another blunt. He'd like an Asian bitch— they said their pussies were nice and tight and sideways.

Kevin felt they were all losers. Friendless. Going nowhere. Guy was a beautiful dumbbell. How many weeks had he been reading that novel, *Sapho*? And why a novel? You couldn't learn anything from a novel. He loved Guy, but his life was vapid and empty and was careening toward a certain destiny and bitterness. Nor did he have the initiative to become a photographer or agent himself or to make an exercise video or to start a day

spa or to learn hairdressing or to design men's clothes—he'd
never bothered to learn any of the ancillary arts of fashion.

Chris was just treading water working as a dishwasher until
he went back to Ely to take over the family business. Why
wasn't he studying bookkeeping or getting a degree in business?
Betty was so jaded, so knowing, so cynical that she couldn't be
a good influence on Chris. She wasn't even that attractive.
Maybe he couldn't do any better with their small dick. He was
glad he'd chosen to be gay, or if not chosen, at least ended up
that way. Guy didn't despise him for not being hung—and he
could always take it up the ass. Chris was sitting on their
"million-dollar ass" (that's what Guy called it) and wasting it,
just using their two-bit cock.

And Vicente? He was nice enough but pathetic, always
stoned and always horny. (Kevin could hear his bed creaking
through the locked door as he jerked off day and night—deep
into the night.) He could smell the burning weed. Did Vicente
want to go back to Spain, to what was surely drab little Murcia?
What would he do there, in the unlikely event he landed a job?
Air-conditioning repair? Garage mechanic? But even these
careers needed some training, didn't they?

How did they get saddled with this loser? That's what Chris
asked, and Kevin didn't know how to answer him.

Kevin didn't want to be held back by this band of layabouts.

He hated fashion. He hated its insistence on what was new
rather than what was attractive. He was enough of a good
Midwestern Lutheran to despise worldliness, especially in its
most restless, nagging form: vanity. You could never be young
enough, thin enough, trendy enough. He thought we should all

be focused on serious, ultimate philosophical questions, and on the train he listened sneeringly to a long, loud conversation between two guys his age about the best watches or the most advantageous terms for a credit card. They seemed totally, hopelessly immersed in the here-and-now and all the tedium of late capitalist material culture. Guy was no better, in fact worse, because he brought to bear on his bad values his immense accumulated sophistication and at intelligence (superior wiliness, good memory, quick social navigating skills, the idealism of his passionate appetites). He obsessed over how to update his image, he, whose beauty was eternal and could span decades, and who should be pondering his immortal soul, not his next haircut.

And yet, Kevin reasoned, *I am young and handsome, and I won't be always. This is the time of my life for sex and beauty, and Guy is the living symbol of that. People see his swimsuit shots with his body sparkling with water (and glycerin), his hair pushed back, the comb lines visible, an angry look widening his eyes and searing his mouth, and they think he's . . . deep, powerful as Jupiter, ready to hurl a thunderbolt, vengeful as Wotan—and it's just silly old Guy, well, no, he has his moods and thoughts, sure, but they're not as profound as his appearance. He looks so interesting, so full of passion, but he's—well, not that.*

When Guy tried to foist off on him the silly frippery he'd picked up at photo shoots, Kevin just handed it back wordlessly. In the past Guy had complained about the vacuity of his profession, but now he spoke of it defensively. "It's an industry worth billions of dollars. It's like food or tourism. Everyone wears clothes and eats and travels. At least everyone we're likely to meet. And there aren't any generic clothes."

"Jeans? T-shirts? Sweatshirts?"

"Designer jeans are a huge market, perhaps the biggest. The same basic design is changed slightly and branded with a famous name and the price is quadrupled. Come on, you've read your Roland Barthes."

In fact neither of them had read Barthes, though Guy had had an admirer in Paris years ago who frequently quoted the *Mythologies* at him, and Guy imagined he'd got the gist. Now, apparently, Barthes was démodé, though students in America still referred to him. American profs didn't keep up to date but clung to the thinkers they'd known since they got tenure: Derrida, Foucault, Barthes . . . America was the attic of French culture, and Guy was worried that over here he'd fallen behind, surrounded by all this old stuff.

Their old, lazy ways had changed. Now they awakened at seven in order to get both boys—Vicente and Kevin—fed, caffeinated, and off to school. Kevin suspected that Guy went back to bed, since he subscribed to the superstition that he could preserve his looks by sleeping eleven hours a night—like the Mexican movie star Dolores del Río. Well, he'd earned it. But there was something about the way he lay as rigid as a king in his pyramid, cucumber slices on his eyes, dried mud on his face, plugs in his ears, glistening cream on his knees and elbows—oh, he wanted to take a picture of that, Narcissus in his counting-house! That would startle his fans and his clients. But why? Surely they didn't think it was all spontaneous and natural, no matter how often photographers showed him on the beach against storm clouds, the fan blowing his straightened and lightened hair, his perfect teeth exposed in his hourly-rate smile, everything out-of-focus except the Rolex on his wrist or whatever product he was hustling. You could say about Guy that he looked great—and looked like himself!—from every angle.

Betty told them in a casual, amused, almost indifferent way that Vicente wasn't going to school but hanging out at a pool hall she walked past every morning on Forty-first Street on her way to work. He was usually wearing a goofy, stoned smile at ten in the morning and seemed overdelighted to see her—or maybe anyone he knew.

"Boy, he's going to get it!" Guy exclaimed, trying to be very American. (Rage in French sounded feline and perverse; only in English did it sound unaffected and tough.)

"Why?" Betty asked innocently. "Poor kid. He told me he doesn't understand anything at Sacred Heart—trig and essays on Native Americans and Shakespeare. At least he has some friends at the pool hall."

"You've obviously given up on him," Guy said. "I haven't! I promised his uncle I'd educate him."

"Oh, his uncle? The jailbird?"

Guy wanted to strike her, but he just bit his lip and left the room. "Did I say something wrong?" Betty asked Kevin.

"About ten things. But he'll simmer down."

Guy hired a tutor for Vicente, a shaggy, thick Columbia student named Henry, gay but masculine in an unconscious, unstudied way, a young man who seemed mature because black lustrous hair was sprouting over his white T-shirt. He sounded as if he had a permanent cold or allergy in his immense nose, as though it were too large to function properly. He was a nice guy studying architecture who had a very male lack of interest in people, their foibles and interests and background stories. He discussed late Renaissance churches in Venice, for instance, with no curiosity about when or why they'd been built or by whom; he concentrated only on the volumes and the solutions to problems, as if San Giorgio had been built yesterday.

His indifference to everyday dramas was useful, as it turned out, since he wasted no time on Vicente's sad tales about his dying mother or his uncle in prison or his black aunt in Lackawanna. He just shrugged with his heavy shoulders and wiped his huge nose with a dirty handkerchief and went back to the math homework. Vicente was usually too stoned to understand what he was saying so patiently. He'd figured out Henry was a maricón too and he even asked him about that, but Henry said, "We could talk about that, but it would lead us rather far afield. Now, let's look at these numbers." He was even indifferent when Vicente staged getting out of the shower at the moment Henry arrived one day.

One Friday, Guy accompanied Vicente up to the Otisville prison in the bus. He knew that only Vicente was slated to visit Andrés today but he hoped to coach the boy on what to say and what to omit. "Andrés doesn't know anything about Kevin. Certainly not about Chris. Don't mention them. Just say you and I spend evenings alone looking at your homework. You can say I've hired Henry to help you. You can say you're working for Pierre-Georges a few hours a week—he'll like that. Don't mention Betty—that will just trap you into talking about Chris. Don't mention the pool hall—that will be our little secret. Don't discuss maricóns with him. That will only irritate him."

Things went smoothly, it seemed, but Vicente was by turns evasive and taciturn, and finally he admitted that Andrés accused him of being stoned, with pupils as big as quarters. He'd lectured Vicente about the importance of working hard with a clear head and being grateful to Uncle Guy for all he was doing for him and making sure he didn't end up like him, Andrés, a loser jailbird. They had talked briefly about Andrés's sister, Vicente's mother, and how she was suffering, and Andrés had had to wipe away a tear. Vicente had liked his uncle and had specially liked his way of speaking Spanish in such an educated manner that reminded him of his mother—and then Andrés would break into a real ghetto English for a phrase here and there, and English that sounded like his own, which he'd picked up from Mohammed in Lackawanna. Andrés spoke Spanish like a maricón but English like a man.

For a few days after the trip to Otisville, Vicente tried to straighten himself out. He didn't wake-and-bake, he wasn't late for work with Pierre-Georges, he actually did the homework Henry assigned, but he just couldn't understand math or write an essay on Native Americans. (He'd never met one, though he'd seen plenty of cool Indians in the movies scalping everyone.) Soon he was softening the blow of failing by smoking again and rattling his bed dreaming of pussy, and bopping around through his day with his lopsided grin. He would try to stay in with the two maricóns in the evening to do his homework, but he never knew where to begin, and besides, he couldn't concentrate. Studying was so maricón.

He was amazed by how much money the maricóns wasted— how they'd buy exotic fruits and vegetables. (He'd never even heard of white eggplants before, which Guy liked to leave in groupings on the dining room table as "décor," or tiny, translucent champagne grapes.) They never cooked meat and potatoes or rice, the only things Vicente liked to eat other than burgers or pizza. They were endlessly serving raspberries without sugar for dessert and unbuttered popcorn for snacks. Vicente was always hungry!

And yet Guy was fond of the impossible boy. After all, in his veins ran Andrés's blood; his long, skinny body was a rough draft of the Spanish Christ his uncle had become. When Guy stuck his head in Vicente's room he was overwhelmed by a stronger version of the family stench.

Whereas Guy hovered over Vicente like a parent and worried he wasn't dressing warm enough or taking his vitamins or concentrating when Henry coached him, Kevin appealed to the boy more because he was categorically indifferent. Between the gym and his studies and the long, grueling nights of fucking Guy, Kevin had every second budgeted, and when Vicente would launch into a rambling story about his job delivering paella on a motor scooter back in Murcia, Kevin kept glancing at his watch—oh, sorry, it was his turn to shop and cook tonight and he had a twenty-page paper due on Friday, something about George F. Kennan's interpretation of the inevitable U.S.-Japan conflict in World War II, and Kevin was out the door, abandoning Vicente in midsentence. The boy was trying to grow a mustache and he studied it for the next half hour in a mirror, then got stoned to see how it looked if he was high. (Pretty cool!)

If Kevin never took a break and hurtled through his days, Vicente ambled through his, only occasionally realizing he was late for school or his office job. He was hoping his mustache would be a pussy-magnet and he couldn't wait for it to grow in. Vicente was troubled by Guy's entranced staring at him, when the Frenchman would get tears in his eyes; the maricón wasn't falling for him, was he?

The tears were due to Guy's tender concern for Andrés's nephew and his fear that he wasn't being strict enough or affectionate enough or stern enough or indulgent enough. And what kind of example was he setting for a provincial Catholic Latin boy? Discussing *fripes* (clothes) and *pipes* (blowjobs) with

Pierre-Georges and makeup innovations with Lucie, the things she was doing to her female models. ("A carmine smudge at the middle of the mouth and then a fade toward the corners, a very high ponytail wrapped in a sheath, bleached eyebrows, and blue shadows above the upper lids.") She said she was longing to make Guy's hair wet, *wet*, as if he'd just emerged from the shower. Vicente had to listen to all this the way a scholar's son might have to hear a Greek classic being discussed or a broker's nephew might listen to the relative merits of stocks and bonds— or as a priest's nephew might hear of the spiritual nourishment afforded by the Eucharist. And then to see Guy and Kevin embrace and kiss—that couldn't be a healthy influence on a normal teenage boy.

Vicente always hung around when Lucie came over. He liked black women, though he'd never been with one; apparently they were as passionate as men and their pubes were as rough as steel wool—and the guy at the pool hall had said they had big purple nipples and liked it up the ass. The only thing that irritated Vicente was that Lucie treated him like a lovable kid; she went so far as to ruffle his hair and tickle him. Sometimes he thought she saw him as a miniature collie—loyal, attentive, not very smart, always smiling, ready to go. He wanted her to see him as a big, sexy man with a mustache, but she'd hug him and nuzzle him and talk baby talk to him.

When Guy went to the Bahamas for a swimsuit shoot, Kevin realized he'd become addicted to his lover's body. He'd jerk off three or four times a day picturing his wonderful face with his look of being a surprised, truant lad, as if his father had just snapped on the basement light when he was about to steal a shot of whiskey. Or he looked like a poacher caught in a cop's flash, with his little jug ears and violet slash of a mouth and startled face, everything flattened out by the scorching light, his hand aiming the shotgun at the large, furry, unidentifiable ruminant. And Kevin would mold in the air the perfect curve of Guy's ass, its unexpected warmth and give, the way his own hand looked so tan and masculine against that trim expanse of plush buttock. And he'd nuzzle it and feast on the hole that tasted bitter but smelled calmly rural.

He was young, goddamn it, and it was only normal he'd trick with those hot numbers in the locker room who sprang boners as he toweled off—but he dared not. He had to be faithful, for the sake of Guy's health and his own. If he cheated he'd have to tell Guy, and there would go his unimpeded access to that glorious dark muscled glove, which had become the lodestone of his days, the sanctum he longed to breach and enter and lodge in. What did they say in art history class that Courbet called his cunt painting—*The Origin of the World*? Maybe Guy couldn't give him babies, but Kevin would keep trying. He knew that with his small dick gays would typecast him as a bottom. (The guys in the gym stared at his ass, and one fellow even whistled looking at it when he dropped his towel.) Only Guy turned over for him or lay between his strong, gold-dusted legs and licked his balls. Crazily enough, Kevin was certain his cock had gotten thicker and longer since he'd been topping Guy. Whereas as a fat boy of twelve and thirteen he'd seen his body as womanly, Rubenesque, and in the bathroom he'd posed with his dick squeezed and hidden between his legs, a towel-turban around his head, his mother's lipstick smearing his mouth, and had considered this zaftig caricature as his only option and found it at once excitingly transgressive and depressing, now he saw himself as a stud with narrow hips, a prominent, muscular chest, a thick neck, and took consolation in what he'd heard a straight guy say in the gym: "It's not the size of the nail that matters but how you use it."

Important as his new manhood was to him, Kevin acknowledged that Guy held the only key to it. When he went alone to a gay bar—Ty's on Christopher, for instance—men who were a little sauced chatted him up and automatically reached for his ass. "That's some caboose you got on you," while guiding Kevin's hand to the hardness behind the fly. Even younger, shorter boys ended up gliding a hand down the back of his jeans and fingering his hot hole; he wondered if he was emitting the wrong pheromones, and all this in a gay world where he'd heard 90 percent of the guys were bottoms. How did he attract all these tops? The worst of it was that if he ever were to disregard the health risks and bag a bottom of his own, the guy would probably laugh out loud at his little dick.

He liked being the man but he suspected only Guy could take him seriously in that role. He was wedded to Guy—for his health, through love, and by his determination to be the top. Guy was always available, a heady, expensive flower he could pick and inhale anytime, day or night. One time out of ten Guy would fuck him, but even then Guy wanted to flip at the end and feel Kevin in him. Just as Kevin seemed more and more addicted to Guy, in the same way Guy seemed increasingly besotted with Kevin's cock, unimpressive though it might be. In the morning Guy would back up against him; Kevin would bop up to piss and then return to his waiting man.

For he never thought of Guy as anything other than masculine, albeit a refined, European, pricey version, and it was Guy's generosity of spirit that kept his body constantly on tap. There was nothing slutty or depraved about Guy. He was a man without affectations or irony, someone who studied the world with the same simplicity with which he posed for the camera.

To be sure, he knew at all times how he looked, the impression he was giving, how he came off. That was his genius, to know what he looked like to other people. Most guys, even models, waited until strong inner feelings bubbled over, then they flailed about or trembled or hee-hawed with lots of sincerity but no objectivity. Guy was objective; he could triangulate himself through someone else's gaze (or the camera's). He didn't care about what he was feeling. He cared about only what he appeared to be feeling. Just as gifted actors, bland airheads in real life, can appear philosophical, troubled, or tragic on-screen, in the same way Guy could come across as leonine, contemptuous, or seductive to the camera, even if he was only worrying about having clean laundry for tomorrow's trip to Milan.

Kevin and Guy flew back to Ely for Thanksgiving. It was a nuisance to get there, with two stops (Philadelphia, Minneapolis) and ending up in Hibbing, an hour away from Ely.

They were traveling with Chris. They now looked so different no one stared at the resemblance. Chris was ten pounds heavier and had long shaggy sideburns and had put on a bright yellow jacket, an old one from high school days, so that he looked as if he had never left the Boundary Waters and was escorting his younger city-slicker cousin and his friend to northern Minnesota for the first time.

The brothers scarcely spoke on the plane but it felt good to let their knees touch as they sat in adjoining seats. And it felt good in the Minneapolis airport to order cheeseburgers with ketchup and mustard and cheddar cheese. (Guy ate a salad.) The people who boarded the planes at their two stops were progressively stouter and louder and more guileless.

Ely seemed so quiet and empty after New York—it had just four thousand people and Kevin noticed that they couldn't hear the loons calling over the lake as they did all summer. The birds had already migrated to the Gulf Coast. Snow was a couple of feet deep, and just a hundred yards from their house was a dark, tall, massive wall of delicious and nostalgic fir trees eating up all the light. Their youth was in that smell, as redolent as rosemary crushed between fingers. Their canoe trips in the summer, their portages across the rocky isthmus, their tents and campfires and instant mashed potatoes, the fish they'd caught and eaten, the musty smell of sleeping bags, the wait for Chris's heavy breathing so that Kevin could jerk off unnoticed, the scary sound of branches cracking. (Bears? There were so few blueberries that season that the animals were dangerously hungry.)

The air was so cold now it froze the moisture inside Kevin's nose and laid a marble hand across his forehead. Their roly-poly mother and taciturn father sat as always in the front seat of the Buick and the boys and Guy in the back. The heat was blasting in the car, the radio was tuned to a country and western station, the windshield wipers were clearing a steady accumulation of snow, their mother was full of local gossip. Her sentences were punctuated by her surprisingly high and light giggles, as if the girl she had been were imprisoned below in this oubliette of flesh. She was reeling off her small talk confidently, but every once in a while she turned around to glance at them with questioning eyes, as if she could no longer be sure of how her boys—and this handsome foreigner—were responding.

Guy wondered if he'd made a mistake coming. It all seemed as crude and hopeless as Clermont-Ferrand, though the landscape was more beautiful. Kevin was holding his hand in the darkness of the backseat, but this "coziness" of Kevin's had become tiresome—almost as tiresome as these Midwestern pleasantries. And then Kevin had a chance of marrying a local heiress—shouldn't he seize it? It seemed this Gunn girl wanted a sexless marriage—so he should go for it. If he gave her up for Guy and then Guy left him a month later—wouldn't that be perverse?

He knew that Andrés would finally be getting out of prison one of these days. Andrés had ruined his life for Guy—didn't he deserve to get Guy? Kevin was young, had a brilliant career ahead of him, whereas Andrés would have no career at all.

And Guy couldn't get out of his mind the sight of that stiff erection pressing against his orange prison uniform. Guy withdrew his hand from Kevin's.

Once they were in their old room, Kevin relaxed. Same old Parcheesi board. Same old childhood brass lamp with the glass chimney and a bulb that brightened when a side stem was twisted. The red Hudson Bay blanket with the big label in black letters on white fabric. The old round space heater with its heavily lashed red eye. The cedar closet that was always ten degrees colder than the room. Their old schoolbooks from high school.

Kevin and Chris took turns showering and then, hair washed and waxed and combed and doused in Canoe cologne from an old bottle in the tin medicine cabinet smelling of high school sex and heavy petting in a parked car, they went downstairs to the kitchen, where their mother was making biscuits in the narrow wood-burning oven as, on the modern electric stove, she fried up a ham steak, hash browns, and cooked apple slices. Guy was already downstairs, nodding through their mother's monologues. It wasn't even five yet. "Why are we eating so early?" Kevin asked.

"I thought we'd get it out of the way—aren't you boys hungry?—because Sally Gunn is coming over for some pie and coffee."

"Gee," Kevin muttered, "you don't waste any time, Mom."

She decided to take it as a compliment. "Yessiree! That's me: Miss Efficiency! Anyway, Sally really wants to see you boys." She looked confidingly at Guy: "Sally is an old childhood friend of the boys. Kevin was in love with her."

Guy wondered what he was supposed to do with this information. Americans were stiff and puritanical—and then they made these shockingly intimate confessions, as if alternating mumbling with an earsplitting blast. They never spoke in the usual quiet, discreet way.

Kevin winced and darted a glance at Guy. Guy thought that Kevin's mother—was she called Marie?—wasn't any more embarrassing than his own mother, and just as endearing.

During their early supper they sat at the low, almost square white wood table in the kitchen. It was still covered with the old oilcloth of their childhood, red roses printed on a tan trellis, the whole thing curling up along the edges as it had for at least the century long of their young lives. They watched TV throughout the meal, as they had for years. Guy thought the TV a particularly barbaric touch.

Sally arrived on her snowmobile, wearing a knit hat from the Andes with pigtail earflaps and a synthetic insulated jacket, red to match her cheeks.

She had her Attic beauty intact—her blue eyes, veiled and mysterious, her curved bow of a mouth, her wide face. She made no effort to talk, to act, to engage. She simply displayed her beauty as she'd always done. It was enough. Their mother turned off the TV and they all sat up and smiled and quipped with a

new animation. It occurred to Kevin that years of admiring Sally
had been good training for admiring Guy; he'd already grown
up awestruck by great beauty. She smiled and nodded and turned
her face slightly to take the light, as a model is trained not to give
repeats, but she seemed to be far away, lost in another language,
uncomprehending though benign, somehow "blessing" them
with the wonder-working properties of her looks. When she did
murmur a few courtesies she struck Kevin as fractionally coarser,
as if her decision to skip college and to help out her dad here in
Ely had made her not vulgar but more common. After all those
evenings drinking at the Log Cabin with other locals slapping
the waitress on the fanny, hee-hawing, and soaking their winter
beards with beer. And her face had aged, at least there were lines
around the eyes and mouth now and creasing her forehead like
an egg that's been boiled too long and has started to get tiny
cracks in its perfect surface. Kevin's father, usually so silent,
perked up around Sally until their mother shooed him into the
back living room. There they watched the big TV. Chris looked
reluctant to leave them but eventually headed upstairs, probably
to call Betty.

When he was alone with Sally and Guy, the big TV talking
to itself in the other room with its insistent laugh track, Kevin
watched her shrug her way slowly and deliberately out of her red
coat—and there was the splendor of her big breasts cradled by a
plum-colored sweater. Only she would have risked red and
plum. Even back in high school she'd always seemed indifferent
to what other people thought of her. Maybe because her dad was
the town's richest man, she acted as if no one else mattered. Or
maybe because even then she'd reputedly dated older men and
she felt superior to her gaggle of high school admirers. Now her
indifference risked becoming a trait, a philosophy, something

unchangeable. She'd never left Ely, though she said she'd taken an accounting course at the local community college.

Guy barely recognized this Kevin—affable, joking, full of American-style anecdotes, not reluctant to say cretinously obvious things. Guy had heard so much about "beautiful" Ely and "beautiful" Sally, but there was something depressing and a bit squalid about both of them.

She waited for Kevin to ask questions and introduce topics. She'd always been like that, like a thirties movie actress who smiled and laughed and nodded, but always at one remove, always through a scrim of starlight (or through a lens thick with Vaseline), a beauty who glimmered and sparkled. Their nickname for her had been "Ice Out," the day in May when all the ice finally melted in neighboring lakes and they were at last navigable. It was funny, because it acknowledged that she was frigid but navigable.

"You and Chris don't look exactly alike anymore," she said graciously, like a monarch introducing a bland subject of conversation.

"I guess we're going our separate ways in life," Kevin said, glancing at Guy. People out here, Guy noticed, mainly chitchatted and joked around, but every once in a while said something serious about life in the same loud innocent way. Guy smiled at Kevin, but he was sick of so much forced smiling; his cheeks ached. And wasn't it awfully middle-class to be half of a couple?

Looking at Sally, Kevin remembered how he'd once been in love with her. He'd written her a heartfelt love letter and she'd written back a note full of smiley faces in which she'd said she'd always think of him as a friend, if not a boyfriend. He'd been so hurt and had wept for days whenever Chris was not around. He'd played "their" song, something they'd danced to once. And yet, if he was honest with himself, he'd never imagined them in a future together. She was too beautiful, too remote, like a goddess who becomes a constellation, like an old-fashioned screen star who's photographed in black-and-white, her head tilted, her hair rhythmically curled, highlights planted in her eyes and on certain teeth. He'd never imagined them together, strolling hand in hand and bending over their baby's carriage, much less sleeping in each other's arms. He knew her as a deity but not as a girl, though once he'd walked outside past a basement rec room and spied on her and three other girls in a perfect squalor of giggling and innuendo—his one glimpse of her as human, less than ideal.

She did almost nothing, never had. She wasn't a cheerleader, didn't play the flute in the school band, didn't go out for yearbook or a play, didn't debate free trade or assume an allegorical role in the annual pageant. If she was a deity, she seldom manifested herself. Someone said she was shy, but Kevin didn't buy that. In democratic Ely anyone who was aloof was deemed shy, the default excuse. But how would a shy woman turn up at his house in her snowmobile on the very night of his arrival? Maybe what his uncle said was right—she wanted a sexless marriage with a childhood friend that would unite Ely's two biggest outfitters. Maybe she knew Chris wouldn't accept her terms of abstinence. But why did she assume he, Kevin, would?

They didn't say much. He'd never been able to draw her out. A woman like her didn't need to talk. She was a beautiful catatonic—another selling point. In high school she'd thought she was too good for everyone, at least everyone local. She'd had her heart broken by a Swiss anthropologist from the University of Minnesota, who'd spent a summer studying the Ojibwe reservation nearby. He'd studied Sally, too, as if she were part of the indigenous fauna. Apparently she'd admired his strong thighs, always visible in shorts, and his gold granny glasses perched on features as classically regular as her own. What she hadn't foreseen was that he'd consigned her to one of the vitrines in his memory, along with a few arrowheads and a sketch for a birch bark canoe.

When she and Kevin were adolescents she'd never made the least effort, but now she seemed marginally more cordial. Had her parents put her up to it?

Guy could see she was pretty but top-heavy, with her big breasts and narrow hips. And not that pretty—Kevin had spoken of her as if she were Garbo or Miou-Miou. Nor did she have much charm—but why should she, in this godforsaken place? It would be wasted on the woodchucks. It seemed odd to think that Kevin had once been in love with her. Guy wondered if he should go upstairs and leave them alone.

Kevin invited her to dinner the next evening and her instincts made her hesitate but her interest made her accept and volunteer to bring the wine.

That night in their bedroom, Kevin said to Chris, "I think Ice Out wants to hook up with me. Permanently. I'll have to say no." Chris was scratching his ankle. He was naked. He had always slept in the nude, whereas Kevin liked to wear underwear and a T-shirt—did Kevin feel more vulnerable because he was gay? Chris looked up and said, "Why no? She's beautiful and rich and you used to have such a crush on her. More than that. You really suffered over her. I remember."

"Yeah, well—why don't you marry her? I'm gay."

"Are you sure you're not just making that shit up? Are you going to let a whim ruin your life?"

"So you think my love for Guy is just a whim, whereas your love for Betty is some big deal?"

"Don't get your panties in a wad. Anyway, I'm not in love with Betty. That's just a whim, too."

"Are we going to end up together?" Kevin asked. He then heard what he was saying and wanted to head off any suspicion of incest. "I mean, as two old grumpy bachelors?"

"God, no, I hope not," Chris exclaimed, with such vehemence it was obvious he'd thought of it.

"So then why not marry old Ice Out?"

"What makes you think she wants me?"

"Well, she wants me, at least Mom says so."

"We're not exactly the same person."

"More or less," Kevin said, and wondered if that idea would make Chris uncomfortable. "Anyway, I'm sure as hell not going to marry her. I don't want to live here, but you do."

Kevin looked at Chris in the soft light of their old bedside lamp, the brass one with the glass chimney Chris had dialed down. He looked at Chris's button-big dick like a white mushroom in the straw of his pubic hair and at the glabrous chest with its small, confined plantation of hair at the base of his neck. *That's the way I look, given ten pounds difference and no farmer tan. That's what Guy has to look at, this white slug with the whiter button-cock*—and Kevin found this funhouse mirror image disquieting, certainly off-putting. He felt a new surge of gratitude for Guy's loving him.

Kevin was lonely in his single bed. It was thoughtless of their mother to put Guy in his own room as if she didn't understand they were a couple. Kevin wished Chris would sleep with him as in the old days, just for company. Kevin didn't dare to climb into Chris's bed, now that he was officially "gay" and Chris had decided he was "straight." Chris had turned off the bedside lamp. They'd always been able to hear their parents' late-night voices through the heating vents. Now the voices at last subsided, replaced by their father's snoring.

Without a word Chris joined Kevin in his bed, which calmed him down and made him smile in the dark. He turned on his side with his back to Chris, who wrapped his arm around his waist. Kevin noticed that Chris was no longer nude but had slipped on some briefs. The next night Kevin visited Guy in bed, but he was afraid to have sex with him—what if they got the sheets dirty? What if the creaking bed could be heard through the treacherous heating vents?

For the first two days in Ely, Kevin was able, at least in his own mind, to maintain a sense of himself as a New Yorker, as a brilliant Columbia undergrad, as a bystander to the international world of fashion, as someone soft-spoken, civilized, self-deprecating, and kind. The Minnesota boy he was impersonating was one seen through the eyes of a French model in New York—fresh, innocent, spunky.

But by the third day at home he'd regressed to his old self—sleepy, idly cruel, loud, vain. He hated this transformation, but it was stronger than he was. Just as his homosexuality seemed tenuous when his twin was straight, in the same way his New York self seemed very fragile, if he could revert to his Ely boorishness so quickly. He liked to take walks with Guy every day at least once, hoping fresh injections of civilization would awaken his slumbering new identity. Guy didn't pick up on any change in him, but after talking to him Kevin felt more alert, more refined, more alive intellectually, as he did after reading Nietzsche, as if he weren't just a rube but a thoughtful, gentle man, sensitive to paradoxes and denser, finer distinctions. Even if Guy wasn't that smart, at least he was sophisticated.

He tried not to be a snob who missed the point of Ely—its

towering pines, its frank bonhomie, its easygoing acceptance of all kinds of people. His parents, Sally, his other high school friends, were slow to criticize anyone. Were they really that tolerant, or did they just think it was rude to point out jarring differences? Were they moral or were they polite?

Guy wanted to see the nearby Indian reservation, but when they drove there he was disappointed. As a child he'd played cowboys and Indians, but on the reservation there were no feathers or horses or peace pipes, just humble little houses and nearly empty streets and a few old, rusted-out parked cars. Guy looked at Kevin and fluttered his hand in front of his mouth and gave a feeble war whoop with raised, questioning eyebrows. Kevin shook his head.

When Kevin criticized his parents for being hicks, Guy pretended not to understand. "They're lovely people," he'd say, getting a faraway look in his eyes. In truth Guy was bored and wished Pierre-Georges would phone recalling him to New York and a "fabulous" new assignment.

Guy worried that his career was slowly coming to an end. He'd been up for a McDonald's commercial in which he'd been paired with a new, hot girl, a Slovenian eighteen-year-old. She had a porcelain complexion, lustrous hair, tiny hands—and in the test shots Guy looked much older. Not his age, but older. The cameraman remembered him from years ago, his first U.S. commercial for Pepsi. The female stylist said, "They don't really ... go together." He hadn't gotten the job. Pierre-Georges muttered that the Slovenian was a "cow."

Kevin rode behind Sally on her snowmobile down the obliterated roads, visible only because of the clearings through the trees. He clung with his gloved hands to her strong body in its red coat and he enjoyed the mindless sensation of speeding through the glittering cold and banking for a turn in the path. He felt nothing erotic, as he might have if the driver had been a man (as he'd once felt in high school holding on to a handsome motorcyclist he barely knew), but he liked that Sally was in control and was steering them through this white paradise, half of which her family owned.

When they came back to his house for lunch they were quick to shed their gloves, boots, and outerwear, and Kevin's mom handed them each a stein full of mulled cider—sweet, hot, and fragrant, with an immersed cinnamon stick. As they sat around the square table with its oilcloth covering, Kevin could see Chris was looking at Sally with a new acuity, as if she were no longer a habit but a possibility. She was even polite to Guy—or polite in a Midwestern way of asking him lots of personal questions, which usually made the French bristle. Was she extending herself toward Guy because she thought he was going to be a permanent part of their lives? "What's it like to be a model?" she asked. "To hang out with some of the world's most beautiful women?"

10

THE YEARS WENT by. Chris moved back to Ely, married Sally, managed the conjoined family businesses, but they kept separate bedrooms and had no children. This seemed to be according to the terms they'd worked out. Kevin and Chris called each other every day at least once, sometimes just to say, "How are you keeping? Nothing to report on this end," and hang up. Every two months, at least during the winter months when they weren't that busy, Chris flew to New York and stayed with Betty. Kevin assumed his brother was supporting her, now that he was rich. At least he couldn't see how she was surviving otherwise. Now that she had her degree in film from NYU, all she seemed to be doing was to write one or two short movie reviews for *Interview*. How much could that pay? A hundred bucks? She was also giving a literary tour of the Village once a week, visiting Edna St. Vincent Millay's skinny wooden house, and pointing out E. E. Cummings's and Djuna Barnes's entranceways on Patchin Place. But her tours seldom had more than ten paying clients.

Chris seemed happy enough. His fingernails were always dirty and ragged and his palms callused. He said he was busy all winter long repairing things—the canoe shed, the outboard motors, the dock, their house and their parents', the cabins they rented out in the summer. He had a lean, energetic old Indian fellow to help him, especially with the canoes. Chris liked him because he didn't talk much and stayed busy all day long and knew outboard motors. Sally kept the books and did all the ordering of the staples and tents they sold or rented out to canoe parties entering the Quetico-Superior country. Their Indian helper would drive the hundred miles into Duluth to load the trunk up and bring it back.

Sally, Chris said, was affectionate and would let him stretch out on the couch, his head on her lap. Once she'd said, "I love the way the firelight plays on your golden hair. It lights it up in front and back here on the crown. I can see where people got the idea of haloes."

As far as Chris knew she was still a virgin, and on their anniversary each year she wore her white wedding gown, but only for him. Their business was flourishing. Fewer and fewer people actually wanted to paddle these days; more and more relied on outboards. The weather was getting warmer year by year, which was good: It made their rental season longer. More and more first-timers were renting; it was hard to convince them to clean up after themselves after they broke camp, and the Indian traveled once a week in his power boat filling up three or four plastic garbage bags. Some folks from New York had actually shot a loon and tried to eat it; they'd even complained it was all oil and bones. Sally told them killing a loon was illegal.

With Chris out of his life (except for the daily calls), Kevin felt lonely. Yes, he had Guy, but Guy was—what was that French word he'd learned—insaisissable? Elusory?

Kevin graduated from Columbia and Georgetown at the top of his class. It had always been assumed that Guy would accompany Kevin on his first diplomatic assignment.

One day, a week before Andrés was meant to be released, at eleven fifteen in the morning, he walked through the door to the Greenwich Village apartment. He found Guy asleep in bed beside a beautiful blond guy who had his head on Guy's chest. Andrés looked at them for a full minute, without making a sound—he'd learned to be stealthy. Tears poured down his impassive face, scorching lines over the tattooed letters on each cheek, the *G* and the *Y* on his face, the *U* on his forehead, Guy's name. He felt so stupid having expected a joyous surprise and welcome at his homecoming. He'd not been smart enough to realize that a star (an ageing star) like Guy would need some trophy boy in his arms. Sure, he himself had not been that faithful in prison, but *coño*, he'd had no other pleasures except working out and jerking off over and over till he went limp. And talking for hours to his idiotic cellmate about the guy's wife and making dumb things in shop.

He'd cheated because he had nothing else to do or have. But he'd always thought that Guy was *fiel* since, *damn!*, he owed him something, Guy had his freedom and this big bed, sheets white as foam, the right to walk around the world as he wished, to see movies and eat Italian, Chinese, Cuban, whatever he wanted, and to stand under the hot shower for hours and to use all the products he wanted or might just slightly want. The least Guy could have done was to stay faithful, *shit!*, this little punk had probably been around for years and years. He wanted to wake them and shoot them both between the eyes or in the balls, there was no decency in the world!

He left the room and wandered down the hall to the guest room where he hoped he'd find his nephew studying but no, the kid was asleep too, asleep at eleven in the morning! Guy had promised he'd look after Vicente, make him work, stabilize him, discipline him—but here he was with two roaches in the ashtray by the bed, a skinny naked body, not a book in sight. He'd heard so much from Guy about the boy's workout routine, his weight-gaining diet, his sober habits, his regimented day. *Fuck!*

Andrés dragged the boy out of bed onto the floor, not caring if he broke his back or injured his flopping neck.

"Hey! *Ay!*" Vicente yelled, startled into English and Spanish, his red eyes traveling up Andrés's jeans leg in a bewildered rage—and then he melted into a smile upon recognizing his enraged uncle.

"Don't fuckin' smile at me, you little shit!" Andrés shouted. He kicked the boy, who looked confused then terrified and rolled away.

"What the hell you doin' here? I thought you weren't being sprung till next week."

"Guess I surprised you and the little lovebirds next door. Thought you'd pull a fast one on ol' Andy." It took a minute for Vicente to realize his uncle was referring to himself.

"Don't kick him," Guy said quietly, confidentially; he was suddenly standing in the doorway and reaching out to touch Andrés's shoulder.

Andrés shook off his hand, tightened his fists and turned to look at Guy. Somewhere in the sun-drenched background was the other guy's naked body, slightly bent over—in shame? Fear? Modesty?

"Sorry if I woke you guys up at eleven in the morning."

"How did you get out early? Who drove you into town?" Guy asked.

"Sorry to fake you out before you hid the evidence and had Vicente all washed up and combed and your trick in the closet."

Guy smiled wearily as if in response to a bad joke or corny pun. His heart was beating with alarm but all he wanted to do was to fold Andrés in his arms. If only Kevin weren't here or would put on some clothes. Guy looked around. Kevin had disappeared and Guy could hear water running. Maybe that was what he was doing, preparing to leave.

Vicente had pulled on some week-old boxer shorts and a dirty T-shirt, which clung so tightly to his body he looked even skinnier. "Let's all chill," Vicente mumbled. He couldn't meet anyone's eyes. His nails looked badly bitten, which Guy realized he'd never noticed before. Those dirty little nails, bitten down to the cuticle, made him feel guilty.

Had Andrés seen him in bed with Kevin? *What a disaster*, he told himself, as his mind scurried around searching for alibis.

Andrés folded his arms, widened his stance and rocked back on his heels.

Guy shrugged and almost whispered, "I'll make some coffee."

Andrés said, "I'll tell you what I'm going to do. I'm going to walk around for ten minutes and when I come back I want to see you bums dressed and the trick gone."

"What's a trick?" Vicente asked.

"It's whores' slang," Guy said wearily, "for a one-time client."

"But Kevin isn't—" And Guy kicked him.

Andrés stormed out. Guy said, "We're up shit creek," a saying he was proud of, since it was both American and manly. "Jump in the shower and get dressed."

"But I'm still tired . . ."

"Now!" Guy barked, which was so unusual for him that Vicente headed immediately into his bathroom to get ready.

Guy hurried off to his own bathroom, which Kevin had filled with steam. Kevin was as pink as a boiled shrimp. "Did you get rid of him?" Kevin asked over the roar of the water.

Guy turned the shower off, which seemed to vex Kevin since he still had soap all over. "He's gone out for ten minutes but he'll be right back." Even after all these years—and especially in an emergency like this, Guy felt as if he were in a dream when he spoke English and he was mildly astonished that he was making sense. He was almost offended that Kevin could talk about getting rid of "him."

Guy said, "Would you mind leaving us alone for half an hour till all this blows over?" He was speaking in his most intimate indoor voice, soft and kind.

Kevin said, "It's not going to blow over. We got to have this out. You're either mine or his—which is it?"

"Let me get showered and dressed," Guy said tonelessly.

A fleeting look of fear crept into Kevin's eye. He rushed off to dress without saying a word. Guy hadn't reassured him.

By the time all three of them were fidgeting and formal in the living room, pretending to be at ease as in a posed, "casual" photo, Andrés had returned. Guy noticed his hand was shaking slightly—from anger? Tension? "Looks like a committee," he said. Then he turned to Kevin and said accusingly, "Who are you?"

"I'm Guy's lover, Kevin. I've been living here for years. I'm surprised you never heard of me."

"How could I? I wasn't exactly free to investigate. And God knows Guy would never have told me anything. He'd sooner die." Andrés looked at Guy menacingly. "All along I thought you were waiting for me. I shoulda knowed you had your pretty blond butt boy in your bed every night. You're not decent, nobody's decent. You didn't mind if I suffered as long as you could fuck a boy every night and get a two-hour rub-down and travel to Europe whenever and wherever you wanted. It ain't decent."

Guy inventoried Andrés's envies—sex, massage, travel. He wanted to buy off Andrés's rage and wounded feelings with all these things.

He wondered how all this would end. He hoped it wouldn't be up to him—that he wouldn't have to choose between them.

And then the focus shifted to Vicente, who was living in the States illegally, since he'd outstayed his original three-month visa by years. Guy had hired a lawyer to sort it all out, but it seemed hopeless, unless Vicente went back to Spain, found an American woman to marry, could prove it was a legitimate marriage, applied for a green card, waited six months . . . Or he could stay here, never break the law, never try to work, stay off the government's radar. That was the problem, Guy explained: Andrés wanted him to work, but he couldn't unless it was off the books. Or Andrés wanted him to go to a university, but he didn't have a student visa. Nor the grades. So he just ended up sleeping till noon, biting his nails, playing pool, trying unsuccessfully to pick up girls, getting high.

Guy tried to explain all that to Andrés, but even though, as a foreigner himself, Andrés understood visa problems, he shook his head and said, "This has got to change. I owe it to his mother, my poor dead sister," and Andrés made the sign of the cross and kissed his thumb, which Guy had never seen him do before.

"But, Andy," Vicente said, using the new prison name, "I help out around the house . . ."

"Not!" Kevin chimed in, which only drew the unwelcome attention back to him.

"Who are you, kid? Guy fuckin' you regular?"

"Actually, I'm the one who does the fucking," Kevin said.

"Oh, yeah? A little punk like you's Guy's man? Guy's your bitch?"

Vicente piped up. "I'm hungry. Anyone else? C'mon, Andy, you must be ready to chow down."

"We don't think about sex like that," Kevin said primly.

"Why don't *you* chow down, Vicente?" Andrés asked angrily.

"Vince."

"Your fuckin' name is Vicente. *Te llamas Vicente*," and he said his name with a Castilian lisp.

"Get out of here!" Andrés shouted. "Let the grown-ups, the *men*, talk."

Looking down, side-swiping them with uneasy glances, Vicente shuffled out but hesitated at the door in case it was all a joke.

"*Salir de acqui!*" Andrés shouted and the boy flew out of the door.

"Great work you're doing with him," Andrés said bitterly.

"That's not fair," Guy said. "I've done my best. He's a bad seed, won't work, always gets high."

"Bad seed? Bad seed, huh? Like his uncle?"

"That's not what I meant, it's just—"

"That's what you said."

A grim silence set in.

"You've gotten so big. So strong and muscular," Guy said in a matter-of-fact and, he hoped, not-too-oily way.

"Scare you, huh? I could fuck you both so you couldn't walk for a week."

Then some evil thought dawned in Andrés's mind—you could tell from his sardonic smile. He looked at Kevin and said, "Don't count on Monsieur Guy stickin' with you through sickness and health, good times and bad. He ain't got a very good record."

"He loves me," Kevin said.

"Oh, yeah? How can you be sure?"

Kevin stood beside Guy and bent his earlobe forward to reveal the infinity tattoo.

Then he revealed his own. And then Andrés revealed his. Kevin looked with confusion at Guy. And then his eyes gleamed with tears and he began to shake his head in denial.

"Trust me, buddy," Andrés said, "he's no good. He's a fuckin' som-bitch."

Oh, *merde*, Guy thought. *Putain!* And for a second he thought he might end up alone—he'd always been alone, that was his natural habitat, loneliness, he could deal with it better than disappointing everyone. He'd lived so much of his life for sexual love, which was a filthy thing, really, all that saliva and semen and anal smears, filthy! Much better to live alone and watch TV in bed or talk to Pierre-Georges as he was in his bed and watching the same movie. Both of them spotlessly clean. Guy felt it was unfair that his fate was being decided in a language not his own.

They talked and talked all afternoon and both Kevin and Andrés cried, though Guy remained dry-eyed (*I'm a monster*, he thought). Guy ordered in two pizzas, one with black olives and anchovies (Andrés's favorite) and one of quattro formaggi (Kevin's), and Guy sampled each one impartially.

At a certain point Andrés slammed the side table so hard that it caved in and fell apart. When Guy brought him another

cup of coffee, he wrapped his hand around Guy's leg. Kevin
stared accusingly. Guy just stood there though the hot cup
was burning his hand. He felt so awkward. He was used to
being admired by more than one man at a time; on Fire Island
different drunk men would grab at him on the dance floor
and he would just laugh and walk away and join his friends on
the deck.

But these guys? He knew them. He loved them. He owed
them something. He'd nurtured their love for him. In Andrés's
case, he'd ruined his life, if inadvertently. Andrés had committed
crimes for him and served years in prison, which had brutalized
him; he'd gone from a sweet, willowy art historian to a tank
with a buzz cut and a foul mouth. He'd learned English in
prison but the worst kind. He'd sunk a dozen social classes—
what would his poor parents think? They sent off a gentleman
scholar to America and got back a gangster brute.

Sexy, though, he thought. *Very sexy.*

And Kevin? For once Guy had had a good influence on
someone. He'd pushed him all the way through university. He
was more confident, more polished, but still Minnesota-pure, if
no longer Minnesota-*naïf*. And yet, the young man was fearfully
in love with him. That's why he'd cried. His love (which he
believed Guy betrayed) was hurting him.

Guy suddenly wanted to scald his face, gain fifty pounds,
shear his hair. He was sick of his beauty, his "eternal" beauty.
People thought he was purer, more intelligent, kinder, nobler
than he was because they ascribed all these virtues to him.
What if he were stripped of his looks, if he stabbed the
grotesque painting in the attic? If they saw him for what he
really was—empty-headed, *vicieux* (how did you translate that?
"Riddled with vices?"), *narcisse*? Used to being indulged and

pursued, terrified he'd outlive his fatal appeal and yet longing to be free of it?

Finally Kevin went out to meet a school friend for dinner. Andrés, with his face branded with Guy's name, took his faithless lover in his arms (he smelled of ammonia from the prison). Guy's body remembered, awakened, though they did new things; Andrés had changed, not the urgency to get the very last millimeter inside him but their practices, those were all new and for a second Guy was jealous of that black guard. Andrés came a lot and quickly, but he kept searching Guy's face and for a second even mimed strangling him, then reached up and closed Guy's eyelids and placed his hand over his eyes.

Andrés couldn't stay in America; he was a criminal alien without papers. Nor could he leave Vicente in this idle, decadent state. Guy bought them both a ticket to Barcelona, with a transfer to Valencia and then a bus ride to Murcia. Andrés was convinced that his nephew would find a job in Murcia. The idea of returning to Spain and working (didn't they have a twenty percent unemployment rate?) didn't appeal to Vicente, though he was mildly curious about what Spain held in store for him. He could remember the glassy, smooth marble pavement around the historic center in Valencia, so polished you could see your reflection in it.

When Kevin understood that in less than a week Andrés and Vicente would be leaving New York, he surprised himself by how gracious he became, couch-surfing at the apartment of a grad student friend way uptown and leaving Guy, with his legibly guilty conscience, to lavish Andrés with love. Yes, Kevin was jealous, but he knew Guy belonged to him. And besides, jealousy wasn't a manly feeling. Men were better than that. They thought of their lovers as their best friends and wanted them to be happy, whatever it took.

They agreed to meet in Miami. For a long time Kevin had wanted to stay on South Beach. He'd seen so many TV specials about it, and it had always looked so glamorous, with its palm trees, art deco hotels, wide beaches, and European bathing beauties. Two nights there were Guy's graduation present for Kevin. The room was decorated in serigraphs by Georgia O'Keeffe—like vulvas or cacti.

But Guy didn't come. That was so unlike him. He lived by the clock and was always perfectly on time. Kevin's mind raced. He talked to his brother three times in a day expressing his fears. He went for long walks where the hotels bordered the beach. Evening was just washing in and the vacationers' cars were already lined up along the little road in front of the hotels. People were spilling out of convertibles and parading past the pedestrians with their slicked-back black hair, flashing white teeth, tans so old they looked like rammed earth dried and watered a dozen times, everyone thick and dressed in neon-blue Lycra, everyone vulgar and chattering and oiled. He thought this was the ideal, Miami Beach, for all the Latins. This was their paradise, these salsa-emitting vehicles and these oil-stained bikinis. That everything was at night made it all the more grotesque, the quality of a bruise, a tanned bruise.

He kept checking with the hotel reception to see if a letter had arrived for him. He realized that after all these years he didn't have Pierre-Georges's number or that of Guy's mother. He thought, *Does this mean I'm alone in the world? Have I lost Guy? Has he just vanished? Surely he wouldn't do that to me. Has he been in an accident?*

Kevin only permitted himself to ask if there was anything for him at the front desk four times a day; he hoped a new shift of clerks would mean the same person wouldn't witness his abjection. One of them, a guy, seemed Cuban or Puerto Rican, and Kevin tried out his Spanish on him successfully.

At last there was an envelope in Kevin's box. Guy's handwriting. He sat on the edge of a salmon-pink tabouret right there in the clamor and confusion of the lobby.

My angel,

I'm not coming. I'm going back to Andrés and we're returning to Murcia with Vicente, who may stay with us for a while. Vince's mother passed—but you already knew that.

I realized that I didn't really want to go to South America. The harsh climate would destroy my already fading complexion, which is wilting rapidly as you may have noticed. And despite the attentions I receive from the same man in Chelsea who keeps Renée Fleming eternally young, a few gray hairs have pushed through, hardy things!

You'd wake up one morning with an entirely gray and faded Guy beside you. The Curse of Quito! To live with a man is already a handicap, as your doctor Blumenstein pointed out to me at the graduation party, but to live with an *old* man never helped anyone at the dawn of his career.

You say that you don't care about age and that you're ready to push the wheelchair and hose down my bum, but how can you be sure? I may not look my age, but the age I look is the one you've fallen in love with. And real old age is no joke; it demands stoicism and commitment on the part of the caregiver.

Andrés sacrificed seven years of his life to me. Anyone who loves me that much deserves to have me, even though the prize may not be worth much after all. Because of me he never finished his doctorate and he's sunk an entire social class. Worse—he's become a criminal, not just poor. His life in many ways is over. You may not understand this. As an American you imagine anything is possible and cannot see that every year another dozen possibilities are closed to us. As two Garlic Belt figures, Andrés and I are realists—about our status as an ex-con and a former beauty queen. We just want a quiet, nearly anonymous life now. Picture us with Vince as three tall sad men who go out walking through Murcia every night after dark.

I've always felt the life force throbbing through you—that and your extraordinary intelligence, your ability to analyze and synthesize everything you encounter. I worship you and the more I've known you the more I've come to revere you. You are the Perfect Young Man: honest, clean, virile. If you ever feel like it, cut a thatch of your pubic hair and mail it to me in Spain so I can smell it while jerking off. I'll send you an address.

Pierre-Georges once said I was like a black hole in space. What does that mean? That I shape the outcome of events but don't really exist? That people project whatever they want onto me, which works since I'm such a nullity?

You may hate me but you shouldn't. I made a man out of you, or rather found the man in you lurking behind the boy and nurtured him in a world given to stereotypes. I made you my man. I even taught you some French. And I kept you safe from AIDS—and kept you, fed you, sat on your dick. I'm most proud of you of all the things and events and people in my life—I gave you the right setting to survive and prevail.

Please forgive me for disappointing you. It won't be long before you find some black-haired hidalgo. They go for blonds down there, whom they call rubios.

Your Guy

Kevin wept for an hour and then called his brother. He felt older and wiser—but in what way wiser?

ACKNOWLEDGMENTS

I want to thank Keith McDermott and Leo Racicot for helping me prepare the manuscript; Michael Carroll for advising me on every word; Brad Gooch for sharing his memories of modeling with me; George Miscamble for giving me an insider's view of modeling; my editors at Bloomsbury, Michael Fishwick and Anton Mueller, for their unfailing wisdom and enthusiasm; my agent, Amanda Urban, who is a great editor in her own right as well as the best representative a writer could ask for. I am also grateful to my copy editor, Dave Cole, for saving me from a thousand embarrassments. I alone am responsible for the mistakes of fact, chronology and understanding in the book. Didier Malige was kind enough to give me his responses, not always positive.

Rick Whitaker and David McConnell kept me going with their encouragement.

ALSO AVAILABLE BY EDMUND WHITE

INSIDE A PEARL

My Years in Paris

Edmund White was forty-three years old when he moved to Paris in 1983. He spoke no French and knew just two people in the entire city. White fell passionately in love with Paris, its beauty in the half-light and eternal mists; its serenity compared with New York.

Intoxicated and intellectually stimulated by its culture, he became the definitive biographer of Jean Genet and wrote lives of Marcel Proust and Arthur Rimbaud. Frequent trips across the Channel to literary parties in London begot friendships with Julian Barnes, Martin Amis and many others. When he left, fifteen years later, he was fluent enough to broadcast on French radio and TV, and as a journalist had made the acquaintance of everyone from Yves St Laurent to Michel Foucault. He'd also developed a close friendship with an older woman, Marie-Claude, through whom he'd come to a deeper understanding of French life.

Inside a Pearl vividly recalls those fertile years, and offers a brilliant examination of a city and a culture eternally imbued with an aura of enchantment.

'In the end, this dazzling memoir isn't just a love song to a city… but a profoundly moving elegy to a friend'
SUNDAY TIMES

'Paris may well be White's pearl, but he is in fact the real pearl … Entertaining and wry, White is worldly-wise and wise'
IRISH TIMES

'At once artfully canny and beguilingly innocent … You want to hold on to him, will him to live more, live longer and write about more years'
INDEPENDENT

ORDER YOUR COPY:

BY PHONE: +44 (0) 1256 302 699; **BY EMAIL:** DIRECT@MACMILLAN.CO.UK

DELIVERY IS USUALLY 3–5 WORKING DAYS. FREE POSTAGE AND PACKAGING FOR ORDERS OVER £20.

ONLINE: WWW.BLOOMSBURY.COM/BOOKSHOP

PRICES AND AVAILABILITY SUBJECT TO CHANGE WITHOUT NOTICE.

WWW.BLOOMSBURY.COM/AUTHOR/EDMUND-WHITE/

B L O O M S B U R Y

ALSO AVAILABLE BY EDMUND WHITE

JACK HOLMES AND HIS FRIEND

A moving, expertly-crafted novel from one of New York's most well-respected authors

Jack Holmes is suffering from unrequited love. It doesn't look as if there will ever be anyone else he falls for: the other men he takes to bed never stay for long.

Jack's friend Will Wright comes from old stock, has aspirations to be a writer and, like Jack, works on the *Northern Review*. Jack will introduce Will to the beautiful, brittle young woman he will marry, but is discreet about his own adventures in love – for this is sixties New York, literary and intense, before gay liberation; a concoction of old society, bohemians rich and poor, sleek European immigrants and transplanted Midwesterners. Against this charged backdrop, the different lives of Jack and Will intertwine, and as their loves come and go, they will always be, at the very least, friends.

'This comedy of sexual manners may be White's finest novel'
SUNDAY TIMES

'There's a sleek, close-shaved quality to White's prose that in passages gives it the warm lubriciousness of early Updike and the dry martini sting of Cheever'
FINANCIAL TIMES

'Lucid and powerful ... White is a novelist of great insight'
PHILIP HENSHER, DAILY TELEGRAPH

ORDER YOUR COPY:

BY PHONE: +44 (0) 1256 302 699; **BY EMAIL:** DIRECT@MACMILLAN.CO.UK

DELIVERY IS USUALLY 3–5 WORKING DAYS. FREE POSTAGE AND PACKAGING FOR ORDERS OVER £20.

ONLINE: WWW.BLOOMSBURY.COM/BOOKSHOP

PRICES AND AVAILABILITY SUBJECT TO CHANGE WITHOUT NOTICE.

WWW.BLOOMSBURY.COM/AUTHOR/EDMUND-WHITE/

B L O O M S B U R Y

ALSO AVAILABLE BY EDMUND WHITE

CITY BOY

My Life in New York During the 1960s and 1970s

In the New York of the 1970s, in the wake of Stonewall and in the midst of economic collapse, you might find the likes of Jasper Johns and William Burroughs at the next cocktail party, and you were as likely to be caught arguing Marx at the New York City Ballet as cruising for sex in the warehouses and parked trucks along the Hudson. This is the New York that Edmund White portrays in *City Boy*: a place of enormous intrigue and artistic tumult.

Combining the no-holds-barred confession and yearning of *A Boy's Own Story* with the easy erudition and sense of place of *The Flâneur*, this is the story of White's years in 1970s New York, bouncing from intellectual encounters with Susan Sontag and Harold Brodkey to erotic entanglements downtown to the burgeoning gay scene of artists and writers. It's a moving, candid, brilliant portrait of a time and place, full of encounters with famous names and cultural icons.

'*City Boy* seems effortless in its tone; it is seamless, wise, funny and charming'
COLM TÓIBÍN

'An open-throttled tour of New York City during the bad old days of the 1960s and early '70s... it's all here in exacting and eye-popping detail'
NEW YORK TIMES

'This splendid book is at once fascinating social history and sublimely detailed gossip'
JOHN IRVING

BLOOMSBURY

ALSO AVAILABLE BY EDMUND WHITE

CHAOS

A novella and collection of short stories that are at once hilarious, sexy and heartbreaking.

What happens when a life implodes? When a respected older man, a product of the liberated 1970s, is incapable of cleaning up his act for the twenty-first century? When he pursues sex with a rabidity his body and his reputation can no longer sustain?

In this collection, which features two new, previously unpublished stories, Edmund White explores different aspects of ageing, romance and sex. Taking an unsparing look at gay midlife, these stories are not fiction devoted to the dim splendours and miseries of the past but rather to the unsettling, irresistible claims of the present. Age remains one of the great taboos of gay culture, but Edmund White, as iconoclastic as ever, writes about maturity with the same precision and insight he brought to adolescence in *A Boy's Own Story*.

'Edmund White is one of the three or four most virtuosic living writers of sentences in the English language'
DAVE EGGERS

'An open-throttled tour of New York City during the bad old days of the 1960s and early '70s... it's all here in exacting and eye-popping detail'
NEW YORK TIMES

'This splendid book is at once fascinating social history and sublimely detailed gossip'
JOHN IRVING

B L O O M S B U R Y

'40   Salope !